THE CITY

S.C. MENDES

ISBN: 978-1-940250-33-5

Artwork by Andrej Bartulovic

Printed in the United States of America
Second Edition

Visit us on the web at:
www.bloodboundbooks.net

To Mom

Thanks for your unending love, guidance, and sacrifice.

PART I

1

MAX RECLINED ON a Ming-style bed in the back of Ku's laundry house. Even though most of the building was secretly cordoned off for smoking—leaving little space for an actual laundry business—the room still felt cramped and gloomy. The yellow tar stains on the walls spoke of loss and promised nothing but temporary escape. Mix in the few beds and dilapidated night stands and Ku's was a far cry from the lavish days of the late eighteenth century, when opium smokers were treated with dignity and the rooms offered a glimpse into exotic adventures of the East. Nevertheless, Max didn't mind a little filth. Once the mind drifted away on opium clouds, what difference did it make where the body was?

Beside Max, a young Chinese host prepared a pipe and oil lamp. With his smooth doughy face, Max pegged him for fifteen. His nimble fingers moved with deftness, and Max's eyes were drawn to a point within the hypnotic twirl created by the boy's swift movements. Almost trancing out, Max gazed into the center of those working hands, then *through* the physical matter, until he was caught somewhere in the teen's life. Wondering what choices had brought him here, and what would happen if he stayed at a job like this.

It's not easy working certain jobs. Opium host is on that list. It's the kind of job that sucked you in until it ceased to be a job and became a lifestyle. Such transitions always happened in degrees so small they were almost unnoticeable. When you finally realized your mistake, it was too late. Then, much like quicksand, it's best not to fight the inevitable. To struggle would only speed up your demise.

Hopefully the boy would quit the job before it pushed away everything good in his life. Before the smoke damaged his body as it had the walls, aging him prematurely, and before a wake of despair left by the endless stream of lost souls dulled his own ambition and sentenced him to a wasted existence. But as the boy got closer to completion, anticipation of the impending euphoria washed away any further wonder Max had on the boy's future.

"Detective Elliot?"

Max looked up at the well-dressed American, confusion wrinkling into his forehead. "McCloud?"

When the man slipped off his gloves and removed the black bowler hat he became more recognizable, and Max chuckled. "Can't believe they let you in here. If you'd shown up more than five minutes from now, I'd have thought you were a hallucination."

"Yeah. Lucky me." John McCloud scanned the meager room.

Max saw the building's owner, Leo Ku, standing a few feet behind McCloud. His lips were pressed firmly together, head bobbing—a nervous tick Max had noticed on his first visit. "Buy yourself a pipe, John. Loitering makes 'em nervous."

"I know." McCloud's smile was dry. "Took a while to convince him to even let me back here. I need to speak with you, so how about we leave?"

Without missing a beat, the host finished preparing the opium, and Max brought the wooden pipe to his lips, maintaining eye contact with the young criminal investigator of the San Francisco Police Department, a man he'd only met a few times before. The oil lamp below vaporized the opium and he filled his lungs. Max lowered the pipe, breath held; McCloud stared back.

Max released the poisoned air and McCloud's eyes adverted from his. A slight sway took hold of his legs and Max enjoyed watching the man's discomfort. Max lowered his voice so Ku couldn't hear. "It must be terrible to witness criminal activity and not be able to do anything about it."

"Can we leave?"

"*You* can leave. I've already paid for this. I'm not leaving till I smoke it all."

McCloud sighed and his uneasy gaze settled on an object under the bed.

"It's a *Himitsu-Bako*, a Japanese puzzle box," Max said. "*Secret box*, to be more precise. I buy a new one every few weeks." Sitting up with all the speed of a turtle, Max slid the box out with the tip of his shoe, then paused before grabbing it. He envisioned two tiny hands wrap around the sides of the box—the fingers slid over the edges, pulling with as much force as such slender digits could muster. Max remembered telling Leigh Anne that force alone would never solve a puzzle box...or any other enigma.

Max kicked the box back into its hiding place and sunk into the bed, the ghostly vision fading. He took a second puff, hoping the opium would block any further memories of his daughter. "Might as well speak on why you're here. This could take a while."

"I'm here because Lieutenant Harris said you were the best homicide detective in San Francisco."

Max's laugh emerged as quiet sighs from his nose. "This dope might be making my body slow, but the mind's still sharp—Harris wouldn't say that."

"Listen, Max," McCloud lowered his voice, "I didn't come here to play games with you. I came because Harris thinks you'll be able to help on a case. Apparently, you're a great detective."

"I wasn't a great *detective*. I was great at solving puzzles, but I don't belong with the department. And even with my talent, Lieutenant Harris knows I don't have what it takes to serve the people of San Francisco." After a third puff, the silent host took the pipe and oil lamp and retreated into the shadows. "So if Harris sent you down here, what did he really say?"

"There's been an incident, similar to..." McCloud paused.

"Something similar to the…the tragedy six months ago."

Max opened his mouth but hesitated.

"The circumstances seem linked…perhaps," McCloud continued. "You must have been great at something once, because Harris feels you're the right person to take a shot at this one. Put it to rest. His orders were to find whatever rock you were hiding under and kick it over."

"That sounds more like Harris."

"It's at a housing complex just past Broadway. Tenants complained to the superintendent about noise. He called us." McCloud shifted again. "We…we walked into quite a crime scene. Children were…I'd rather not go into it here."

Despite the possible link between his family's tragedy and this new one, Max knew a smile was emerging on his face. After months of non-communication, Harris realized he needed Max to handle these types of cases.

Max's composure in the face of such extra-brutal murders was mistaken by others as the sign of a great detective. But being a so-called great, dedicated detective wasn't what had allowed him to succeed in closing the books on heinous crimes where others had failed year after year. It was something else. And Harris knew what it was. "Well, then. You have my interest, McCloud. But before I'll let you take me from this fine establishment, you need to tell me what Harris *really* said."

McCloud ceased his uneasy shifting. "Fine." His look hardened on Max. "He said you were the best, but that you were also the sickest. That none of this bloodshed would make you bat an eye. You would follow the trail anywhere, blend in with scum, and absorb everything in this case if you had to…because you could. No one else on the force would be able to go to the same lengths. And since you have nothing left, you'd be that much more willing to step forward."

"Thank you." Max smiled and looked at the young host now working with a new patron. Opium host wasn't the only profession with heavy hooks waiting to sink into your will. Homicide detective assigned to the grisliest murders in San Francisco had to be somewhere near the top of that list. Max held out his hand. "Well get me the hell out of here, Officer McCloud. We've got sights to see."

The scene outside the tenement complex McCloud brought Max to was painfully familiar to that October night six months ago. Throngs of onlookers flooded the street. And the memory of that night fought through his opium haze and took center stage in Max's mind.

Despite the cold winds that night, Max had sweated heavily as he walked home—the night of *the tragedy*. His perspiration mixed with the cheap perfume that still clung to his body, creating a sickly-sweet aroma. Satisfaction and guilt mixed in his mind about as well as the sweaty perfume. It made his heart pound.

First and last time. That's it, I'm done.

Of all the drama he had expected to incur when he returned home that evening—the accusations from Eve, severing the final shred of her trust and love for him, hiding things from Leigh Anne—Max could not have fathomed what he found at the entrance to his apartment building.

Harris had been there, and a slew of officers questioned the crowd that had gathered. Harris's face and the fact that no one could look him in the eye said it all. Max pushed past Harris despite his supervisor's pleas to wait.

The east wall of his living room was splashed in crimson, the liquid drying in macabre patterns. Only severed arteries left blood stains like that. And arteries took you quick—every beat of your heart pushing you closer to death.

Max saw the remains of his wife next. Eve Elliot couldn't even be described as a corpse. She was a pile on the floor. Some mad hunter or surgeon had taken great care in skinning her like an animal, preserving the flesh with expert incisions. Leaving her sloughed off skin behind, like some ghoulish snake.

"My daughter?"

"We're not sure yet," someone replied.

There was a lot of blood on that wall. Max had hoped it wasn't enough for two people.

Tonight, John McCloud led him through crowds that looked

almost identical to that night. Two uniformed officers, doing their best to hold back the nosey people, allowed the duo to pass through the front door. Lieutenant Harris and three other officers stood inside the lobby. Harris's face was puffy and stoic as usual. Like his face, his sack suit was too baggy and wrinkled, adding to the impression that he had not slept well in days. "Max, thanks for coming."

Max nodded, taking off his gloves—his fedora and trench coat stayed on. His eyes and jawline no longer felt as slack as they had at the den. The adrenaline of the situation had sobered him up and left him with a different kind of high. It'd been so long, he had forgotten how much he missed the thrill of a new case.

"Consider this reinstatement from your leave." Harris waved him forward and they began up the staircase. "It's bad, Max. Two of our men already lost their dinner."

"Can't wait."

They reached the second-floor landing.

"Neighbors reported screams and loud banging to the landlord. When he finally got around to checking, there was no answer from the tenant. Landlord entered and...well...contacted us immediately. That happened about noon. The homicide team has been poking around all day. Taking shifts while McCloud tracked you down." Harris stopped at a paint-peeled door. The number 213 was etched into a brass plaque screwed into the wood.

"And all this has something to do with Eve and Leigh Anne?"

"Perhaps. All I know is that your place...that was...that was something I've never seen before. I'm sorry that Eve had to go through that. And dammit, I wish we could have found a lead for—"

Max held up a hand. "I know." He pointed to the door. "But what about this?"

"What's behind that door is the only thing that comes close to your place six months ago. And I need to believe they're related. How could the city produce separate lunatics who murder this way?" Harris shook his fat, red face. "I don't know what the hell happened in there or why. But I need you to find out."

Max put his hand on the brass knob, chills down his back reminding him that the last murder and abduction scene he walked into had been his fault.

He pushed away the regret of his infidelity and opened room 213, noting that there were no signs of a forced entry.

The cloying odor of blood filled the room. It was metallic and fresh, but Max knew that the smell would change soon. A putrid twinge was detectable—to a sensitive nose—just under the copper. In less than an hour, the whole apartment would reek of rotten meat if the bodies were not removed.

He stood in front of the door and scanned the barren room. There were no pictures or paintings, not a single plant, nor bookcases or knickknacks in the ten-by-ten-foot living space—only splintered wood and a poor paint job. There was something about the sparseness that told Max it was more than just poverty keeping the room void of personality—maybe a flop house.

The single piece of furniture was a couch, centered a few feet from the far wall. In it was a man. A dead man. His head hung backward over the top of the couch. At first glance, age was indeterminable. What was apparent though was the gaping hole in his chest. The wound tunneled through the dress shirt—stained a dark red—past the flesh and ribcage, to where his heart should have been.

Max moved closer, careful to not step on the patches of carpet still wet from the copious amount of spilt blood from the excavated chest cavity. His eyes moved from the chest to the tilted head. Circling to the back of the couch, Max observed the ashen face—dried blood against a shattered nose. The zygomatic bones forming the eye sockets on both sides of the victim's head looked to be fractured and driven inward, leaving the skin swollen and bruised a dark shade of purple. The eyeballs themselves had bulged slightly from the orbital walls. A watery fluid mixed with blood leaked from the corners of each eye—he assumed a bone shard had ruptured the vitreous chamber of the eyeball.

"So we assume the man knew his attacker..." Max looked at Lieutenant Harris who remained in the doorway. "And we're thinking this is a botched deal."

9

"Good of a guess as any," Harris said. "No forced entry, no signs of a struggle—just a sudden attack." Harris breathed through his mouth. The air was turning worse as they spoke. "Maybe while they sat to negotiate, the attacker stunned him with a blow to the head, then went to work on the chest."

"Well, that's some crackerjack work, Lieutenant. Gruesome—and the stealing of a heart does lead to some questions—but it's nothing your boys can't figure out. I had a real nice Tuesday going before McCloud stole me away—it is Tuesday, right?"

"Christ, Elliot. I thought you came here to help."

"I thought this had something to do with my family. Turns out you just want your black sheep back because this is a—"

"They're in the bedroom." Harris gestured to the narrow hallway. "It's a massacre."

Max turned to the short hallway from the living room. The walls, yellowing from years of no cleaning, were narrow. Their claustrophobic effects added to the ominous tone Harris set. Max passed the bathroom and the smell got worse. He stepped into an eight-by-eight room. Like the entire apartment, the room lacked any character or decoration. This was definitely a squatter's pad. A hideout. Not a home. The only furniture in this room was three army cots.

The victims were on the cots.

Three young bodies—mutilated sheaths of skin—each laid out on top of a canvas bed. Max's jaw trembled and he fought to keep it from dropping. The long hair and the height of one of the bodies suggested they were females in their early teens. One of the three young girls—the one most intact—had an iron shackle affixed to her left ankle. Bloated flesh, blood, and tendons soiled the clamp and chains that led to the frame of the cot.

The two other victims were something Max had only seen once before: piles of flesh, the husk of the body.

Eve

Their hair and skin flayed with expertise so that it remained in one connected piece. The removed organs were clumped together under the cots. Similar chains were fitted to the legs of their cots as well. But nothing solid remained within their shackles. The bones were missing entirely.

Max felt a knot of pain twist in his stomach, and he suddenly wished he was back in Ku's opium den. He didn't need closure; he needed a fresh pipe, a pull of whiskey or even just a new *Himitsu-Bako* puzzle.

Let's just give this a try, he bargained with an unstable mind that threatened to remind him of his fatal shortcomings. *Please. And if it doesn't work, Chinatown isn't going anywhere.*

The promise of future ecstasy was enough to calm the internal craving and suppress the flashes of Eve's empty skin suit and his missing daughter.

Max turned off the feelings associated with the images and clues of the real-world puzzle box and stared into the empty-sockets of the girl-suit, long blonde hair still attached to the skull-less face. Her eyes resided in a pile with the spleen and liver and intestines. Ignoring the immeasurable pain the child must have endured, Max played out scenarios in his mind. He saw the girls as possible kidnap victims of the dead man in the other room; or perhaps they were daughters of the man and chained up by the killer, or maybe daddy was the killer.

After several minutes, Max's trance was broken by Harris, who entered with nose and mouth buried in the crook of his arm. "The man on the couch has been confirmed as Jeffery Poppens. The girls are still unknown. This is the only thing we found." A small leather pouch hung from his fingers.

And the first piece of the puzzle slid into place.

II

MAX WAS PART of something again, and the excitement had revived him. Forgotten were his qualms with Harris and the force. A mental deal had been struck with his inner demons, and memories of his family receded to their temporary hiding place so that a new escape could fill his mind's eye. A case that horrified everyone else. Max may have hated most aspects of homicide work, but he loved those first moments after leaving a crime scene. It was like the briefest caress with a new lover. Everything was still possible, and curiosity ran high. Success felt close enough to grasp, as long as the hunter kept up the momentum.

Which was why Max wasn't about to slow down.

It was almost eight thirty under the spring moon when Max found himself in the lavish compound of Shin Sho, the leather pouch Harris gave him in the pocket of his trench coat. A woman in a floral-print *changsam* led him through the house whose upstairs doubled as a high-end brothel, the soft sad twangs of a Zither Zheng Harp audible through the quiet halls. Though Max didn't see the musician, the notes were growing louder. He didn't see the incense either, but its pungent smell was detectable throughout the entire house, same as the music.

Despite the soothing atmosphere, flashes of boneless, splayed-out skin danced in Max's mind. The patience and skill needed to carry out such mutilation meant the act itself was a message, to prove a point. But who was the intended audience? And what about the missing bones, were they trophies?

The woman stopped at a beaded curtain, the sad cascading plucks of the harp coming from just beyond. She gestured him through and Max parted the beads, stepping into Shin Sho's low lit office. Below the one electric lamp, a woman sat on a silk pillow, her dress, low cut and vibrant, reminiscent of Tang Dynasty outfits. In front of her was the harp. She drew out a long final note as Max stepped up to the desk.

"Mister Elliot." The ancient voice came from behind pools of shadows and pipe smoke.

The musician stood up and moved from the glow of the lamp into the hazy darkness of the voice. Max's eyes adjusted to the meek lightning, and he saw the woman walking back, a hand-carved pipe in her palm. She went past him and out through the beaded curtain, leaving Max and his host alone.

Now able to see better, Max approached the long wooden table that Sho sat behind. He wore a *tang zhuana*, black as his braided hair, fitted with gold trim. His face was still as lean as the last time they'd spoken, and Max was impressed that the few lines running down his cheeks never denounced him as old or feeble; they just solidified his air of wisdom and power. "Shin Sho, thank you for seeing me on such short notice."

Sho opened his hand, gesturing for Max to sit. Max obliged and knowing his time was limited, he removed the pouch from his trench coat pocket. He laid it on the table and pulled the drawstring wide, offering a look at the grayish powder. "Have you ever seen this substance before?"

Sho took the pouch and studied its contents. The muscles of his lean cheeks flexed. "Did you buy yourself?"

"What is it?"

"Most call it *sǐ fěn*." Shin Sho drew the bag closed, cinched a tight knot, and tossed it on the desk between them. "Best to leave alone."

Max's neck and cheeks flushed with anger first, then shame. "It's not for me."

Shin Sho studied him with intense green eyes that had never dulled over all the years Max knew him. Max could feel his past drug choices being remembered and scrutinized in those wise orbs.

"I found it at a crime scene," Max said.

"I suggest you look for 'nother clue."

"Three young girls were butchered. Chained up like animals in a dead man's apartment. I can't walk away."

"Max, this like nothing you ever experienced. I—"

"It may have something to do with Eve and Leigh Anne." Max leaned into the sweet aroma that still clung to Shin Sho from the pipe; he ignored its siren call. "No cryptic warnings. Just tell me what it is. Please."

Sho closed his eyes for a moment, breathed deep, then opened his lids and fixed a penetrating gaze on Max. "It is a drug. A drug I have never sold. Powerful, though. Well beyond what you find in opium den."

"It was hidden under some floorboards. Maybe the man was a pimp controlling the girls through addiction. If this is some new drug, then I'm guessing only a few people know how to make it. Should be easy to track down."

Sho shook his head with slow deliberateness. "It is old. Very old. But you are correct; only a few know it. I am surprised *they* would have overlooked this when finished with the murder."

"Any idea who *they* are?" Max said.

The answer came out thin and wispy as breath. "The Mara." Equally as soft, Sho said: "The only chemists who can make *sĭ fĕn* are The Mara."

"Mara," Max said, as if repeating the foreign word would somehow expand its meaning to him.

"Your victim—pimp—no doubt had dealings with Mara. The Others, they are sometimes called. This man cheated them in some way. Sold this—" Shin gestured to the pouch that sat on the desk between them "—without authorization. The Others have an unforgiving nature. The deaths are retribution."

Max pulled out a small, leather-bound notepad, the lead of his pencil etching into the paper. He looked up from his hastily-scratched notes. "Seems like new Chinese gangs are coming out of the woodwork every month or so. These Mara: are they a Tong?"

"They are not a gang."

"Fine." Max dared a bit of sarcasm. "Where do these *non-gang* murderers meet?"

Shin Sho pressed his lips together.

"Interesting." Max picked up the pouch. "If I pursue this, will I find it has something to do with you?"

"Not at all." Shin Sho smiled. "Some things are simply not discussed. You'll learn that if you follow this path."

"Can—"

Sho extended his hand, index finger long and slender pointing to the exit.

Max turned and saw the servant girl in the floral *changsam* beside him. He looked back at Shin Sho. "Thanks for your time."

The painted lips of the woman who brought him to Sho still held the same obedient smile as earlier, yet Max knew his face was lackluster compared to the enthusiasm he'd arrived with.

Unfazed by Max's change in demeanor, she led him back down the hallway. In the large foyer two young women lounged on a puffy couch, conversing in whispers. From the office, which now felt so far away as Max and the female servant approached the house entrance, the Zither Zheng's song resumed.

"Mister Elliot." A soft voice from halfway up the sweeping staircase.

Her voice vibrated into him with the same sad frequency as the Zither Zheng's notes, and Max stopped, the front door not more than ten feet from him. The void created by the pause was filled with the harp's distant song of beautiful longing and Max's hesitation to answer.

He finally looked to his right and up the staircase at a thin Chinese woman.

"Yanmei." He murmured her name as quiet as a secret.

Max watched the robed woman descend, then stop at the second to last step, waiting just above the floor. He could imagine her naked flesh just beneath the thin white fabric, the softness of her hair bun in his hands.

Smiling, always smiling and cordial, the host woman at his side asked Max: "Stay tonight?"

At his right Yanmei waited, silent and beautiful.

Before him, the exit.

But what was through that front door anyway? More dead ends? Harris had provided only *one* clue, and if Shin Sho refused to speak on the powder's manufacturers, Max had nothing. Just like there was nothing left at his house. Maybe if there had been a single lead, Max would have continued the case. Exerted further effort.

A sudden feeling of defeat sunk into his bones, extinguishing the fire of the chase he'd experienced earlier. Yanmei's presence had simply clarified what he already knew, and it was time to come to terms with that truth. These three girls were no different from his family's tragedy. It was an American Ripper story. And as such, this Chinatown Jack's identity would never be discovered. Just as certain mysteries were destined to remain hidden.

Max looked back up the stairs. Yanmei's room sounded more inviting than Ku's laundry den.

"Sure," Max said. "I'll stay."

Max watched—a glass of whiskey in his hand—as Yanmei finished drawing the bath. She had brought out a pipe, oil lamp, and opium with the alcohol, but he'd stopped her from preparing it and asked for the bath show instead. The paraphernalia sat, unused, beside a cross-legged Max, surrounded by pillows on a large rug.

With slow movements, Yanmei parted the kimono and let it slip to the ground. She made a spectacle of dipping her pedicured foot into the steaming, sudsy water. Max watched her slender, pale body submerge into the tub. The tops of her small pointed breasts enjoyed brief visibility as the displaced water sloshed around them. Though his eyes were focused, his thoughts were elsewhere, and Max downed the rest of the whiskey, hoping to anesthetize his mind and bring his attention back to the concubine.

Her black hair was pinned up with chop sticks. Her powdered and painted face also managed to stay dry as she made a show of raising slender legs out of the water, one at a time, caressing the soapy bubbles over their smooth skin. It was how she'd gotten Max to lower his defenses the last time he'd been here.

You were supposed to be done for good after that night.

But those words were sworn back when Max had thought his wife was still alive.

He stretched up and over to the coat rack next to him—not fully leaving the comfort of the velvet pillows—and pulled the leather pouch from his trench coat. He opened it and, though the powder was odorless, he gave a sniff, confirming the fact to himself once more. The whiskey spun his resistance to mush, and he looked back at Yanmei. This time his testicles twitched with desire. Max thought about replacing the opium in the pipe with the *sǐ fěn*. Of course, he wouldn't allow Yanmei to partake. Not with all the mystery surrounding the drug. But why shouldn't Max test out the high? Who was Shin Sho or anyone to tell him what he could handle?

Sloshing, dripping sounds guided his attention from the pipe and back to the tub. Yanmei had risen, water cascading down her nude body, as she reached for a towel hanging from the bamboo and silk changing divider. She patted herself dry, then went behind the screen and put on a different kimono.

She sat on the rug in front of him, knees and legs together underneath her bottom and out to her right side. "I love baths. I pretend I come out of the ocean. That I am fresh and alive. Do you like the beach, Mister Elliot?"

Of all the questions to ask, why the beach?

The tiny hands that had emerged in Ku's den were back. But instead of wrapping around his puzzle box, they were parting the muddled clouds inside the detective's head. The hands tore through the wispy coverings created by alcohol to blind Max from all memories that threatened him with pain. Envisioning Leigh

Anne endangered his pact with the darkness inside, making Max sick to his stomach, and the longer he forced himself to look at Yanmei's alluring smile the more his daughter's face transposed on the prostitute. The ensuing nausea worked to sober him.

"Everything okay?"

Just fine. My missing daughter's favorite place to visit is the beach. Did I mention she's probably dead—

Or perhaps she wasn't.

Yanmei looked anxious, but Max could think of nothing to say that would assuage her concern. How could he explain his musings to this adolescent, when it was a battle to understand them himself? Over the past three years, the regularity of his mood shifts from elation to despair had increased. The frequency of occurrences reached its apex after the tragedy, and clearly, he was still riding the crest of the phenomena. A void had formed where his sense of purpose and direction should have been housed. The vacuous longing hadn't formed overnight from any single event; it had grown over time. And Max was now a servant to his unhinged, unfocused will, cognizant that he was a victim to passing whims yet unable to stop it.

"Mr. Elliot?" Her voice trembled a bit and it only served to remind Max of her age.

Disgusted with himself, Max pushed up and staggered against the rack, retrieving his coat and fedora. "Sorry, Yanmei. I have to go."

"Why you always leave this way?" She pulled the kimono tighter, covering the errant exposed flesh. "You say I'm beautiful, then run. Have I offended you?"

He regarded her eyes that were glossy with sadness, not anger. "You are beautiful," Max said. "I'm the one who's ugly."

III

Max nodded to Kevin Tourville as he entered the station. The front desk watchman and overnight receptionist appeared a bit surprised but raised no fuss as his former colleague headed to the offices. It was ten o'clock, but Max figured someone could get him the tintypes from the crime scenes. If he didn't keep his mind focused on the case, regardless of the hour, there was no telling where Max would find himself. Only two desk lamps still burned in the dim room, but before Max could bother checking which officers now resided at those desks, he saw the light on behind the tempered glass of Harris's closed door.

Max went right up to the door, held his breath and listened to the rustling paper, envisioning the mountainous piles shifting about the lieutenant's desk. Max could remember the days when he was in charge of keeping files organized for his then partner. Harris's version of order had always been chaotic. Unlike Max's methodical precision, Harris could step outside the box and return when necessary. The fluidity had helped with their cases, and Harris's open-mindedness had led to his advancement. When you're willing to absorb anything though, one must be careful who and what they choose to associate with. In the unfortunate case of Harris, the former detective's mind absorbed the poor idea to slowly shut down to being open-minded.

Ironic.

"Someone there?" Harris barked, clearly seeing Max's shadow through the opaque glass.

Max knocked twice. "It's me."

"Well, you gonna stay out there all night?"

Max opened the door. "Didn't think you'd be here so late."

"As a detective, I thought sleeping was hard. As a lieutenant, I can say my former self didn't know what poor sleep was."

"I'm not so sure your former self would agree." Max regretted his choice of words.

"Is that where your animosity is coming from? Over some case that we ended nearly five years ago?" Harris said.

Of course it was about that case, and the night where they'd been forced to make a choice together, a choice that both bonded them on a deeper level than ever before, but one that also dissolved their partnership. Yet at the same time, that moment had nothing to do with today. It was minor in the larger scheme, simply another thread woven into the hangman's noose.

However, the current thoughts sweeping through him didn't care for that logic. Max was ready to make his speech razor sharp in its attack.

"Maybe it is. Maybe you made a mistake with this murderer." He shrugged. "Now you need me to clean up your mess again."

"A mistake?" Harris's voice rose with indignation. His lips parted, but whatever string of berating comments he had pushing for release were swallowed in silence, and Harris lowered his volume. "You know what your problem is, Max?"

"Please tell me, Ted. 'Cause for years I thought it was covering for you, so you could leave me in the dust, and take your cushy desk job."

"Cushy!" Harris threw his hands up in frustration. Then he chuckled, sarcastic and clipped. This time Harris looked to be the one speaking before thinking, and Max delighted a bit in watching the man's temper flare. "This has nothing to do with me. This has nothing to do with that night. You made your choice—"

"As did you," Max reminded him.

"The problem is you're never satisfied, Max."

"What do I have to be content about?"

"I don't mean recently. I'm talking about your life prior to the last six months. It also has nothing to do with the night Cullen Smith died. Your struggle was constant before that, always coming and going at a whim." Harris was flustered and the words seemed to tumble out of his mouth with no real cohesion, but Max grasped what his former partner was struggling to articulate.

Harris's emotional state left little point in Max arguing that Cullen Smith did not simply die that night. Known as the Digger, the serial killer was fatally shot by the jumpy trigger finger of Harris four years ago. But a back and forth volley of cheap ego shots wouldn't improve the situation. They'd covered each other that night as partners. And neither one of them had gotten what they deserved. Or perhaps they'd both reaped exactly what they'd sowed. Either way, Harris was right: Max had not been happy prior to or after their testimonies.

"Fair enough," Max said. "I suppose there's no point in hashing up the past."

"None that I can see."

"Then what's the deal besides me cracking the case and getting the mayor off your back?" *One more jab won't hurt.*

Anger flashed in Harris's eyes, but Max could see the shame there too. The truth reddened his face and made his words seem fake despite their good intentions. "It's not just for me, Max. I swear to God I thought this might bring you some peace. Justice seemed to help balance you in the past. But now—" Harris opened his hand at Max "—look at you; it's gotten worse. You're a wreck. Nobody wants to see you like this." He took a deep breath. "*I* don't want to see you like this. Not after everything we've been through together."

"Those days are long gone."

"Be that as it may, I don't wish the type of misery you experience in any friend, current or past."

"You really think that if I crack this one I'll be happy?"

"If you gain something in the process, beyond justice…yes, I believe you could be. At least it's worth a try."

"If I find Leigh Anne… I'll be happy."

21

Harris nodded, though his face looked skeptical. "What do you need from me?"

"Is this really all you've got?" Max held up the pouch.

The anger flared again in Harris's eyes over the implication that he was hiding evidence from Max, but the flame was extinguished just as quick. "We didn't find anything else. Did you?"

"Just give me the tintypes," he said. "And some time. I need to study everything."

"We'll start bright and early tomorrow."

"It's been six months, Ted. I don't do early anymore. If you want me back, I need to ease into my return. Fly solo for a bit. I can't have you breathing down my neck every day."

"The mayor is breathing down mine, Max." Harris gestured in the air. "Children have been skinned alive. This is going to shock the community."

Max kept his calm. "If you think I can do it, then let me do it my way."

Harris conceded with a light sigh. He opened a drawer, removed a manila envelope. "I do believe in you," he said. "Johnston will remain lead on paper only; this is your case. You're on a special task force, unofficially in charge. Report back here as you find things. But try not to let your absenteeism around the station become a habit." He held out the envelope. "I just have to know that you won't lose yourself out there."

"If I do, it's not your fault." Max let the manila envelope hang before his face. It seemed that their roles had changed over the years. Suddenly it was Harris who was calculating and rational, and Max was the unsure rookie who was on the brink of a crisis, grasping at anything to stay afloat.

"This is where you belong." Harris extended the envelope closer.

Max accepted the package. "Well then this is the deciding factor too," Max said. "If I can't solve this one, I'm hanging it up for good."

After the precinct, Max returned to his apartment with the envelope of crime scene tintypes and sat in his living room. The same empty, quiet living room that had squeezed him in a painful embrace for the past six months. The loudest sounds were now the occasional clink of ice in the highball of whiskey or the howl and curse of a stubbed foot or dropped implement as a result of too much said whiskey. Tonight's glass of amber gold was raised to Max's lips more frequent than usual, only to be set down again beside the drug-filled pouch and the sealed parcel of photos on the coffee table. He'd been drinking fast and staring at the pouch for the better part of two hours.

Sǐ fěn.

The whiskey calmed his aching stomach and quieted the voice in the smallest recess of his brain.

It's like nothing you've experienced before.

Sho and he played a similar song and dance every time they met. Max had gone there before to watch the women, experience the opium, and gambling. He'd even received information on criminal activity. Vague was always the order of the day with Shin Sho. The Chinese kingpin gave no details so concrete as to incriminate himself—only the competition—*but* the answers would always be there, even if coded at first. Tonight, though, he had built nothing but curiosity.

Max planned to keep the new knowledge to himself. Lieutenant Harris may have reinstated him—the particulars to be worked out in the next few days—but Max wasn't about to share his cards yet. The department needed Max more than he needed them. He was the one who could stomach the diseased shit the city produced.

It had been bad today in the Broadway apartment. And October 13th, 1909, six months ago, that was another day when it didn't just rain filth. It poured.

Rather than think of that October night, Max took another sip of whiskey and opened the parcel. The tintypes spilled across the table and Max was thankful that the gore could only be captured in black and white—it helped him shut off the emotions. As far as he was concerned, the walls and cots were just painted in thick, black paint. When he reached the snapshot of the young victim who was no more than discarded skin, Max wondered what the organs' owner was like in life. No matter how many examinations he gave each image, the photos refused to divulge anything new. He pushed the violent pictures aside and picked up one featuring the outside of the apartment. The badly chipped door. In his mind's eye, his own apartment corridor in Eden Plaza shimmered ghostly over the snapshot, and his own room number blocked out 213.

Max finished the highball and this time couldn't stop his thoughts from pulling him back in time. Back to the cold October night and the long walk to this apartment. Not one of the officers could look him in the eye that night. Max often wondered what he would have seen in their eyes should they have looked at him. Or what they would have seen in Max's. Would they have registered the shame he felt at being with Yanmei just hours before his wife was murdered? Would the guilt he felt for choosing the youngest possible prostitute still be on his face when the Lieutenant told him his daughter was missing? At twelve, Leigh Anne was just six years younger than Yanmei.

Max remembered his stress levels had reached maximum capacity that evening. The dams of patience were stretched, the raging tides created by juggling work and social politics with parental and husband responsibilities had broken through, and he felt some primal force guiding him. Max had just wanted a quick fling. First time, last time. Eve hadn't touched him in months anyway; what was the harm in one time? The lack of physical affection had driven him further from her each day, and it seemed he was going to lose Eve regardless. In a twisted way, this act was an opportunity to relieve the pressure, avoid a breaking point, and provide a chance to work on their marriage fresh.

The harm, it turned out, was coming home to a bloodbath in his living room. All his wife's killer left was a pile of skin. Flayed from the bone like she was a fish. Just like the two girls he saw today, the killer had managed to keep Eve's face and body in one piece while the incision ran downward from the skull through the spine, and the innards and bones were essentially pulled out the back.

Nothing his fellow officers could have said would have prepared him for the shock of looking at the eyeless mask that was once Eve's face. Dead skin, lying upon a pile of mangled meat, tendons and muscle and organs strewn about the room.

"My God," he'd heard someone mutter that night. "Who steals bones?"

All of Eve's bones were missing, along with his daughter. Nothing indicated that Leigh Anne had met the same fate. But there was no ransom note, no clues. Just questions and a room that reeked of shit and vomit. The vomit he found out later was that of the two officers who arrived at the scene first. Max hadn't thrown up that night, not even when they used a shovel to transfer the heaping pile of dead tissue into a cadaver pouch.

Max tipped the highball back, but only a solitary drop of whiskey remained.

I should have been there.

He hadn't been there though, and after learning of his daughter's disappearance, Max did nothing to champion the cause of finding her either. He had helped himself instead, continuing his selfish pattern.

But he couldn't let those memories get in the way of his work now. He had to focus. Decisions made when emotions were high led to mistakes. If he proceeded rationally, he might be able to find out what happened to his daughter. And perhaps, if he was real lucky...

Maybe I'll find her.

"Charlie." The name came to him like a brilliant idea. Though the thought of Charlie Willis agreeing to be his lead was more of a crap shoot than genius brainstorm, it was potentially Max's last resort before he lost the trail.

IV

Max Woke On the couch with whiskey's calling card of pain throbbing at the base of his skull. He checked his watch with indifference. Four pm. Since the murder-abduction of his family, time hadn't mattered much. And Max wasn't about to start making it a priority now. For the time being it looked like he had a free pass with the lieutenant. It was nice to know he could skip checking in at the precinct in lieu of hitting the streets as soon as possible.

After putting away his breakfast—or what time would have dictated as an early supper—Max headed to Chinatown. It was a ten-block ride by trolley and during the short trip Max made a mental list of places to find Charlie Willis. There were only a handful of establishments the man deigned to hang his hat. And if Charlie wasn't high, he was usually gambling; so when Max found him playing some version of dominoes in the back parlor of the restaurant Lee's, he wasn't surprised.

Charlie opened the black pieces on the table between him and his opponent, looked up from the white and red markings, and let out a small cheer as he collected his winnings. Max clapped his hands together, slow and long, drawing the attention of the disappointed Asian as well as Charlie.

"Max Elliot." Charlie stood up. Like Harris, he wore a wrinkled sack suit that had seen better days; worse than Harris, Charlie's faded, plaid gray jacket did not go with the mismatched brown trousers. Charlie picked up his off-white gambler hat—completing his destitute ensemble—and uttered some words of condolences in Chinese to his opponent. Then he turned to Max and strolled over. He pulled at the sleeves of his rumpled suit jacket, and the smile below his pencil-thin mustache, though full of grimy teeth, seemed genuine. Max was thankful that Charlie had won—he stood a better chance with him in a positive mood.

"I know things ended poorly between us last time. Hell, 'poorly' is an understatement. Can we talk? Privately?"

"Sure, sure." Charlie pointed at a small, unoccupied table in the corner and they sat down. "Wow, Max Elliot. It's been awhile. What's on your mind?"

It was unsettling to see Charlie so jovial.

There were only two things Max ever needed from Charlie. And if it wasn't one of those, that meant Max was arresting him. And that had only happened once.

"I need you to tell me about *sĭ fĕn*."

"That's a bit outta my league." Charlie's volume dropped. "It's a rush though. I've tried it before. Used to know a connection, but it ran dry."

While he spoke, Max saw a twinkle in the man's eyes. "Maybe we should go somewhere else to talk," Max said.

In minutes, they were walking the streets. Those passing by gave Charlie's outfit a second glance, though no attention seemed to be given to their conversation.

"So this connection you knew, did they happen to live just off Broadway?"

Charlie's beady brown eyes shifted back and forth. "Yeah."

"Well, I believe I have your buddy's last shipment." Max opened his coat and flashed the drug-filled pouch.

Charlie's eyes grew wide.

"I'm guessing you've heard what happened to him."

"I did. He ain't my buddy though." Charlie's head swiveled

from left to right as if a mistakenly-perceived association could deal him a similar death. "It was a business connection 'sall."

"Relax, Charlie. That's why I brought us out here. This is just between you and me."

They turned down a small alley and stopped in front of a decaying brick wall. Overflowing trashcans blocked their view from the main street and walkways.

"I need some answers."

"I don't know nothin'."

Max held up the pouch and studied Charlie's eyes. "I think you *do* know something, Charlie."

Charlie shuffled back and forth, his expression indecisive. "Look, I had nothin' to do with that stuff. If I get roped in, I get taken care of, too."

"Nobody's roping you in, Charlie."

"I heard that before." He glared at Max, eyes hot with accusation.

"Look, I just want to know why The Mara decided to rip out Jeffery Poppens's heart. And why in God's name three girls were chained up in his bedroom."

"Fuck sake." Charlie paced. "Jeff was my hook-up. I used a few times…way back. Since then, I just sent him buyers. That's all. Nothin' more. I got a cash cut for sending customers his way. I had no access to the powder. Jeff is the only person who sold; you can't find that stuff anywhere—"

"So I've heard," Max said.

"Yeah, well, he must have chaffed the chemists bad to get killed like that."

"Chemists?"

"Like you said, The Mara chemists."

If Charlie knew about these Mara too, how the hell had Max never heard of them? "What about the three girls? Was it a sex thing?"

"That's part of it, I'm sure, but with the Mara it's always more than just sex. Women—people—they're used for everything."

"Everything?"

"Yeah." Sweat beaded on Charlie's forehead. Almost half a foot shorter than Max and fifteen pounds underweight, Elliot had always considered Charlie a squirrely little man. But now he seemed even more nervous. His skin appeared clammy, his brown hair slicked back with perspiration. Charlie's lips must have been dry though because he kept licking them. Like he was hungry. Hungry for what? The powder or to stop talking about The Mara?

First Shin, now Charlie. What is it about this topic that makes people clam up?

"Look, man," Charlie said, "people come down here to blow off steam, right?"

Max nodded.

"Of course they do. It's Chinatown, it's a blast. They got the dens, the women, the gambling. Tongs run the show, it's like a city within a city; you know that. It's why people come here. You can find things on these street corners that you can't get anywhere. Cops only breeze in when somethin' bad happens, real bad."

"That's the Chinatown *you* know. But there's somethin' else here—under the surface. Somethin' more than the prostitutes and drugs. It's got nothin' to do with the Tongs or the immigrants. It's here because it can be here. This area is already marked 'cause the rest of the city views Chinatown as full of outsiders; 'cause 'normals' turn their backs on things until it can give them somethin' in return."

"And this *other* Chinatown…this is where I find The Mara?" Max asked. "The child murderers?"

"This is where you find everything. Including stuff that would make your skin crawl."

"I want to make my skin crawl, Charlie. Tell me how to get there, and I'll give you some of this…" Max removed the powder from his jacket on his hunch that Charlie was craving.

The cold flash of desire gleamed in Charlie's eye for an instant then vanished. "It ain't like directions to a store. You need to be brought in by someone they trust. Like an exclusive club."

"Then I want you to introduce me."

Charlie shook his head. "Not even *fěn* is worth going back to that scene." The man had a slight tremble in his extremities.

"Why'd you mess with Jeffery Poppens, then?"

"Easy money. I ain't exactly a hirable candidate in the job market. I never had to see the *fěn* or that world. I'm different than the guy you used to know. The joint straightened me out."

Max doubted that. He knew firsthand that people rarely

changed.

"Walk away from this one, Max. Trust me. If there's anythin' left that you care about, walk away."

"There isn't," Max said. "In fact, this all may have something to do with my kid's disappearance and the murder of my wife."

"You want revenge?"

Max remained silent.

"There ain't no closure in this other place; only a cycle. It can't be stopped."

"Are you denying me a chance to get my daughter back? I said I was sorry for the way things went down. I—"

"I'm over that shit."

"Then help me just once more. For old time's sake. And whatever happens afterward is up to me, right or wrong."

Charlie sighed. "It ain't easy. But I can start you off somewhere, and I suppose I'll vouch for you."

"Max shook his hand. "I appreciate this."

"You won't," Charlie mumbled.

Max took a bill from his pocket and, using origami, fashioned it into a bowl of sorts. He funneled a healthy supply of the powder into the makeshift container.

"Come to my place tomorrow night," Charlie said. "Eight pm."

V

LIEUTENANT HARRIS WAS closing things up at his desk, ready to head home, when Max strode into the station. Harris checked his watch: seven pm. "Everything okay?"

"Yeah." Max smiled and casually sat in the chair across from the lieutenant.

"Okay." Harris tried not to let the irritation show in his already strained face. "Is this how it's gonna be from now on?" Harris asked.

"What do you mean, sir?"

"There it is again." Harris threw up his hands, then sank back into his chair, leaving the briefcase open on the desk. "That tone you add to everything, hoping to get under my skin. I haven't seen hide nor hair of you all day. Is it not reasonable to ask if everything is okay, if you've learned anything new?"

"I thought we were doing this my way."

Harris rubbed his fingers over the wooden armrest, calming himself. He wished he could flip a switch to get Max leveled again. Those moments of centered clarity seemed to be fleeting for Max, though when the detective reached them, Harris knew the man could accomplish anything. The trick was keeping him balanced. Sometimes Max reacted best to tranquil talks, other times hard truth and authority did the trick...Harris choose to remain calm for now. "I thought we were still all a team despite playing this one a little looser than normal. That means reporting back sometime before the day shift ends."

"The kind of information I get doesn't just appear between the hours of nine to five. Besides, I don't remember coming to you and asking to be put on this case. You found me."

"I honestly thought you would want to be a part of this."

"Why? Because I'm the sickest one on the force?" Max said. "Because I can blend in with scum?"

Harris felt his cheeks flush. "I told McCloud the truth because he would have seen through us anyway. Hell, I doubt he even likes me much."

"Seen through me? Whatever do you mean?"

Keeping calm wasn't working. Harris took a breath and leaned forward, mustering up his authoritative tone. "Just because everyone else here regards your little drop into the abyss reasonable due to the circumstances, I know the truth." Harris tapped his meaty finger against his own chest, then pointed it at Max. "You gazed into that vice-filled abyss long ago. And goddammit I know you loved them both, but you had always been waiting for a reason to throw it all away and jump into that pit of depression. The murderer just gave you an excuse. It doesn't make you evil, just human."

Max closed his eyes.

Harris leaned back. "The boys around the station consider me a straight shooter, always going by the book, by the law. I'm a hero to them, just like you: the great detective who can solve the most heinous of crimes. But you and McCloud know that my decisions are politically-based, panders to the press and the state officials. And McCloud doesn't care for that; that's why I doubt he'll succeed here, especially now that he wants homicide. But he's a good man."

Max chuckled. "Yeah, well I still don't like him."

"You don't like anyone." Harris grinned, and he could feel the balance shift back into Max.

"Fair enough." Max pulled the leather pouch out of his pocket. "Ready?"

"Yes." Harris nodded. "Thank you." Relief washed over his body to know the storm had passed and they could finally speak business.

"Turns out this little gray powder is a pretty intense drug. And it's so rare that there are only a few people that can manufacture it."

"What are we looking at? A new form of heroin? Cocaine?"

Max bit his lip, shaking his head. "I don't know yet. Everyone I spoke with has been cryptic and paranoid. All they'll say is that it's powerful. I have one new lead which I'll start on tomorrow. If I can find out where this stuff comes from or what it is, maybe we can start piecing together why it was at the crime scene."

"Perhaps he was using it to dope up the girls, bring them up addicted so they could be coerced into turning tricks."

"Maybe." Max pushed the pouch across to Harris and stood up. "I'll let you know as soon as I get more information."

"So...you're back, right?"

"For now." Max took a deep breath. "Look, I'll give you all I can."

And Harris knew it was the most reassurance he was going to get from the unorthodox detective. He'd give Max time and keep some faith in his former partner. "Be careful."

After Max left, Harris picked up the pouch of the powdered drug. It felt lighter than when he gave it to Max, and it took effort subduing the voice that reminded him Max Elliot did not mix well with narcotics of any kind. *The voice that whispered: He's not coming back.*

After the encounter with Max, Charlie slinked home to his cramped tenement housing on the outskirts of Chinatown. The ratty conditions seemed to exist in the perpetual glow of twilight, of gloom and hopelessness—the mortar that held every ghetto together. The city had put about zero effort in reestablishing his neighborhood after the big quake. They'd pumped something like ninety million dollars into the city in the first nineteen months. But they carefully left pockets of destruction peppered throughout San Francisco. This way in a few years there wouldn't be much opposition when they decided to tear down the slums for better housing that Charlie still wouldn't be able to afford.

With each step over trash and past huddled shadows begging for change or offering sex, Charlie drove another mental nail into Max's coffin. And by the time he made it to his second-story apartment he had an idea—almost as ingenious as the last plan.

Charlie closed the door and crossed the few feet of living room into the kitchen, ignoring the human slumped on his sofa like a pile of dirty laundry. Charlie was looking for a glass in the cabinet when he heard the sofa creak as Chris Barnes—who smelled like a pile of dirty laundry too—stirred to life and stood.

With thick stubble on his cheeks, Barnes ambled into the kitchen. "What's the word?" he asked.

"I think we're home free," Charlie said. "Been to all the old haunts, played dominoes with the boys, and I ain't heard no chatter to the opposite. And since you and I are still breathin' then everyone—and I mean *everyone*—thinks Jeff acted alone. He—"

"He did," Barnes said, eyes fearful. "Just 'cause we spread the word, I didn't do anything—*we* didn't, I mean."

"Yeah. *We*," Charlie said. "Don't forget that you're a part of this too."

"Yeah, I mean…*we're* gonna be fine," Barnes said, though his eyes searching around the room betrayed his lack of faith in the statement.

Charlie finished his water and they both went back to the sofa, taking a seat. "Got a present for you." Charlie dropped the origami pouch onto the scarred wooden table. "A little *fěn*, courtesy of the SFPD."

"You talked with the cops!"

"Christ, Barnes. We went over this. You knew they'd round me and the usual suspects up for questioning."

Barnes pointed at the origami pouch, wild-eyed. "But where would the cops get *fěn* from?"

"Max Elliot is back with the force—he's the only one I spoke with and he knows we had nothing to do with it. He just wants info."

"What are you telling 'em?" His voice trembled with fear.

"Shit, man, get a hold of yourself. I'm sending 'em on a wild goose chase."

"And the *fěn*, where did that come from?"

"Relax. It was at Jeffery's."

"How? *They* don't leave clues."

Charlie forgot that sometimes Barnes had a functioning brain. He'd always been the muscle, but every now and then a light switch turned on. "I'm sure—"

"You!" His fanatical eyes fell on Charlie. "You went back after *they* were done and planted—"

"Don't' be an ass. I want this over with as bad as you do. Jeff must have hidden the batch; it took the police a while to find it. And for helping him, Max gave me some of Jeff's last batch. Nothing more to it." Charlie opened the origami folds, exposing the powder to Barnes. "And it's all yours."

The last few months with Barnes had been like watching a train wreck in slow motion. The man had outlived his usefulness. And his only saving grace at this moment was the new development with Max Elliot.

"Really?" Barnes's eyes went wide again, this time with hunger, not fear. He reached for the makeshift pouch, hand shaking.

Charlie gripped his wrist just before Barnes's fingers wrapped around the folded bill. "Remember, this gift is to remind you to keep your mouth shut. With my help guiding this case, Max Elliot might run into problems. And if that happens, the department will probably check all his informants trying to find him. Don't worry if they approach you. It's all textbook. If anyone asks, you just keep sayin' you know nothing. Understand?"

Now that he'd seen it, Barnes could barely tear his eyes away from the drug long enough to nod.

Charlie released his grip. "Good. Now, I need you gone tomorrow—just for the night. After that, come and go as you like."

"Where will I go?" Barnes was already preparing his smoking pipe.

"Once that stuff hits, who cares? Stay at a den for the night." Charlie chuckled. "I'll be gone for a week, maybe less, but when

I come back, I'll try to bring more of your precious powder."
Barnes nodded and returned to the *sĭ fĕn* ritual.

VI

THE FOLLOWING EVENING, Max found himself on Charlie's soiled couch. He kept his trench coat on as a layer of protection, though it did little to eliminate a lingering stench of dirty laundry. "So how do you want to do this?" Max eyed the dingy room that was nearly as sparse as the Broadway crime scene save some shelving and the coffee table between them.

Charlie sat in a chair across from the couch. "I miss the days when you'd ask me questions about—"

"Why? So you can give vague answers and tiptoe around the issue? Just tell me everything you know, starting at the beginning."

"Nah, I'm a sucker for tradition." There was a twinkle of mischief in his eye.

"Fine. Who the hell are the Mara?"

Charlie winced and pumped his palms at Max. "Why so loud?"

"You can't think someone will hear us—"

"Somethin's always listening when it comes to them. Best not to call attention to one's self." For the first time in a while, Charlie's eyes held a note of authority. This was something secret that he was imparting on Max, a role they hadn't played out since before Charlie's arrest. "There are certain words you don't go spoutin' off about. They deserve a little...tact. Little reverence."

"See, this is why I wanted you to...fine." Max lowered his voice. "Who are the—"

"The *Others* have been here for a long time—well before us. Least ninety-eight percent of the population know nothin' about 'em."

"Before us?" Max raised his eyebrows. "Like Indians? Are you telling me a bunch of savage Indians scalped those girls?"

"Oh, they're much worse than savages. But they ain't Indians. They ain't human."

Max focused on his breathing and kept the anger from his voice. "Okay. I see what's happening. You want to waste my time to get back at me. That's fine—"

"I told you before, I ain't screwing with you."

"You're just claiming that the killers are a bunch of...what—*creatures*? Intelligent creatures?" Max stood up and headed toward the door.

"You came to me 'cause no one else is willing to give you shit on these things. Bet even Shin Sho turned you down, huh? No way you'd visit me before him."

Max turned from the door. "You got thirty seconds to change my mind."

"You don't really think Shin Sho could be scared of somethin' human. He's a master, and even he knows not to divulge information," Charlie said. "Makes my claims a bit more plausible, eh?"

Max walked back to the soiled couch. "So non-human monsters killed those girls?"

"Didn't say that. But I did answer your question. Next!"

"Okay. Let's say I believe you. How could such a thing be kept under wraps? You're talking about humans dealing with *non-human creatures?*"

"They're lizard-like, and only a few humans deal with 'em. Those with the mark." Charlie flashed his right palm and Max saw what he had always thought was a birthmark become clearer. It was a circular image scarred into the flesh of his hand. "And you know very well why this knowledge don't get out." Charlie smiled, his thin cheeks sallow and grim. "No one wants to end up like Jeff Poppens."

"Then why are you risking a similar death to tell me?"

"I don't know. Gut feelin' says I have to share this with you. Next question."

Max placed his hands on his knees, reminding himself to remain receptive. Maybe this was all symbolic. Perhaps somebody *was* listening to them somehow and Max had to decipher what Charlie was saying between the lines. Though that was becoming more doubtful with each question. "Where do these things reside?"

"A City buried below us."

"Is this some kind of riddle?"

"No. Literally. A giant metropolis carved into the rock with earth above and below. Have you seen the crowded streets of New York? Chicago?"

"I did go to university. Studied history my whole life. Of course I've—"

"And yet you still wound up a cop."

He almost stood back up, but leaving wasn't going to change the situation. "Yeah, I've seen photos of those places."

"Well, that's what it's like 'cept minus the high-rises. Not much different from Chinatown either. A giant bazaar, home to humans and Others alike, shops, peddlers, and street performers. Brick housings built high toward the surface, crammed with tenants. Delicacies and shows. Stone temples of architecture. Old and new machines. And lights. Lights like ya never seen before, a constant glow fakin' daylight, allowing life to thrive."

"They mirror us?"

"Somewhat," Charlie said. "Primitive in some ways. Advanced in others. Hell, I seen devices there—inventions—stuff nobody on the surface has seen yet...then a few months later, bam!" He pounded his fist in his palm. "A company releases a patent for something new. Like there's a store house feedin' technology to people. And in The City—just like here—there are safer places and dangerous places...you have to know where to go for what you're lookin' for. And man's law don't apply. The

Others maintain order."

"How can there be peace with no laws?"

"They maintain order. You can find peace there. You can also find hell. They just maintain the balance."

"I…" Max shook his head and sighed. "I can't—"

"It's madness, yeah?" Charlie laughed.

"I'm glad you can see my predicament." Covering his face with his fingers, Max massaged energy back into his tired, dry eyes.

"It's all true. And when you finally see them…" Charlie got a far off look in his eyes. "They're like humans but covered in scales. Almost reptilian, snout-like noses. Not green, though. More like every tint and shade of red. And their eyes… You'll never be the same."

Max kept his eyes closed, envisioning these lizard people. "Assuming again that I believe all this, how do I gain access to The City?"

"That's the fun part." Charlie held up his scorched palm again.

Max opened his eyes. "I suppose that's the mark?"

"You sure you want in?"

Max gave a soft chuckle. If he walked away from this lead—not that there was any other path to follow at the moment—the fiery momentum would extinguish, and the three girls would fall into a cabinet with all the other cold files. All the cases that ran dry from lack of leads, the same void in which his family resided. Max needed something to believe in if he was to continue, and Charlie was all he had. "As crazy as this sounds, it beats sitting on my ass and a slow death in Chinatown. I have a few debts to pay back with this one. I'll get the mark. I'll do whatever it takes."

"In two days—Saturday—you're gonna join me at this location." Charlie slid a piece of paper across the table. Max picked it up and studied the address. "Meet me there no later than noon."

Max nodded, still looking at the paper. Lost in the chaos of his thoughts, Charlie's voice sounded muted and watery. It took a backseat to the musings of what The City and its denizens looked like.

Charlie snapped his fingers. "Are you listening?"

Max snapped back to the present, glaring at the rude gesture.

"Yeah. I'm listening."

"Good. 'Cause you don't want to screw up down there. There's no luxury of walking away. Now listen…"

"Thomas!" John McCloud took off his gloves as he approached the table and slipped them in his pocket.

Thomas Proctor rose from his seat, his signature grin already stretching across his face. He reached out and shook John's hand, clasping his forearm. "It's good to see you, John."

"Indeed." There was comfort in Thomas's embrace, and after the last few days McCloud needed that.

Thomas sat down and picked up his neat bourbon. "I'm gonna get you one of these," he said still smiling. "You look like you could use it." He burst out in a short round of laughter. And McCloud chuckled too, but more at the fact that Thomas always laughed hardest at his own jokes.

"But to be serious, John. How are you?"

McCloud looked out over the boisterous pub. Lots of ale, lots of smiles. Jerry's Inn was never a sad bar in McCloud's opinion. And Thomas had never been a pessimist in all the years McCloud had known him. "I could tell you I'm fine. But you wouldn't believe that, would you?"

"Not really."

"I guess my life is at a point where I need some of that patented, cure-all and motivating Tom Proctor tonic."

"You make it sound like I'm selling snake oil." Another laugh, then he signaled the waiter for two drinks.

"Well, the minute your speech's spell wears off, I'm back knee-deep in problems."

"You still working as a criminal investigator for the city?"

"As always, you know what's ailing me."

The waiter set down the drinks, and McCloud raised his glass in appreciation.

"Well give me the details and I'll see what magical word concoction I can create to cheer you up."

"I feel like I'm hitting unreasonable obstacles in the department. I'm a good criminal investigator. But I want homicide detective."

"You've been saying that since you left the juvie circuit," Thomas said.

"Exactly." McCloud took a sip, the liquid burned and relaxed his stomach at the same time. "My requests are getting passed over. The few times they give me a shot at a missing persons gig, they give me the coldest cases. Then when I can't dig anything up, they use it against me." He tried to imitate Harris, puffing out his cheeks while he talked: "Well, we gave you the Rodgers case, and Matthews's too. You had some trouble, didn't ya?"

"What makes you think homicide will be any different?"

"Tom, the cases were over a year old. I can't work a miracle."

"What I'm saying, hypothetically, is let's say you do transfer to homicide. What if they stick you with similar cases? Give you a workload with a small success rate?"

"Then I figure out how to get fresh cases," McCloud said.

"If you can figure how to get fresh cases in homicide, just use that same technique in your current position. You'll be assigned to new missing persons cases and problem solved."

Tom's smile widened, but instead of calming McCloud, his rational way of looking at the situation annoyed him. "It's different." There was only a wet ring left in his glass, and McCloud waved to the waiter for another drink.

"Maybe you just *think* it's different," Tom said. "What's your end goal? What is it you want from your career? Because five years ago, I thought I knew what you wanted from your career when I hired you for the juvie department."

"I just want to help as many people as possible."

"You sure you want to hear my response? You probably won't like it."

McCloud sighed. "You're right; I won't. But I contacted you because I need your answer, even if I don't like it…or don't particularly want to hear it."

"You'll help people no matter what you do, John. Helping people isn't a career goal though." Tom gave him an emphatic smile. "It's what happens when you dedicate yourself to something you love. It's the result."

McCloud started on his next drink.

"My point is," Tom said, "It doesn't matter if you're in homicide or criminal investigation, or you design a fingerprint system that the department can use to expedite processing. Your role will be helping people."

"See, when you put it like that, it sounds simple. That's the snake oil." McCloud smirked.

"Why is it snake oil?"

"Because even though it's that simple, my mind doesn't accept that. And no matter where I go, I feel like I'm being hindered. Like I'm not allowed to give my full potential."

"Maybe you need to figure out *how* you want to help people. And perhaps you're being thwarted because crime and homicide is not where you belong."

McCloud closed his eyes, nodded his head with all the speed of a sloth. "Perhaps."

"Feel better?"

McCloud opened his eyes. "I actually do. Like I said, if nothing else you're uplifting for a brief moment. Now enough about me. How have you been?"

"You mean beyond the day job?"

"Does anyone have time for a life beyond our jobs?"

Tom's smile didn't bother him this time. "Most men don't," Thomas said. "Which is why you better pick something you love doing."

VII

Two DAYS LATER, Max put a shirt on over his long underwear. He had to break into the winter clothes box, but it was necessary.

First thing's first. Dress warm. You're underground. It's gonna be cold and damp in places, Charlie's voice reminded him.

Max grabbed his thickest pair of gloves from the box too, slipping them into his trench coat before putting on a white button-up over his two previous layers. Next came his gray vest. Then he picked up his holster, hesitated, and returned it to his drawer.

If you bring a gun, it's on your head. They don't want weapons in The City, unless they supply them.

Max felt this tidbit of information was offered to make him less cautious, more vulnerable by leaving behind his best form of protection. After all, whatever complicated cop/snitch relationship they held a year ago was now as dead as the flesh taken from room 213.

Ignoring the advice, Max picked up the leather holster again and strapped it about his shoulders, then slipped in the revolver.

His tailored jacket was next.

Max then opened the small safe he kept on the floor. He removed a few bundles of cash and filled the new inside pockets he had sewn into his trench coat. He put it on over his suit and studied himself in the mirror, checking the outfit for suspicious bulges and obvious giveaways of the gun or money. It felt surreal having his wife's inheritance—and the last of his savings—strapped inside his coat.

Everything is available to you for the right price. Dollars, pounds, yen. Doesn't matter. The Others deal in all forms of currency. It's the individual's belief on the monetary system rather than the money itself that creates value.

On the dresser beside Charlie's handwritten set of directions to The Edge was a bottle of Express Blended Whiskey. Max took a swig.

With gun, cash, trench coat, and his fedora pulled low, Max left the house. He took the trolley to its last stop, then weaved in and out of ghettos and parts of town he had never seen before. Although he was following Charlie's directions, Max felt lost. The deteriorating neighborhood he walked through didn't help put his mind at ease, either. These were the forgotten towns after the quake; the ones that survived off the limited-governmental aid, but in the end, supported themselves. They answered to no one except their neighbors, and as much as they seemed to hate their lives, they didn't want it any other way. And as a general rule, these kinds of people didn't like outsiders.

When the anxiety had built to a nauseating knot in his stomach, he finally saw the address. 618 East Rippen stood out from the rest of the blight. It looked like an oversized theatre house, the kind that use to run vaudeville shows over the weekends and single plays at night. The structure was by no means immaculate, but it was in better condition than the surrounding buildings. Though that fact didn't exactly put Max at ease. Now that he was standing at the front door, a double-cross seemed like a real possibility.

It was easier to believe that Charlie was finally seeking revenge for his prison sentence than it was to accept a tale of a club that led to an underground world filled with vices and beastly humanoids. Max doubted that the six-month jail stint was equal to murder, but it was probably worth paying thugs in a crappy part of town to beat the tar out of Max and steal all of Eve's insurance money. And he couldn't put such a ruse past Charlie.

Max eased a hand inside his trench coat. The icy claws of paranoia sunk into his mind: one way or another, he had a feeling this case was going to be his last.

With his free hand, Max opened the front door. He stiffened, but didn't draw his weapon on the large man who waited a few feet inside the well-lit building. Around the tweed suit that hugged the man's muscular frame was a lobby that was the day compared to the night of the ghetto it resided in. Red carpet led to a window ticket booth on the far left wall. From the ticket booth, the carpet turned to a small staircase leading to a set of double doors. The walls were barren for a theatre. Absent were the large posters and flyers for upcoming shows and beautiful starlets. There were plants and baroque wallpaper of what could have been gold *fleur de lis*—though the design was too tiny for Max to see—and a gorgeous chandelier in the center of the ceiling.

Max nodded to the man, an uneasy half-smile on his lips. "I'm here to meet someone at The Edge. He and I have an appointment with Goodfellow."

The man considered Max with cold eyes. Max remained passive, but he couldn't shake the thoughts of being patted down and exposing his weapon. With grace, Max moved his hand from the butt of the revolver to a stack of money in his jacket. "I can pay of course." Max slid a bill from inside the bundle and produced it.

"It's ten to the box office." The man nodded toward the wall of ticket booths.

Charlie hadn't been kidding about needing money. Max walked as confidently as he could past the man, and approached the middle booth—the only one with someone behind the glass. *Ten dollars*, he thought, still unable to shake the thought of a setup.

The ticket booth attendant was a skinny male, too skinny. His face resembled a bare skull. Bloodshot eyes bugged out against sunken sockets. His stringy gray hair was thinned to the point that it barely covered his scalp.

Max slid ten dollars through the slot before the repulsive man could say anything. The living skeleton retrieved the money unenthusiastically and lifted his frail arm, one bony finger extended.

Max turned, followed the path of the digit to a wide set of stairs—maybe a dozen steps high. At the landing was a small figure standing beside a set of thick double doors.

"Do I need a ticket or receipt?"

Again, the boney finger raised in silence. The man's lifeless eyes gazed through Max.

Taking the hint, Max headed to the staircase. As he ascended the steps, Max could hear the muffled sounds of revelry pulsating from behind the double doors. He paused halfway up, shocked by the one painting in the whole lobby. Hanging above the double doors was a Hindu painting of a naked, headless woman. A scimitar in one hand, her own severed head in the other, and from her cranial stump spurted three arcs of blood. Two of the blood streams were collected in bowls held by two wild looking women dancing below her headless body. The third fountain landed in the mouth of the severed head. The vibrant colors were splendid in their beauty, yet the image left an unsettling impression on Max at the same time. *Chinnamasta* was printed across a small plaque below the painting.

Reaching the top, Max stopped before a short man who reminded him of a dwarf he had once seen at a traveling carnival.

"Welcome to The Edge." The man offered a twisted smile and tugged one of the doors open.

Max stepped into a giant theatre. He stood in awe as the heavy door creaked closed behind him. A smiling woman stood at a podium a few feet in front of him, her hair a fiery orange. Her body clothed in a silk and satin dress with embroidered net overlay—which looked far too expensive for anyone living in this side of town. Max looked past the prim host, his eyes straining through the smoky haze and dim lighting at the spectacle before him.

The floor had been gutted of the generic stadium seating from which plays were generally viewed; in their place was a sea of round tables. They were draped in black tablecloths, a candle burned on each. Men and women of various races occupied the seats, most dressed elegantly, though even those who were least prestigious still had on their Saturday best. At some tables it appeared that the patrons were playing cards and dominoes. The only lighting in the audience, as far as Max could see, was the candles. They created a mass-like ambience of the old Roman Catholic days. But there was something dark and unwholesome about the type of prayers offered up in a place like this.

The stage, like the theatre seating, had also been modified to something unlike any stage Max had ever seen a play on. A long catwalk extended from the mainstage about twenty feet in between the tables. From there, it split again, this time left and right, creating a cross. The wooden modifications cut runway paths through the round tables. They were lit by red and purple stage lights. The lack of sufficient white lighting created shadows and an eerie-colored haze to the tobacco smoke that drifted overhead.

Max couldn't be sure from his vantage point, but it appeared that there were women dancing upon various locations of the stage. The music that filled the theatre seemed to be sitar or other traditional Eastern tunes; perhaps Egyptian. He knew of cabarets and burlesque shows, seen the pictures of the Moulin Rouge and the famous Grand Guignol, though Max never thought he'd experience something so fantastic and unique in person.

Over the music the redhead behind the podium said: "A table, sir?"

"I'm meeting someone. The reservation should be for Charlie Willis."

She looked down at a list. "Ah, then you must be Mr. Elliot. Please, follow me."

Max kept pace just behind the woman as she weaved them between tables, stopping at one to the far right of the main stage. Charlie was seated there, dressed in the same mismatched suit, hat on the table.

"Here you are, sir. Enjoy." She left with a smile and an unobstructed view of the main stage and one of the adjacent runways. Three women danced in time to the music, gyrating, seductive. Their two-piece costumes accentuated deep tanned flesh and slender abdomens. While the billowing silk pants, bras sparkling with all manner of jewelry, scarfs, and veils showcased their exoticness, the garments covered much of their bodies, leaving Max's imagination to wonder what they looked like below those painted eyes and lips.

"Damn." Max sat and it took a moment before he could break his gaze and look at Charlie.

"Welcome to The Edge." Charlie lifted his arms. "This club here is your last stop before the underground. Once a week they celebrate The City with a twenty-four-hour festival. It's the only time they accept new visitors."

"Impressive," Max said. "Let me guess, today is that day?"

"Sometimes ya get lucky, huh?"

"Here you go." A waitress took a highball of clear liquid off her tray and placed it on the table in front of Max.

"What's this?" he asked, though in her evening dress with plume motifs, more French than American, she did not seem like a waitress.

"It's *mogjiŭ*," she said, the hint of a laugh creeping into her voice, then she moved back into the pulsing music and crowd to deliver more drinks.

Max lifted the glass and smelled it. There wasn't much of an odor. He looked at Charlie. "*Mogjiŭ?*"

"Yeah." His laugh was high-pitched and nasally. "It's all they serve here. So don't waste your time asking for whiskey."

"Is it alcohol?"

"Sort of." Charlie raised a glass of his own clear liquid. "To new experiences."

Their glasses clinked, then Max took a sip, the liquid cold as it slid down his throat. Though slightly bitter, it was not unpleasant.

"How is it?"

Max felt a bit lightheaded. "Not bad." Almost immediately a sense of calm confidence seemed to wash over him. "Mogjiŭ, huh?"

"*Mogjiŭ* is what most people call it. Sure it's called by other names too. You learn that once ya stick around for a while. People come from all over and each with their own words for things."

Charlie took another sip. "But it does the trick, same as all alcohol."

Max found the glass rose to his lips more frequent than he intended. He savored the sip longer than anticipated too. Before he knew it, the highball was empty. "It does seem to be working." He was loose. Very alert still, but whatever the drink was, he felt good. "If there's so many different people, do they speak English?"

"Because of the location, yes, they do. I wonder if there are other cities around the world though." Charlie stared off, fixated on the girls.

Max looked at the beads of condensation rolling down the sides of the glass. Fears of a revenge plot by Charlie dripped away with the sweating surface. Then the waitress was back and a drink was once again in his hand; Charlie's too.

"To old times," Charlie said, returning his attention to Max.

Guilt welled up like a lead ball in Max's throat and made his voice crack, jaunting the pronunciation of the words. "To old times." He almost apologized for last year but caught himself and swallowed a large gulp of *mogjiŭ* instead. Nothing good could come from stirring up the past.

"You feel relaxed?" Charlie said.

"Yeah."

Charlie looked at his watch. "Good. They'll be coming for us soon. And you'll thank a painkiller like *mogjiŭ*." Charlie read his face. "You gotta do it; only those with the mark can move back and forth. One must choose to be marked."

"I just don't get it; how can this place remain a secret?"

"I'm sure there's lot of things you just don't get, Max." Charlie leaned back in his seat. Lowered his voice. "Don't mean they ain't real."

Max kept his mouth shut.

"Did you bring money?" Charlie asked.

"Plenty."

A dark woman in her thirties approached the table. She wore a black mourning dress; her face was placid. "Mr. Elliot? Mr. Willis? It's time for your appointment."

The following events were a blur. Partly because the *mogjiŭ* made him focus less on his body, as if his head was simply floating through the crowd, but also because things were moving fast…or maybe the time distortion was just the *mogjiŭ* too. He couldn't be sure.

In what felt like mere minutes, the woman led Charlie and him away from the cultural dance and music show and up to the next floor. Before Max knew it, they were in a small office, the dying embers of a log in the fireplace, and a larger than life man seated behind an equally large desk. The office had an oriental feel to it, with Japanese paintings of bonsai trees and lengthy scrolls lining the bamboo-plated walls. The hodgepodge of international influence, from the French-inspired theatre to the Victorian dresses and now this, felt like a preparation for the melting pot Charlie spoke of below.

Past the man and desk was an electric elevator. Max did a double take at the lift. Electric elevators were unheard of in a building this old.

Before Max could question, Charlie flashed his palm at the large man and headed to the back of the office, to the open elevator doors. "Some things you gotta do alone," he said over his shoulder. "Goodfellow'll take care of you." The gears of the lift doors groaned to life and before they closed Charlie said, "Meet ya on the other side."

Max was left alone with the bulky man and the metallic clanging of the elevator.

The knot of unease twisted back into his intestines. Max fought off the sedating effects of the *mogjiŭ* as Goodfellow motioned to a chair in front of the desk. It didn't help that the width of the wooden chair and the straps built into the armrest conjured stories of hopeless asylums and painful electrocution therapy.

Max took slow steps, scanning the corners of the room, paranoid thoughts of a double cross continually springing up in his mind. The closer he got, the more stoic Goodfellow looked with his dark eyes and the unseen expression beneath his bushy beard. When he sat in the chair, the butt of Max's own pistol pressing into his side was comforting.

"You are here to conduct business with those known as The Mara?" Goodfellow's voice was emotionless, the simple recitation of a script that had lost meaning to him long ago.

"Yes."

"Only those with the mark can do business with Maras. You are here to be marked?"

Max glanced at the chair restraints. "Yes."

"Do you understand the commitment that comes with knowing the Mara?"

"I believe so," Max said.

"Do not make any attempt to bring The City's existence to the public eye. Do not attempt to bring contraband from below to the surface without permission. Realize that you have complete freedom of choice within The City. Understand that every decision you make comes with a consequence."

Goodfellow took a strip of leather from the desk drawer and tossed it to him, then stood. Max couldn't appreciate his size while seated, but when he walked to the fireplace, Max could feel the gravity of dominance that a six-foot-four man built like a brick wall carried to a situation. Goodfellow pulled an iron from the burning embers. Max felt his balls tighten and tingle in his stomach.

"Strap your left hand into the chair, palm up."

Max's blood was rushing, and he felt the pounding most in his throat and eyes. He could accept being branded for life—a permanent reminder of the lengths he went to save Leigh Anne—but tying his hand left him at the mercy of this brutish stranger.

Goodfellow held the iron before him, waiting, its circular head glowed orange, wafts of smoke curling off its metal emblem. "You don't want to jerk around during this."

Max thought of the dirty bars and dens he'd frequented over the last six months. The strung-out gamblers. His empty home. Those were the only things he seemed to have left, and they didn't define him. They masked his final fear: death. And when he thought about it, death was the one thing he shouldn't fear. It could be his ultimate escape.

Max laid his arm down and used his right hand to bind the leather strap at his wrist. Goodfellow started toward him and Max could better see the thinly cut intricacy of the metal, like a wax seal, not thick and clunky like a cattle brand. He clenched the leather hide between his jaws.

The giant now hovered over the left side of the chair, and Max tensed, ready to receive the searing pain.

Goodfellow disappeared behind him and before Max could evaluate the change, Goodfellow grabbed the detective's right wrist from behind, using his body weight to drive Max's whole arm into the chair. At the same time, he pressed the brand into Max's left palm.

Max grunted, chomping down on the leather. Flinging his head back, he connected with Goodfellow's massive chest and stomped his foot on the ground.

"Done," Goodfellow whispered.

Max felt his body released, but it didn't soothe the pain which somehow burned both cold and hot at the same time. The smell of burnt skin tickled his nose, and Max looked at his fingers, gnarled in anguish. A painful throbbing pulsed in his ears. Over its roar, he swore he still heard the sizzling sound of flesh.

Goodfellow returned with a glass bottle of clear liquid. "This will help keep it clean." He pulled the cork and poured a generous amount onto Max's palm.

"*Jesus.*" Max gritted his teeth as the burn flared up again. He fumbled with the wet strap, and, once freed, brought the tender hand to his chest, breathing deep, trying to ignore his senses, and focusing on calming himself.

While Max wallowed in silent discomfort, Goodfellow returned to his desk and produced a leather ledger. He undid its metal clasp and opened the book to the middle using a red ribbon marker. Taking ink and quill from the drawer, Goodfellow scrawled in the book.

"Name."

"Max Elliot."

"Sign, please." The ledger was pushed to Max and a pen was put into his good hand.

The burnt nerve endings of his left hand were receding into a constant, dull ache and Max scrawled his signature as best he could, biting his lip. When he finished, Goodfellow closed the ledger and removed two glasses from the desk drawer. He uncorked the bottle again and filled both cups.

"This will ease the pain." Goodfellow actually smiled as he raised his own glass. As impossible as it seemed, somehow, the *mogjiŭ* was still cold, even being stuck in a drawer. Ingestion was more fun than topical disinfectant, and it took only a minute for the liquid to untangle Max's intestines. His breathing became less labored, and calm took the place of the ache. A sense of victory surrounded him. He was branded, accepted into this bizarre new order. Now he could finally investigate The City.

VIII

Max stood in the same electric lift as Charlie had earlier. Goodfellow nodded a farewell and the doors creaked shut. Max lurched with the start of the descent, but he felt quite pleased and confident. His hand even felt good now; strange considering that the flesh had raised to a red welt that resembled a circle widened at one point with intricate designs.

Five minutes in, the elevator ride became less smooth. Pressure built in his ears, then dissipated after bouts of yawning. The lift car began to rock and Max gripped the handrail. Another two minutes slipped by. He flopped from excitement to fear; he was truly under the ground. It wasn't possible; it was insane. What if—

The lift came to a jarring halt and Max fell against the back wall. The electric hum was gone; all that remained was the echo of his breathing. No movement, and Max was sure the elevator was broken. Panic enveloped his mind like a cloak, the thought of being stuck underground, buried alive and forced to die one shallow breath at a time...

Then the doors parted to darkness, and a damp, chill air greeted him. The dim elevator light bulb penetrated just enough to see a room of sorts, wood walls and floors, the planks warped with age and moisture. Granite shards and dirt reached out through the fissures between the wood—earthen hands attempting to push away the foreign material. Max thought of the gold rush and the miners, the men who excavated the earth, breaking for lunch and rest in such a room.

He took wary steps from the elevator, pausing, watching, but Charlie was not waiting for him. Nothing was waiting for him. The rollercoaster of nerves inside his body that had revved up after his branding now plummeted into another pit of self-doubt. Every bested obstacle was a dizzying high of success, but each peak was matched by an equally deep well of uncertainty.

He forced himself to banish doubt and thoughts of failure. He had to view this as just the next challenge, and Max knew it was better to push forward rather than sit still and analyze the ups and downs until it killed him. He embraced the confidence of the *mogjiŭ* and continued full steam, making his way to the corner of the tiny room where a set of descending stairs could be seen. A dull glow reached up the cave wall with tendrils of light from the darkness below.

Max focused on the excavated stairwell, and as his eyes adjusted, he saw cutouts in the rock walls holding kerosene lamps every ten yards or so. With a deep breath, he began down the narrow passage. After a few minutes, the steps molded of earth and clay turned to chiseled rock and the cold nipped at his face as Max traveled deeper underneath Chinatown.

Only the sounds of his breathing and footsteps, bouncing off the cold rock around him, met his ears. Then, after fifty more feet, he heard something beyond his laborious breath. Not just random sound or voices, but the hubbub and cacophony of life. The narrow hallway widened, then completely opened and the darkness retreated as Max stepped into a cavernous world.

Now he was there. And by God, Charlie was right. The stuff of legends!

The earth had been hollowed out and an enormous, blackened stone wall stretched across the cavern. At its apex, the wall ended maybe one hundred yards from the rocky ceiling. Ahead of him was an opening in the wall and an archway built at least thirty or forty feet from the ground. Through the opening, Max saw civilization that stretched as far he could see. If not for the jagged cave ceiling one would never know they were underground. Especially since there was illumination from buildings and light posts, a soft glow that didn't quite mimic the sun but offered almost a recreation of near dusk. The artificial sunlight swelled up over the high encampment around The City and through the archway.

Max shuffled up to the stone entrance, marveling at symbols carved into its bricks. Their meanings were foreign but filled him with a sense of archaic wisdom. All along, a part of him had worried that this would end as a wild goose chase. A set-up to a fantastic lie. But The City was here. It was the truth. And Max had to assume that so were all the other stories. If so, those symbols should probably read: *Abandon all hope ye who enter here.*

He spent another few minutes staring into the walled world, a sense of hesitation consuming him, rooting his feet so he couldn't pass under the arch. There was a feeling of finality, that once he crossed over the threshold, there was no coming back. He'd seen heroin overdoses before and wondered if the user knew that a particular ride was their last. Did they feel it in their gut, their bones? Did they immediately wish they could undo the hit or take just a little less? Was this that moment for Max or had he passed that long ago?

Did it even matter?

Maybe he'd find his daughter. Maybe this would be the greatest puzzle. Maybe not. Max looked back to the darkness of the earthen stairs he'd just come from. Either way, there was nothing back there for him. The option of retreat had been off his consideration list for a while now. His barren apartment wasn't a home. Hell was home to him now, and he'd keep it in his heart.

Stepping under the archway, Max entered The City.

IX

MAX MOVED SLOWLY down the cobblestone roads that branched out from the entrance, crisscrossing in a labyrinth. Every block was noted with a ten-foot obelisk. Some were accompanied by similar pillar stones, but these pillars differed from the obelisks in one way: they were missing the triangular apex, and instead the pillar terminated in a glowing ball—The City's version of light. All the obelisks and pillars had one or more symbols chiseled into them. No wires connected the stone light posts, but each one bathed the street vendors barking at the milling crowds and the people buying inedible-looking food from wheeled carts.

Max passed groups of performers—both young men and women—dancing, playing music, offering tricks and games, all with hats turned up on the ground, hoping for tips. Lining the streets were various brick shops, tall town houses, and shoddy apartment buildings. Clotheslines were strung across the alleys between the complexes. Exquisite buildings of luxury craftsmanship shared space with the flea-market, canopy style of Indian bazaars.

The air smelled of smoke from cooking food and the aroma of the delicacy changed every ten feet. Some shops smelled of boiled meats, others the sinus-stinging cleanse of faraway spices. And the people were just as varied. For every American gentleman and Edwardian Brit Max saw, there was an Asian, Spanish, Indian, or African counterpart. Their clothes were distinct and different, yet most of the purveyors shared a layer of what his grandpa called "elbow grease". When a person put in an honest day's work, toiling in their own efforts, they got this look and feel about them; even their clothes developed a hardworking characteristic.

The customers didn't seem to share much else in common except for the circumstances bringing them together. Max saw shades of skin tone that were unknown to him until now and heard languages that pleased his ear and some that grated at it.

Three children in tattered clothes swooped in, squawking and grabbing at Max's hand, breaking him from the awe of his trance. Two of them rattled off words in a language Max didn't recognize.

"We can help take you places," the third little boy said. "Where you wanna go?"

Max jerked his hand away from the kids, lowered his head, and pushed through the crowds, hustling around a corner to a less populated area. Music and drunken signing poured out from an open bar door. Max slumped against its side wall to orient himself. This was more overwhelming than he had expected.

Where the hell was Charlie?

Max let a few minutes pass, catching his breath and contemplating his two choices: Stay put and wait for Charlie or push on and look for the type of brothels Charlie had suggested they investigate first.

Max took a deep breath and stepped back into the main roadway. Reminding himself to evaluate the environment with detective eyes instead of with awe, the inhabitants of this new land seemed to slow down. He looked at the forks in the paths and the labyrinth of obelisk-style street signs and pillars marked in sigils similar to those on the archway. Precise hieroglyphics like the ruins of Mesopotamia, their carved lines were unknown to him, yet still spoke to an unconscious part of Max. As if prodding him awake, trying to remind him of something that he must have once known eons ago, but had been lost to him through the ages. Steam rose from hot spots battling the underground chill, creating a strange, wispy fog of mystery.

After choosing to go right, Max's confidence grew. *It's just a city*, he told himself. The maze-like streets, shops and homes lining the cobblestone paths were no different in structural layout from the overcrowded European villas or Sicilian towns built into the very rock itself.

Better yet, it was a puzzle box. And he just needed to find the right move to crack it.

Max noticed patterns within the strange bazaar after only three blocks. He stopped a hundred feet before what looked like a rundown theatre house, smaller than The Edge. Instead of the names of plays, the marquee held a medium-sized wooden plaque. The wood had a depression, about three by five feet, cut into the treated lumber. The edges of the panel were carved in elegant, flower-like decorations. The depression itself was painted a deep shade of red. There seemed to be a similar building with a colored marquee every block. Sometimes a foreign word or name appeared too. But they all shared the same wooden panel. The only differences were the colors displayed.

"That's not the show you're looking for." The voice meeting his ear was smooth and confident, and the man speaking them emerged from an outcropping between buildings. He was tall, even with the hunch in his back, forcing him forward just below the shoulders. His left hand rested on a black cane; a top hat sat on shoulder-length hair.

"And I suppose you know what I'm looking for." Max rotated his back toward the brick wall so no one could sneak up on him.

"You desire the forbidden pleasures that a red show can never offer." The man's right hand shot forward, a black business card between his thumb and index finger.

Max looked up at the marquee and its blood red panel, then at the card in the man's hand. "What makes you think I'd want something beyond a red show?"

The man raised his card to Max's eye level. "You want the ultimate experience—Gehanna has no-limit, black shows."

Max took the card, its front a pure abyss of the blackest ink, the back a brilliant white, with an address written in numbers and symbols. "If the red show doesn't give me all I need, I'll be sure to visit."

"I hope you do." The man gave a raspy laugh and slunk back into the shadows.

Max pocketed the business card and looked at the door below the theatre's marquee. He heard light footsteps, then a white form came into his periphery. Max turned, a young girl dressed in a tight white jacket-and-trouser suit, stained gray from years of underground work, stood beside him. He stared at her, but she was looking at the red door that previously held Max's attention.

"Can I help you?" Max asked.

"Nope. But I can help you." She looked at him with a sly grin.

"Everyone down here is a pitchman, huh?"

"You're so fresh even a human can smell the burnt skin on your hand. Without a trustworthy guide, they're gonna swindle you. I'm your best bet right now."

Her features reminded him of the black-haired adolescent host who had prepared his last pipe at Ku's den. But while that kid's soft smooth face had made the boy look almost androgynous, this teen had a feminine quality about her that surpassed her age. Max's years of profiling pegged her around sixteen. But something about the way she held herself and those eyes made her much older. Like she'd already experienced some of the challenges that awaited the Chinese host if he stayed at the opium den.

"I'm fine. Just looking for someone."

"You may have fooled that black-show creep, but you don't fool me. If this person you're looking for *does* exist, it'll be near impossible to find 'em." She stepped closer but was still more than an arm's length away. "This place is about thirty square miles, and you're new here. Face it, mister, you'll be lost in no time without a guide. Not all people and places in this city are as friendly as me."

Max looked out at the complex network of street vendors and brick buildings. He cursed Charlie and looked back at the teen. "So what's your offer?"

"A beginner's tour of The City. You pay me for each destination reached."

"Deal." He held out a hand. "I'm Max Elliot."

"Ming." She stepped forward, grasped and released his hand

in a quick squeeze, then was back out of his reach. She turned, her black braid of hair whipping through the air, and took off down the road. "Let's go."

She moved deftly through the crowds, never pausing to check the obelisk signposts. Max struggled to follow her, mumbling apologies to those he bumped, taking long quick strides to keep pace.

"Doing okay?" She slowed and looked back at him.

"Sure, sure. Just taking it all in." Max gave a weak laugh. "Didn't figure on you being so quick."

"Gotta be fast. Time is money."

Ming led him to a park bench, minus the park, in front of what Max assumed was a hospital. A giant cross, more pink than red from years of weathering, had been painted on the structure's chipped brick wall. They took a seat and she held out her hand. "You're American. You got dollars?"

Max looked around. The crowds and merchants were less dense here as were the buildings. The whole area seemed wider. From the bench, Max could see into the maze at several openings, following their paved walkways as they narrowed into bottlenecks far away.

Max placed a dollar bill in her hand. "So why are we here?"

"Tour starts here. The City is basically a giant market where people live. Most people buy tickets to shows or plays. Colors let you know what you're gonna watch. But you can buy and sell anything here. You tell me what you want, and I take you there." She held up her finger. "But I don't participate. I'll wait outside if you pay me. Many places as you want; when you find exactly what you need, you can dismiss me."

"Sounds fair."

Ming pointed at the cross above them. "Commit this landmark to your mind. The Ward is the border between the East and West Ends. And your first decision." She studied him with dark eyes that seemed to pass no judgement. "What are you looking for here that you can't find above ground?" Her voice was as indifferent as her eyes. But even her strictly-business attitude could not alleviate his anxiety of telling this guide—who only looked to be a few years older than his own daughter—where he needed to go.

Well, before this rat named Charlie hung me out to dry, he told me we'd search the brothels first. Care to take me to a house of prostitution?

"Would you believe me if I said I didn't know?"

"Not a chance. But I'm willing to play along—more money for me in the end. We'll start here on the edge and work our way east." Ming's eyes hardened. "It's quicker and cheaper if you wanna be honest with me though."

"Starting here works fine for me." Max couldn't help being impressed by this fearless girl.

"Suit yourself."

"So what's the deal with the colors?"

"Whenever you see a marquee with long rectangular painted panels, you know it's a live-action theatre. When the panels are small squares, it's an exhibit of pictures or art. And the color tells you what's gonna happen. Gold and blue represent artistic events like music, dance; it's usually exotic. When there's nudity, it's not at the levels of other colors. Burlesque, I think you'd call it."

Max focused on a theatre in the distance, avoiding the girl's gaze. She hadn't flinched when saying *exotic* or *nudity*. Two words that he never expected to come from the lips of a sixteen-year-old, let alone spoken to him. But he didn't stop her; he had to know everything. "What's the red show?"

"A red show means there'll be blood."

He looked back and Max found himself mesmerized by her dark eyes, which still held no tone of emotion.

"And these black shows in Gehanna?"

Ming looked to her left. "Gehanna is what they call the deepest part of West End. Lots of rumors about that place. I've never been and I don't plan on it. The East is often referred to as She'ol. If you want a black show or to visit Gehanna then you don't need me."

Her tone made Max embarrassed he'd even asked. He remained silent, half hoping she'd change the subject while the other half of him wished she'd continue about the taboo destination.

"Purple signifies a *sǐ fěn* house," she said.

"I know a bit about that stuff," Max said. "Powerful drug, right?"

"Ever done it?" Ming asked.

"No. What's it like?"

"I only know what people tell me, mister. I heard it can be different every time because of how the powder is made. But it's like living in dreams…just make sure to clear your schedule. The hangover knocks you out for a while."

"What about gambling?" He thought of Charlie, hoping to ignore that aching allure of the new drug and the itch inside that chided him to take a brief break and smoke some. If he could just keep his momentum though he'd be fine; an occupied mind and new leads would prevent that small voice from turning to begging pleas. Max wasn't a drug addict. He was an escapist of reality—addicted to the relief that came with letting everything go. The vice he employed to reach his escape didn't matter; *sǐ fěn* sounded as wonderful as opium or booze right now.

"Betting is everywhere. The stakes…" Ming's lips formed a thin, contemplative line. "Well, if someone values it, you can gamble it."

That sounded like Charlie's paradise as well as a personal hell. Maybe he'd gotten sidetracked while waiting for Max. "My friend is quite a gambler—I was truthful about looking for someone. Will you take me to the best gambling club?"

"The best? That's all opinion, Mister Elliot. I'll take you to the one with the most varied games."

From there they moved in silence, Ming leading him through winding streets of repetition. There were no automobiles, trolleys, or hansom cabs. Pedestrians rode bikes, rickshaws, or walked. All housing seemed to resemble the shared condos and tall apartment buildings on the surface. Rags trudged alongside tailored suits. The mingling of classes here was something Max had never experienced before. Above ground, status was everything. Eve and he were never invited to black-tie dinners. The Police Gala they attended at the Mayor's mansion was the closest they'd come, and the invitation had been delivered with a note reminding officers to only wear their decorative dress blues. The poor did not rub elbows with the rich.

But in The City, they did.

It was as if the citizen's knowledge of this hidden world, along with whatever vices they enjoyed together overcame any distain they held for one another. And Max figured he'd learn soon why such a place could bond deeper than money.

א

As THEY WALKED, Max was happy Ming didn't attempt small talk with him or ask more about his mission. It was easier to spend the trip in his mind, hypothesizing various scenarios to explain Charlie's disappearance as well as try and formulate a new plan. One that didn't include Charlie Willis.

"Here we are. One of the biggest casinos in She'ol."

The structure was massive. Nothing like the underground clubs in Chinatown. It was a resort. Unlike skyscrapers on the East Coast that were built upward, this casino—a term he'd only heard once or twice before—was built wide. A stretched balcony ran between two floors for at least a thousand feet.

Max gave her a dollar. "I'm not sure how long I'll be. But perhaps wait in the vicinity for a bit or check in later. If I don't find my friend, I wouldn't mind employing your services for a while." He pulled out another bill. "Insurance?"

Ming snatched the extra dollar. "I'll be in the area. Keep my eyes open for ya. No hard feelings if I get a better gig or you find what you're looking for."

"Yeah, no hard feelings." He turned from her, but she caught his arm.

"Another tip: I understand why you don't want to tell me, but the pit boss won't know where to send you unless you speak up about what you really want."

"Pit boss?"

"The Mara in charge." She raised her eyebrows. "You've seen them before, right?"

Max thought of Charlie's unbelievable descriptions of the local race. Creatures born before us, here since the beginning. "I know you don't participate…but any chance you want to take me around inside?"

"You really have a no clue about them. Do you?"

"Thanks for your discretion," Max said, eyeing passersby.

"It's gonna cost more for me to make an introduction."

Max held out another dollar.

"Two," Ming said. "And you gotta level with me about what you're looking for."

"Three," Max said. "And you don't ask any more questions. Just answer mine."

"Look at that." Ming smirked. "You're already learning how to do business around here." Ming pocketed the bills. "Others have names, but humans rarely use them. A consistent title is easier. Casinos have pit bosses. Most shows and brothels have concierges. Their job is to find out what you want, and make sure you're happy."

Ming opened the front door; a narrow staircase ascended to a dim second level. Each step brought a stronger smell of smoke, and a low murmur of activity hummed above them. At the top of the stairs, Max saw a figure behind a wooden podium. Two more steps and he paused.

Ming continued without him and stopped on the landing next to something that shouldn't be alive. It had to be a realistic costume, statue, or a theatre prop from some play about mythology and demons. Ming waved him upward and the humanoid—which was the only term Max could use to describe the figure—stood silently waiting. Max's next steps came slow as he made his way to stand slightly behind Ming.

The creature's mouth parted in a gleaming bone-white smile

and Max hoped his gasp hadn't been too noticeable. The humanoid was dressed in a gray suit. There was no hair on its exposed body parts, just leathery skin, textured like a snake. Max couldn't say that the thing in front of him was light red, but it—he?—wasn't the color of any flesh Max had seen in his life. It was of similar height and weight as Max. The smile revealed two rows of teeth, sharpened almost to a point, like canine's teeth. It had two arms and five fingers—just like a human.

"And what are we looking for, little girl?" The voice, so deceptive in its soothing tones, clashed with the cold, animalistic appearance of the creature. But more importantly, it could talk. Charlie hadn't lied to him yet, and still Max couldn't believe that it was actually happening.

There were such things as monsters. And Max was here to battle them.

"I need to hire him a shadow." Ming hitched a thumb at Max. "A pass for a novice. He's paying in American dollars."

The reptilian creature leaned forward and Max involuntarily shifted away. But the monstrosity didn't attempt to swallow the detective's skull; instead its gaze rose and fell over Max with painful scrutiny. The pit boss Mara, the Other, blinked and an inner set of vertical eye lids closed. He inhaled violently, the slits in his bump of a nose expanding. The inhuman eyes opened and searched deep within Max's, unsettling him on a new level. The Mara stood back.

"Five American dollars for unlimited access and safe passage…within reason." He held out a leathery hand, a short but thick ivory talon curling from each fingertip.

"Give him the money," Ming said.

"What exactly am I buying here?" Max asked as he handed over the cash, dreamlike as his hand passed the bills to something that his rational mind said could not exist on this earth.

Ming answered: "You get to use the club today same as a member would—the full experience. And you have the promise that if you get tripped up or make a newbie mistake, a Mara will step in so nobody gets angry and tries something. They'll shadow you from afar."

"So long as your blunder is due to lack of experience with customs of a game or City etiquette." The Mara placed Max's bills inside his suit jacket. "If you cause deliberate trouble, then we deal with you. Understood?"

"Yeah." Max looked over at Ming. "Thought that's what I paid you for."

"I don't do shows, remember?" She flashed that smirk again and took two steps down the stairs. "Don't worry. I'll be around."

Her footsteps down were swallowed up by noise as the Mara opened the door to their right. Max spilled into the decadence of music and smoke drifting between tables that stretched as far as he could see. If this was what the upstairs had to offer, he wondered what was kept on the ground level.

Max scanned the faces, most human and male. Skin tones from all corners of the world. Grimy teeth and dirty clothes rubbed alongside well-groomed aristocrats. Different dialects. But all with the same greedy hands.

He homed in on the few reptilian faces overseeing the crowd, but none appeared to be more focused on Max than another. Not that identifying his hired shadow would make things less stressful. Either way, he was putting trust in this place, and that in itself was dangerous.

Trust Ming.

Though he had no reason to put any faith in the voice, or Ming, beyond the obvious fact that she had no motives to lie to Max. None that he could see anyway.

He continued along the game tables where men dealt cards and threw dice. Checkers, chess, and dominoes led the way to other set-ups he'd never seen before. There was even a mechanical machine that resembled a mutated telephone that patrons fed quarters to and lights blazed and blared during victories. But there was no sign of Charlie Willis.

Max approached a bar on the far wall. To the right of it was a double door exit. Or perhaps an entrance. All previous doors were on his right and led to the balcony. These were the first inside doors. And they were painted black.

Max leaned against the bar and put a quarter on the countertop as the bartender approached. Thankful to be speaking to a human, Max said: "How much whiskey can I get for this?"

The bartender placed a glass on the counter and pulled a bottle of clear liquid from below. "All we serve is *mogjiŭ*." He pushed the glass and quarter back to Max. "It's on the house."

Max lifted the drink to his lips, tried to smell it without attracting too much attention. "Special deal for a novice?"

"*Mogjiŭ* never costs down here. Neither does *fěn*."

The man retreated to another customer and Max took a sip. He had always preferred the numbness of alcohol to the opium. Opium was too lethargic. But the booze often made him too destructive. As the *mogjiŭ* slithered into his gut, he was finding that this new drink was a great alternative to both.

Max's gaze went back to the watchful forms of the Maras. Several wore the snug tailored vests and suits of the upper echelon, but a few of them who lined the walls wore robes, cinched at the waist with rope. The suits seemed to do the talking, but that didn't mean they held the real power. If there was a pecking order to the species, perhaps the robed clan was superior in some way.

Max studied the black doors. His hand felt for the black business card in his trench coat, his mind replayed Ming's firm distaste of the color.

He raised the glass again to his lips, surprised to find it empty. Perhaps *mogjiŭ* was a dangerous alternative if he drank this quickly.

"'Nother one?"

Max almost told the bartender yes. He stopped his head in mid nod, breathed. "I guess not. What's behind those doors?"

The bartender looked down at Max's scarred hand. The intricacies of the brand were beginning to show as the swelling went down. A circular emblem resembling a snake. Scales adorned its body, a single eye denoted the head and its tail originated from its open mouth. This time the symbol was familiar, something Greek he'd seen when studying history books, but the name eluded him.

"Oughta have another drink if you're planning on going in there," the bartender said.

"That bad, huh?" Max did not protest as the man refilled his glass.

"Or perhaps that good." The bartender laughed. "Check it out. You've got a pass for the day." He acknowledged something over Max's shoulder with a nod, and Max knew it was his shadow.

Trust that Ming set you up to be safe.

Trust was something he hated to place in others. Hell, he didn't understand why anyone ever trusted him. Only pain had come from it for his family.

Max threw back the drink, adrenaline tingling in his hands and feet. "You make a valid point."

Before he let his mind get in the way of the *mogjiŭ* by asking rational questions, Max pushed off from the bar and headed to the black doors. He placed his hands on the wood and swung them open.

The foyer led to a staircase down. He could hear chants and shouting before he reached the ground floor. The smell down here was different than upstairs. Something rotten held sway over all, and it was compiled from various burnt leaves and herbs, aftershaves and sweat and decay all mashed together and lingering about the mass of bodies huddled in rows of stadium seating.

The arena's audience consisted of raised wooden bleachers around a boxing ring without the ropes. Max made his way to the nearest benches, climbed to the top row, and sat in the corner. Below him he observed men and women in matching velvet vests and black slacks pacing the seats, the women dropping off drinks, the men recording notes in ledgers with graphite pencils.

In the ring, a man was strapped by each arm and ankle to a large wooden chair similar to the one in Goodfellow's office, though this seat was high enough that the man's bare feet dangled just above the canvas flooring. His was naked from the neck down, a healthy roadmap of muscle developed from manual labor defining his body. A stitched leather mask encased the man's head; large glass button eyes and a long, curved beak stabbing downward gave the mask a vulture's resemblance. It reminded Max of the seventeenth century plague doctor's masks, only this nose didn't end in a point filled with sweet smelling herbs. This nose hooked downward, and just past the man's neck it turned into rubber hose-like material. The hose connected the main leather mask to a small hookah bong placed on the seat between his legs, the ornate glass blocking his genitals from the audience.

A tall Mara standing beside the restrained man raised his arms. "*Ting!*" The crowd followed as he pointed to an iron clock hanging from the ceiling. A gangplank ran behind the machinery, containing a scoreboard and hangers—a young boy crouched on the walkway at attention, one hand resting on a lever.

"The two-second rule will be in effect to account for any—" the Mara smiled at the boy "—*human* error. There will be a blade and a minute head start. *Iboga* administered after one minute. Feeder at minute three. Freedom regardless by seven."

In front of Max, a British man flagged down one of the employees. "Three quid on this bloke to win." The man received his voucher and turned to Max. "I can't help it. I always root for the underdog." He laughed, his greasy mutton chops spreading wide with each chuckle. "Perhaps you'll let me even it out with you, mate. Three quid says he goes unconscious at six minutes. Aye?"

"No thanks."

"How about which body part the feeder bites first?"

Max knew better than to ask what a feeder was, so instead: "I'm not a gambler."

"Sure you are." He smiled. "You're here ain't ya?"

"*Ting!*" The crowd quieted and, as one, turned from each other to focus on the ring. The Mara placed the handle of a barber's blade in the hand of the restrained man. Then he signaled the boy in the rafters. "Begin!"

The blade glinted in the light as the bound man leveraged it between his pinky and ring fingered, flexed his wrist to an impossible angle, to cut at the straps there. He could only make quick tears in the fabric before his wrist bounced back in pain. But the man repeated the motion, knowing that if he severed that wrist strap, then his whole arm would be free and he could get out of the contraception.

The masked head leaned forward and Max could only imagine how hard it was to see out the glass eyes. The wrist flicked, and the process repeated as the crowd screamed at him. *Give up* chants mixed in with *Give 'em Hell*, the effect of which turned Max's stomach. Half this stadium wanted the man dead based on nothing but money.

Max looked up at the giant clock. The boy dropped a number one onto the scoreboard hooks.

"Time!" the Mara shouted.

A female employee, human, rushed up to the struggling man

with a canister and tongs. Using the tongs, she removed hot-orange coals from the canister and placed them on the hookah. Max looked at the mask-bong contraception and realized that the prisoner would be forced to breathe in whatever substance was in the hookah. The small nostril holes in the mask's beak would keep him alive with fresh air, but it wouldn't be enough to eliminate much of the smoke passing over them.

The man's head jerked a bit, but the woman held the hookah steady, vaporizing whatever was packed into its bowl. The man's movements slowed as the smoke filled his mask, but he continued his attempts at cutting. He missed the mark several times now, though he didn't quit. The employee waited two minutes, then disconnected the nose-hose from the hookah as well. She then detached the beak and hose connection from the mask, taking it and the hookah away.

The man's face was still covered except for his mouth and nose now. The result left him looking like a half-man, half-plucked vulture hybrid—every bit as alien looking as the Mara. The captive sucked at the fresh air until he was coughing. Once he seemed to regain himself, he dropped the blade as if realizing that he'd made as much progress as possible. He flexed his arm, real world muscle pulling against the small incision he'd made in the strap. He tensed further, then relaxed. Wiggled his wrist, tested the structure, then flexed again.

There was a slight tear.

"Time!"

Max cringed at the sharp voice. It was about to get harder for the man again. Beyond being tied in a manner only a contortionist could escape, they'd drugged him with the bong, and now...

The woman returned; this time she held a sort of wild animal by a leash around its neck. The hybrid creature resembled the hellish offspring of a wolf and rat.

"Aye!" The Brit pointed with joy. "Here comes the feeder."

With a few inches of size on a terrier dog, the feeder pulled against its restraints, gnashing drool-covered fangs. The woman attempted to unhook the leash's collar, but the feeder snapped at her hands and she simply let go and hurried out of the ring.

The feeder approached the masked man, who by this time had stopped pulling on the straps, despite the initial tear. The animal sniffed and licked the bare feet and the man's head lolled. He was feeling the effects of the smoke, had to be; he was moaning but showed no sign of pain. Max looked at the timer and scoreboard as the kid changed the number to four. Then a scream ripped his attention back to the boxing ring.

The crowd swelled and shouted along with the man's blood-curdling cries and the feeder's clacking teeth and squeals of delight. It devoured the man's foot in less than thirty seconds. A bone stump poked through the raw, ragged flesh of his ankle, a pool of crimson spreading across the canvas of the boxing ring. His screams were hysterical, but in their thralls, the man resumed the fight and tore his right arm free of the leather restraint.

"Hot damn!" the British gambler in front of Max said. "The sod might just do it."

The tortured man fought through the haze of whatever drug *iboga* was and searched for the razor blade—when he dropped it, he must have forgotten he'd need it to cut the rest of himself free—constantly stopping to push the feeder away over and over again as the creature tried to climb up the chair to the man's belly.

"*Where's the fucking blade!*" His shrieks were knives drawn over steel sheets, sending chills across Max's neck. The man slapped at the wooden chair and Max found himself squirming in his own seat. The feeder accepted momentary defeat against reaching the man's guarded midsection and moved to his other foot. Two bites and the man gave up on looking for the blade; he tried pummeling at the beast but his swings were wild, blinded by pain, drugs, and the mask.

Max looked to the clock. He had endured more than five minutes.

With his right foot eaten off, there was nothing to hold the man's leg in the restraint. He pulled his limb up and rose out of the strap, screaming anew as the mangled nub rubbed against the leather. With half his body free, but in agonizing pain, the man seemed to hesitate, swaying in the smoke. The feeder capitalized. It leapt up into the wooden chair and sunk its teeth into the thin skin on the man's scrotum. His screams, shrill beyond belief, intensified as his testicles popped between the jaws of the feeder. The man spasmed in the chair, choking and sobbing and screaming without oxygen, then coughing.

Like the bloodthirsty crowd around him, Max found himself shouting. There was something in Max that had to come out. He didn't even know if he was screaming real words or if they were just guttural howls to release whatever this twisted game was pumping into him. The whole building shook with energy. But as much as Max yelled, what he really wanted was silence.

The leather head dropped, blood and spit bubbled out his nose and mouth as the rat-thing burrowed its way inside his pelvis.

"Time!"

The boy hit a button and stopped the clock. He adjusted the scoreboard. Six minutes and fifty-five seconds. The crowd settled its debts and Max was disgusted by the money being passed around him. He'd cleaned up every manner of homicide. And in that moment, he realized, he'd never seen a murder committed. He was only called to examine the aftermath. And as gruesome as shifting through remains were, it was an entirely new concept to watch the life taken from a person. Especially in such a display. Fighting to the end, tasting the briefest moments of victory only to have the rug pulled from your feet. Watching the blood ooze out until the arterial pressure receded to zero.

"First time, mate?" The Brit in front of him put a cigarette into his mouth.

"The first death of the day is always a little rough," Max lied with sarcasm.

"Fancy a fag?" He lifted a meaty hand, offering his pack.

Max waved it off.

The man returned the smokes to his jacket pocket. "Don't look so ill, chap. That bloke got 'zactly what he was looking for."

"And what would that be?"

The man took a deep drag, the smoke poured from his mouth and nose. "What every slave wants: escape."

"Slaves?"

"Indentured slaves to The City. Forced labor. Every so often, you get a chance to have your debt wiped away."

"You're saying he won freedom?" Max looked down as a clean-up crew swarmed into the rink. They secured the feeder and zipped the corpse into a bag. "Too bad he won't have a chance to enjoy that freedom."

The Brit shrugged. "Escaping the pain of life can be as freeing as escaping chains most times."

That was something Max could understand.

The Brit took another puff. "In a way, I envy the slaves who play for their freedom. Every man wagers his life to something. But guys like this—" he gestured to the ring where only a bloodstained chair remained— "they place their bets direct. All or nothing, win or lose all in a second's flash. That's the true gambler! Me, I prefer to wager my soul over a lifetime—which in a way, is less honorable to the profession."

Back at the ring, a new set-up was being staged. In the center was now a table and two chairs, no restraints this time. In front of the furniture was a Mara flanked on either side by two men dressed in black and white jumpsuits.

Max lost himself staring into the splotches of scrub-faded stains on the canvas ring. Each discoloration had been a life once. Now they were nothing but a blemish. He scanned the crowd; still no sign of Charlie.

Between the seated men, the Mara held up his clawed hands, a dirty white bandana in each. "Number four." He tied the bandana around the forehead of the man to his left and Max could make out the Roman numeral painted on the cloth. "Or number six." The other bandana went around the man on his right, displaying his numeral. The Mara turned back to the crowd. "Place your bets."

Max was rocked again by the eruption of frenzied shouts and movement. Bills and paper receipts were thrust back and forth.

"Bet the house?" an employee asked him. "Payout drops after the game is announced."

"Not this round," Max said. He looked back at the ring, surprised that he was still sitting here. In essence, he'd watched a medieval execution. Death by torture. Even those who called public hangings cruel would have to agree that this demise made lynching look like a tea party. How much of this could he take? Was he expecting to just sit here and hope Charlie would arrive by some miracle?

"And...*ting!*"

The room settled into quiet murmurs. A male employee walked up to the Mara with a small wooden chest. Smiling wide at the crowd, the Mara opened the box with elegant movements.

"The game: One Bullet." He removed a long-barreled

revolver from the box. Brandishing the polished metal above his head, the room fell into frantic howls again. Max leaned further back into his corner seat, not wanting anyone to approach him for a bet, but not ready to leave this barbaric circus just yet.

The Mara quieted the crowd, then turned to the men. "Begin."

The men sat down at opposite ends of the table, its surface stained a brownish-black. The Mara popped out the revolver's chamber, loaded a single bullet, and spun it back into place. The gun was laid on the dirty space between the men, and with a flick of his wrist, the Mara sent the entire weapon spinning.

Silence blanketed the crowd and Max could hear the metal scraping against the wood finish. The spinning slowed. The barrel loomed at one man, then the next. Slower still.

A murmur went up as the barrel came to rest, pointing at the right arm of number four. The man's eyes closed and Max could see his chest heaving. Number four opened his eyes and reached for the gun. Max cringed against the bleacher as the man raised the barrel to his temple. Besides his initial trepidation, Max could not detect fear in the man's movements. When the steel was firmly planted against his skull, the crowd shifted as one, holding their breath.

Click.

Max felt his body relax. A brief moment of betting ensued as the weapon was placed back on the table and the other man wrapped his fingers around the handle. Unlike number four, six was trembling as he raised the instrument of death. His arm seemed to get stuck about a foot from his head. Max couldn't blame the man; he couldn't imagine pulling his service revolver on himself. He looked at the gamblers around him, their eyes wild with excitement, their lips wet with anticipation.

"Come on, ye fucker!" The voice came from somewhere in the vast sea of faces and it broke the ice. Similar insults were hurdled at the man, urging him to take his chance. The Mara leaned forwarded and whispered something into number six's ear. The man shook his head, closed his eyes, and positioned the gun.

The explosion sent Max jumping from his seat. Number six fell sideways, the white bandana soaked to a deep crimson. Number four, face splattered with brain matter, dropped his head and began sobbing...or laughing. Cries of victory and defeat from the crowd roared over the gunshot's echo.

No time was wasted by the human staff as they carted off the table and chairs. A Mara took number four to the corner of the ring, and looked to be reading off a piece of parchment to him. A canvas stretcher was brought in and the corpse was removed.

Max stood on trembling legs and headed down the bleachers in a daze. It was time to leave; Charlie wasn't here and this deranged sideshow gave no signs of slowing, just a revolving door leading to the next death game.

"Remember what I said, mate," the Brit called out after him. "They both escaped. Method don't really matter."

Max ignored him; he felt like he couldn't even trust his own voice if he tried to speak. Like the words wouldn't be there or it would sound different than he intended. He moved in silence to the staircase and back into the casino upstairs. The air was cooler. He looked down at his blistered hand.

An Ouroboros! That was it. He was marked by the Greek tail eater.

"Leaving so soon?" the pit boss doubling as doorman asked.

"Yeah," Max said, using all his strength to do so. "Saw everything I needed." Max walked past the creature and down the stairs toward the exit. He placed his hands on the door and wished that Ku's laundry house was on the other side. Quiet and peaceful. He'd even settle for his own apartment right now. But he was stuck with the whirling hustle and bustle of a damned city. Even knowing what kind of world was waiting for him on the other side didn't prevent the jarring feeling he was struck by when opening the door and stepping back into the milieu.

Max stood near an obelisk on the casino's corner. Ming was not among the crowd pushing past him. He touched the carved sigils on the signpost; they were not just indecipherable, they were ominous and foreboding. And it added to the unease he was experiencing. As a police officer, he'd come to terms with prisoners being executed. That was called justice on the surface.

But slaves being tortured… He'd looked the other way once or twice during a minor social injustice in San Francisco, but he'd never condoned slavery.

Or the murder of slaves. Or worse, forcing them to compete in blood sports to claim their independence from captors.

But this place *did* allow it. He looked up at the cold rock ceiling. This city didn't mind at all. Not only did no one care that human beings were being exterminated in the building next door, they encouraged it…were enjoying it.

Max was dead and this was hell. The only other explanation that made sense was that he was comatose in Ku's laundry den. His body lay incapacitated by some ridiculous amount of opium, while his brain put together the most intense hallucination ever. Both options seemed more reasonable than the truth.

Max needed to sit, so despite having zero appetite, he found a café and bar and requested a table. He pointed to a menu item that he couldn't even pronounce and choose water over *mogjiŭ*. When the meal arrived, Max could only pick at it with the wooden spoon.

"You find your friend, Mister Elliot?"

Max looked up as Ming took a seat across from him.

He placed the fork on the table, surprised and happy to be distracted from his philosophical contemplation. "He's not my friend. I just needed his help."

"Maybe if you tell me what's going on, I can help you."

"You mean collect the money and then ditch out at the hard parts. I was not prepared—"

"I told you: *I don't participate.* You said that was fine. Can't change your mind after."

Max took a sip of water instead of responding. There was no point in arguing with a teenager. "How long have you lived here?"

"Basically all my·life. I know stories from aboveground, but I don't think I can live up there. Too different."

"I've never met a teenager quite like you. How old are you, sixteen?"

"Almost seventeen."

"Well in San Francisco, you'd be queen of the seventeen-year-olds. I don't know anyone who could conduct themselves around adults as well as you do. Let alone how you talk to a police officer." Max thought of McCloud, interrogating Ming as the crime boss of some underground racketeering gig involving guides. He wondered how smart juvenile criminals were in San Fran. There was no doubt Ming was intelligent enough to run the show though. A stupid person would not last long down here.

"You're a police officer?"

Max nodded.

She laughed. "I've heard of them before. None down here. Unless you count the Others. They enforce what few laws they have."

"Luckily, I'm not looking for a job," Max said. "Is that how they get slaves? Are they arrested and forced to play these black death games?"

"So you *did* want a black show?"

"No, I didn't. I didn't know what the hell that door meant when I walked through it."

"Well, at least I got to know you a bit better." She winked. "You want to continue the tour?"

"I'd say I'm paid up for a few more questions." Her cheeky calmness was getting under Max's skin, and worse, she'd half sent him there as a test. Waiting to see how he'd react if he did see the black show.

Wouldn't you test your mark? his mind asked.

Max knew he would.

"Yeah, you're paid up." Ming scooted her chair in, lowered her voice. "Next tip: slaves can be anyone who owes the Mara a debt. If they don't kill you, they put you to work in the slave shows of Gehanna and the West End mostly, 'specially if you're female. Or they put you to manual labor anywhere in The City."

"I saw a lot of humans working in the casino. Are they slaves?"

"No. They work for the Mara. Slaves only—"

"People are employed by these creatures? As a job?"

"Yeah. And keep your voice down," Ming said. "Plenty of people give themselves freely to the life."

"Fine," Max said. "Can these debts be paid off besides death wagers?"

"You managed to stumble into the only black games arena in She'ol. It's really the only place with slaves in the East End. For whatever the reason, the Mara choose some slaves for these black games, offering them freedom as the wager. But the rest of the shows around here are regular performers."

"What do they do with male slaves?"

Ming shrugged, voice still low. "All sorts of rumors on how this city came to be. All I know is that the place is maintained by slaves. Stuff breaks, wears out, what-have-you, servants fix it. That's what happens with most of the men who cross the Mara. The men who perform in the shows are usually only there to…"

Max knew she was struggling to find the right word.

"To act out fantasies on the women," she said.

Max didn't feel as uncomfortable when the conversation shifted to sex this time. He was in a world where taboo and slaughter didn't seem to bother anyone. And he'd better start taking that cue if he was going to succeed. "So black is always death games?"

"Black always involves death. If it's in a casino, then it's gonna be a game. If it's in a theatre, you may just watch a murder. If you see a black and pink theatre, it's a sex show with death involved. But far enough West the rules start to change a bit…like I said, I don't go there."

"This is a lot to take in." Max ran his hands over his short-cropped hair. "And why are these places not really on the East End?"

"When I said the rest of the shows are regular performers, I meant those people want to be here, doing this. Even if it's a red show. They ask for it. And just because you saw slaves wager their life for freedom, sometimes those contestants are just thrill seekers."

"Wait. Thrill seekers? You mean non-slaves sign up for those insane wagers?"

"Your voice," Ming scowled. "The City is home to all sorts of people. Some want to experience beating the pain and fear, I guess. I don't know."

"You're telling me people *want* to be eaten alive by mutant rats? They want to be cut while an audience watches? They want to be fucked to death in a black show?"

"I gotta go." The chair screeched against the ground as Ming stood up.

"I'm sorry." Max closed his eyes, massaged his temples.

"Please stay. I won't cause trouble." He couldn't risk losing Ming. For some reason, getting answers from her felt more straightforward and truthful than any he'd get from guys like the greasy Brit. Ming could distance herself from the filth, and that detachment surprised Max at first; how could anyone be so indifferent to such madness?

It's no different than you at a crime scene.

Max was used to murder victims. Ming was used to The City.

With the ability to not associate, Ming had maintained an innocence that was lost by any citizen who actually partook in the vices of The City. That made her the only person worth trusting. And he'd need to trust someone if he was going to survive here.

Ming sat down. "Mister Elliot, you're not like anyone I've guided before, ya know that?"

"I can imagine."

"What do you really want here in The City?"

"I need to go to a brothel."

"See, was that so hard?"

Max looked around the small table, but the few patrons inside didn't seem to care one bit about their conversation. "The truth is my daughter was taken and I have reason to believe she was brought here. She's not a slave. She didn't ask to be kidnapped. And the guy who was supposed to help me find her bailed. I just need to find a brothel that has young…"

Ming focused those dark eyes on him. Unlike before, now her eyes were judging. They were piercing through his soul, just like the Mara's had. Max hoped she could see he was honest. He had no more cards to play.

Turns out he was a gambler after all. He'd rolled the dice when he chose work over being a husband and father. He took the risk when he cheated on Eve. When he trusted Charlie after everything that happened between them. Max was an incredible gambler… but now that his debts were due, he suddenly had trouble with the games he'd willingly played.

"Some things are best discussed on the move. Come on," Ming said, leading him from the café.

XI

Max KNEW THIS was his best choice. Ming was probably more trustworthy than Charlie in the end, but he would proceed as Charlie and he had discussed. Explore the brothels and inquire about Leigh Anne from the point of view of a potential client. As perverted as it was, Max realized it was better than the truth. At least Ming wouldn't have to see his acting if she always stayed outside.

Once they were on the streets, Ming pointed toward the hospital. "I know of one brothel near the border that has what you want. We'll try there first. All the other choices are deeper in the West End, and I still need to decide if I'm willing to take you there." She started off and Max stayed close by.

"Thank you. The crimes against my family, they're not things I talk about easily. I—"

"Save it." Ming picked up her pace. "I've heard every sob story out there, and it doesn't matter what happened or if I believe you. I take people where they want to go. Simple as that. You asked for a child brothel—no cover story needed."

Max fell behind her, hoping to ease the tension. She still thought he was lying to save face, and Max couldn't blame her. She was his guide. Nothing more. Even though she had waited around the casino and checked in on him, she was just keeping tabs on a lucrative job. And he certainly wasn't paying her to believe him.

Max allowed Ming to retain a slight lead, letting The City's sounds fill the empty space between them.

"There it is." Ming pointed. Still over a hundred feet away, her disdain of the brothel was clear in her body language.

"Regardless of if you believe me or not, I want to thank you for your help. And answering all my questions."

"Just some friendly advice: don't be nervous when you talk to 'em. Confidence goes a long way."

Show no fear. It was the old adage. How to survive in any wild, be it jungle, desert, or concrete: never let the universe know that you're afraid. "Thanks."

Max stepped into the building. It was similar to hotel layouts in San Fran. There was a lobby with a front desk, stairs leading up to rooms and floors above. Frames lined the walls, and as he walked to the scaly Mara behind the front desk he was enticed by the paintings. Reproductions of famous French nudes and karma sutra sexual acts watched Max approach the short, squat Mara. Besides his height and slightly wider nose, there were no other real differences between him and the rest: hairless, leathery skin ranging from reddish to brown hues.

The creature smiled and with one long finger it beckoned to Max. "Please, approach."

Max stepped forward without a falter, and he stood tall even when the creature leaned close. It inhaled through thin nostrils.

"Are you sure you're in the right place? You smell more like a *sǐ fěn* man to me. Then again, there's no harm in trying something new."

Max went to feel his pockets expecting the touch of the pouch, but he knew the powder was left with Lieutenant Harris days ago. Even still, it had no odor. Yet somehow this thing could smell remnants of the drug on him. "I have no interest in that powder. I'm here for a girl."

The creature smiled. "Been a while has it?"

"Indeed." Max felt his confidence rising. This was a back and forth dance. No different than shaking down a rat back home. "If I'm gonna pay for something, I want to do it big. You know?"

"Of course, of course." The Other clicked his short, thick nails against each other, his voice dripping with more seduction. "Taste the forbidden pleasures, and why not? That is why we are here." The twisted concierge leaned forward. "Tell me: what do you want in your *transaction*?"

Hot fury rose to Max's face. This is where his daughter might be held captive. Where she was possibly being bought—

He banished the thoughts. "I like them young. The younger the better. Eleven, twelve maybe." Max felt his heartbeat increase with the lie. His cheeks still felt flush from his lingering anger and Max hoped the Other would mistake the rosy cheeks for sexual excitement, helping to seal his ruse.

"Unfortunately, I cannot give you what you desire." The grin slackened. "I deal in youth occasionally, but I don't have anyone at the moment. Head over to Belhum's. There you will find what you need."

"I see." The adrenaline shut off, and frustration at Charlie wormed itself into Max's mind. "Thanks for your help."

Max walked out and saw Ming leaning against a brick wall.

"That was quick," she said as he approached.

"Are you willing to take me to a place called Belhum's? I'll pay double."

"Are you serious?" She stood up from the wall. "One minute you're looking ill from the casino violence. The next minute you wanna waltz into the West End looking for child brothels."

"You're right, it makes no sense...unless you believe my story. Then it fits. And you must believe me on some level. You're still here."

"I'll take you to Belhum's, maybe Baabo's too. But that's as far west as I go for now. And nothing past the fires of Gehanna."

"Deal."

Ming held out her open palm. "Pay in advance for this one."

He gave her two dollars. "It's really that bad?" Max asked as they headed down a twisting path.

"For whatever the reason, a different breed of show became popular there. The Mara act different there, and the humans... It just bothers me."

"I could tell."

"Well we won't be going too deep into the territory. Just past the ward."

They turned at an obelisk depicting a ringed circle and three arrows circling each other, and Max saw the hospital-shaped building and bench in the distance. "Why a health ward? This place doesn't seem to care who lives or dies."

"Wards have two main purposes: storing dumplings and storing skin puppets."

"Do I even want to know what the hell those things are?"

Her smile seemed more genuine this time. "Probably not."

They passed under the painted cross.

"Hypothetical question, Ming. If I wanted to buy back my daughter, settle her debt, how would I do it?"

Ming sighed, her smile fading into indifference again. "Still wanna talk about this, huh?" She shook her head, but not in anger, more in hopeless resignation. "I don't know how to free a slave. I told you that. Best bet is to offer something you think is of value. Over the last few years, I've learned that the Mara have a different logic than people. They'll surprise you from time to time with what they accept, they'll make deals and cut bargains that seem counterintuitive to business. So always ask. Worst thing they say is no."

"Got it."

"And here we are." The building, while maybe a bit more neglected, looked the same as the previous brothel.

"I understand if you can't wait for me here. But—"

"We'll see. I hope you find what you're looking for."

Max didn't bother asking for clarification on her ambiguous answer.

Again he walked through the door; again a similar scene greeted him. This concierge was scrawling into a ledger when Max approached. He was in no rush and took a moment to finish whatever he was recording before looking up, a sly smile on his face. "Welcome. I am Belhum." The pronunciation of the name was harsh and phlegmy.

"Thank you. I'm looking for a young transaction." The act came easier this time.

"Of course." The concierge put the quill down and rubbed his leathery hands together. He was professional, and in their smart suits, with their calm, measured way of speaking, Max almost forgot what kind of brutes the Mara really were. They were a glorious façade for a miserable world.

With a new idea, Max took a gamble and held out his palm, raw and red. "Though my desire is quite strong and has been building for some time, this is my first visit to your impressive city. Despite my anxiousness, I need to know how this works."

Belhum looked about the room, perhaps satisfied by the lack of other guests, then he spoke. "After payment, you will receive two hours with your purchase. All manner of coitus is allowed." The Mara's eyes narrowed. "Violence is strictly prohibited in this brothel. Any violence against your purchase will result in swift consequences. Is that understood?"

Max nodded.

"When your time is up, you'll hear a knock at the door. Leave the room promptly. We ask that you exit the building via the back door, and you are welcome to return anytime."

"I understand." Max nodded. "What's the price?"

Belhum leaned forward and closed his eyes. He inhaled Max's scent as the other Mara had done. "For you...American money's fine. Ten dollars."

Max opened his coat to retrieve the cash. "Do you ever deal in non-monetary transactions?"

"We deal in all manner of compensation. That is the law. Some clients have different value to offer us than money." The Mara extended his clawed hand and took the cash from Max. His reptilian lips curled, causing adrenaline to race from Max's head to his fist on waves of electricity. As much as he wanted to punch that snake-like nose, Max hated himself just as much for having to play this perverted role.

With the index finger of his other hand, Belhum pointed to the stairs. A human appeared. "Follow him," the concierge said.

Max trailed the man up to the third floor and down the hall. Room 312 was stenciled in black on a brass circular marker of the room they stopped at. "I will be back in two hours," the man said. Then he left. Swallowing hard, Max braced himself and opened the door.

She was sitting on the bed in a blue dress, frilly white lace around her neck and hemline. A white sash was about her waist with a bow in her hair. She stood as he walked in and nodded a silent greeting. The room smelled fresh and was clear of clutter, only having a bed and dresser and nightstand with water. The girl also carried a refreshing perfume about her. It all seemed too familiar, firing off memories best left buried.

Max closed the door, hand pressed against the wood, willing himself to not walk out. He stood silent, unable to look away from the girl. She kept her eyes on him, like she was staring through him. Still, Max couldn't formulate the words. This girl was practically his daughter. A bit older and taller, but still a blue-eyed girl with her hair pulled up in a ponytail.

The only major difference was the aroma that hung about her. She should have smelt like grass in a field, chalk in a classroom, the salty stench of beach trips. Instead, the room exuded the same scent as Shin Sho's women. A shameful intoxicating fragrance that made it easy for men to say yes.

She flipped the hem of her dress about a bit and finally said, "What do you want me to do?" Her voice was soft, trusting.

Max opened his mouth, but his voice caught and cracked, emitting an unintelligible sound. The aroma-filled air made him think of the sex he'd had in a room last year, a room that smelled the same. The sex that wasn't with Eve.

She moved closer and leaned against Max's frame. Her small delicate hand went up to his chest. "I can do all sorts of things. Tell me—" she looked up at him, eyes bright, "—have I—"

Max broke his paralysis, taking her hand and gently removing it. He rushed over to the bed and sat on the soft mattress, taking a deep breath. "Please," he said. "I'm not here for what you think."

She took a spot on the bed next to him and put her hand on his leg. "It's okay. I don't mind why you're here. It's why I'm here too."

Max cringed, moved her hand away again, and softened his

voice. "I'm just here for information."

"Oh, mister," her voice quavered with slight nervousness. "I'm not sure what you're looking for, but—"

"I..." Max paused. He looked around the room. Would they know what he was doing in here? Were they watching? Max leaned in a bit, lowering his voice. "My little girl was kidnapped."

"I wouldn't know anything about that, mister."

"Are you sure something like that didn't happen to you?" Max chose his tone very carefully. He had to gain her trust and pray she knew something.

The girl shook her head.

"Don't you think your parents worry about you?" Max was hardly aware of the change in his voice.

"I don't have parents," she said. Then with renewed gusto: "You can be my daddy?" A hopeful smile across her face.

"I told you I'm not here for that. I just want to find my daughter."

She looked down at Max's hand, red and blistered.

"I'm sorry to hear about your daughter." Her charming act fell away, and Max knew he was talking to a child blinded to the truth, thinking she already knows it all. "I'm really sorry. But kidnapping doesn't happen often here, mister. I swear. It's not like that at all."

Max's clipped laughter cut with sarcasm. "Are you kidding me? You're what, fifteen? And I just bought you for sex. Kid, this place—"

"No." A little color rose to her cheeks. "I wasn't kidnapped. Their ways may be different from yours, but everyone is given a choice." Her voice softened. "The Others are very clear about that."

Max tried to look beyond her calm demeanor, read the truth in her eyes. What kind of choice was it when the options were self-dignity or starvation and homelessness?

"They outlaw crimes like kidnapping, but sometimes people do it anyway," she continued. "And they are always punished for their actions...in time. But I made my choice. It's not so bad."

"What's your name?"

"Cheyenne."

"Cheyenne, my daughter was taken, by humans, I believe,

who chose to break the Mara's code. Though I don't know exactly who yet, I'm going to find out. I also have reason to believe she was brought here and sold, regardless if the Others knew the true nature of her procurement or not." Max pulled out a crumpled photo from his coat pocket. "I just want to know if you've seen my Leigh Anne."

Cheyenne looked at the photo for mere seconds. "I recognize her."

The excitement balled in his throat and Max could barely speak. "Is she here?"

"No."

The wind left his sails, and Max's body fell with an empty ache. Max knew the odds of her being at this exact brothel were slim, but hope always seemed to get in the way of logic.

Cheyenne looked away as she continued, "She was brought here for help a few weeks back. She was...pregnant."

The image formed as broken fragments in his mind. His daughter. Twelve. Raped. *Pregnant.* The words didn't seem coherent and his brain refused to process them, not wanting to accept the truth they held.

"It happens." Her voice was cold and factual, a tone that should belong to an adult but instead came from someone who had been robbed of a childhood. Were they not discussing his own flesh and blood though, Max would have appreciated Cheyenne's straightforwardness. Her ability to detach. Hell, she was using the same even keel tone Max employed when he talked about the grisly murders he investigated, when he gave insincere condolences to families, and referred to victims as "puzzle pieces".

Now, he couldn't seem to detach for longer than it took for the *mogjiŭ* to wear off.

"They couldn't do anything for her here," Cheyenne said. "I heard they took her to a butcher."

Butcher. The word echoed off the numbed walls of his brain, and it took several moments of silence for Max to muster up the strength to speak. "Is she alive?"

"I don't know." Now Cheyenne looked at the folds in her dress. "That was a few weeks ago. Healing takes time. They don't waste the dumplings on us. It's too expensive. If she gets well, I guess she'll be back."

"Dumplings?" Now he wished he had asked Ming for that explanation.

"It's medicine."

He could tell that there was some sympathy in her eyes. That was when the irony hit Max: Cheyenne was just like him. She cared. She had the ability to empathize. But those traits didn't keep her alive or supply her with the drive she needed. She talked with him, but once Max left, she'd go right back to work. Max recalled countless times he'd placated Eve by half-listening to her stories, nodding at the appropriate times, and repeating the words "I love you" without real energy behind it. Maintaining the family only so he had something meaningful for the few times when he wasn't working. A wave of depression hit him at the realization. "Please tell me how to get there."

Cheyenne gave him directions to a butcher named Lakzo. She put her hand on his thigh when she was finished. This time, her touch was comforting. "Good luck."

"And you're okay? You choose to stay here?"

"Yeah. I mean, it's not bad. I get paid well. Men tell me how wonderful I am." She exhaled a laugh. "And it beats being a street guide or vendor."

He nodded. With the track record of decisions he'd made, Max had no right to argue. He caught another whiff of her perfume and the memory of Shin Sho's prostitutes flashed, purposefully trying to block out the depressing cloud of emotions threatening to attack his psyche, helping and yet torturing Max at the same time.

Sex was another amazing escape.

But it never lasted, Max reminded himself. *And the pain would return, twice as strong.*

He breathed through his mouth, trying to block out her scent. "Thanks, Cheyenne. I wish you the best, too." He stood up from the bed and headed to the door.

He left in silence, the grieving parent. Cheyenne, like the unhelpful police department who'd done their best, given some advice in the right direction, but whose help was now over. The role reversals kept him in a state of turmoil, and Max doubted who he even was anymore.

Max walked back to the closest signpost and looked around. There was no sign of Ming. He shouldn't have been surprised, but a part of him had held out hope she would have waited. Even if she was still cautious of him, she was genuine. Hadn't really cheated him; leaving him in the casino didn't count. She'd made sure he was shadowed with protection.

But Max had more important things to worry about. Like how the hell he was gonna find Lakzo. He ignored the butcher part. Things in The City were not always what they seemed. Wards stored skin puppets, casinos killed people. Butchers could be surgeons for all he knew. She was pregnant. Maybe they just aborted the babies. Didn't mean they butchered the mother. She couldn't mean that. No way Cheyenne could have explained it as calm as she did.

What if she could?

Then there was no point worrying about it now. He'd cross that bridge when he got there.

Not wanting to get lost in the maze, Max walked west in a straight line so he could find his way back if—

Something slammed against a wall just ahead of him in the alley. Trash scattered and he heard a feminine squeal, followed by a gruff, indistinguishable voice. Max drew his gun and leapt around the corner. There she was, pinned against the brick wall by a brute of a man in miner's overalls, his hand wrapped around her thin throat.

"Ming!"

The miner glanced over and in that split second, Ming struck. The man let out a shriek of pain, his hands shot to his crotch and he crumpled to the pavement. She brought an object in her fist down on the back of the man's head and he splayed motionless.

She vaulted away from the body and landed behind Max.

"Christ, are you okay?" Max looked over his shoulder, keeping the gun pointed at the prostrate form on the ground.

"Yeah, let's get outta here."

"What about him?"

"He's marked." She raised a butterfly knife. A light mist of red on its blade. "Whoever finds him can deal with him. I had no choice. That's on him." She stomped east, in the direction of the hospital ward and Max followed.

"Ming."

But she didn't stop until they reached the borderland bench.

"Ming."

"What?"

"I'm trying to figure out what happened back there."

"What did it look like?" She threw up her hands. "Some guy grabbed me and I handled it. That's why they have shows and clubs, so guys can work that shit off. But he chose me instead. If he dies it's not my fault."

Max wanted to put his arm around her, comfort her like some crime scene victim. But that wasn't Max's style. And he doubted Ming would want it anyway. "You're right. It wasn't your fault. He made his choice." Max spoke soft and slow. "Thank you for waiting for me."

"Waiting for you? I just wanted to see if you needed more help. If I play my cards right with you, I can take a whole month off work."

"Fair enough. Well, if you're still willing, I'd love to give you that month off. I could use more of your help."

"Let me guess; you have a lead for your daughter?" She eyed him, head cocked, suspicious.

"Yeah."

She laughed in disbelief.

"Ming, you've taken me this far. I actually have a precise location to visit. If you help me get her back, I'll make sure you can take two months off work."

Ming plopped onto the bench and put her head in her hands. "I must be out of my mind." She looked up at him. "What's your plan?"

Max took out the photo of Leigh Anne. "A girl in there told me she's at a place called Lakzo's. I need to weigh my options, but I figure I offer him all the money I can to buy her back. Can I get room and board somewhere near here, rest and think for a while?"

Ming inspected the photograph in Max's hand. "Yeah. It's been a long job so far. We could use a few hours of sleep. I know a place."

And she led him back into the relative safety of the East End and She'ol.

XII

McCLOUD POKED HIS head into the lieutenant's office. "Sir?"

Harris looked up. His eyes seemed annoyed, though maybe just tired.

"Sorry, sir. I—"

"Come in." Harris gestured for John McCloud to join him at the seat across from his desk. His face softened. "What can I do for you?"

"As you know, sir, it's hard for me to remain idle. As you're also aware, I've been waiting for the right time to join homicide. And after finding Elliot, it seems like the time is here. This case is fresh, and if we double our man power on it—"

"I appreciate your zest for justice, McCloud. But this should not be your first homicide case."

"Time is our greatest adversary, sir. I—"

"You're a fantastic investigator. And we'd be honored to have your skills in the homicide department, but let's wait until promotions next month. I don't believe this should be your first homicide."

Hearing the words from Harris's flushed face sent McCloud's blood boiling. He couldn't tell if the lieutenant didn't want him working on anything involving young girls because he was afraid it would remind McCloud of his sister, Janice, or if he was worried that his skills weren't honed enough for such a prolific case. Either way, it was insulting.

"Well, then not this case...per se. How about the murder of Eve Elliot instead? Let me show you what I can do."

"Dammit, McCloud. We're working off the assumption that Eve's killer is the same person responsible for the girls and Poppens. This madman should not be your first case."

"Just last week you teamed me up with Detective Johnston for exposure. He *was* the lead on Eve's case until you saw the apartment near Chinatown. Then—with all due respect, sir—I stopped being his apprentice in the homicide investigation; I became an errand boy sent to collect Max Elliot."

"I'm sorry you felt overlooked. Don't take it personally. We're all playing for the same team. And we all have a role to play within that team."

"I understand that, sir. But I'm in limbo now that my homicide mentor is unofficially off the one case I was offered. I also understand the necessity to bring Max back and give him lead. I do—whether I agree with his tactics or not. But is it possible that he is too close to this one to be of help?"

"I'll assign you to shadow Johnston on a different homicide."

"I want this one, sir. Team me with Max."

"Max isn't going to work with anyone."

"I thought that was your decision, not his." McCloud paused for a moment, waiting to see if he'd overstepped his bounds.

Harris's face remained red, but he didn't say anything.

"I'll investigate the Elliot tragedy since no one else did," McCloud continued. "I get it: when Max bailed, the department decided to ignore this one. If Max didn't seem to care back then, why should anyone else? But now that the killer has struck again, we can't just turn Max loose and hope he finds a clue. We need to investigate his family. Try to find a link." Without verbal resistance, McCloud's voice rose a bit with the excitement of convincing his superior. "Someone does not brutally murder this way without a strong motive. Learn more about the *original* crime and perhaps I—we—can help Max with the info he is receiving. Same team, we're just running multiple plays in hopes of upping our odds for victory. Besides, Leigh Anne is a criminal investigation. Not a homicide. I can start there."

"I'm going to give Max some time. Maybe we don't have to dig through his life and destroy his family's past any more than it already has been. If or *when* I decide your idea has merit, I will let you know."

McCloud refused to let his disappointment show. He nodded and headed for the door.

"Officer McCloud."

He stopped. "Yes, Lieutenant?"

"He may be unconventional, but the overwhelming lack of control with...shall we say, inebriating substances, was never as bad as recently. I'm talking the last three or four years. And though I sometimes allow my personal frustrations to show in public, even I need to remind myself that Max has been pivotal in helping this city for the bulk of his adult life. But he's his own worst enemy. I also challenge anyone to go through what he's been through and remain unaffected." Harris paused. "I appreciate your contributions to this department as well. You must trust me when I tell you that this should not be your first assignment."

"Duly noted, sir."

When they got to the boarding house, Max looked at Ming. "Stay here. Rest."

Ming leaned against the front wall of the boarding house, arms crossed. "I don't care if I half believe you. I'm not sleeping with you."

"I didn't mean it like that. If I'm hiring you, I have to cover your travel expenses. That's fair." He hoped to coax her off the wall but decided not to press the issue. "Well, let's just meet here in about six hours then."

Ming nodded but didn't move, so Max went inside, relived to

see a human male behind the front desk this time. He bought a room for the six hours, happy that in this land of perpetual dusk, time was measured the same, though he assumed sayings like "this evening" or "in the morning" were meaningless without the sun and moon. Before he received his key, he made a second purchase and gave the man instructions for his guide.

The room Max got was sparse. A small bed. Bathroom. Desk, chair, and lamp. That was more than he needed anyway. He laid down on the bed, still dressed, and closed his eyes. He knew he wasn't going to sleep well, if at all, with what he'd seen today. But he needed to try and recoup from the last several hours. In his line of work, Max thought he'd seen everything. But the drugs, money, sex, and murder of San Fran could not compare to this new madness. A place where monsters were free to rule the streets and life was cheap.

Turns out he'd only scratched the surface of the world's depravity.

Ming was still hitched against the front of the building, debating her next move, when the innkeeper appeared.

"Room for ya," the old, white-bearded man announced. He held a silver key in the air. "Six hours. Paid in full by your pal with the trench coat." The man smiled, yellowed teeth poked out through his dry lips and unkempt facial hair. "He requested a room far away from his."

Ming approached the man and took the key. "Thanks." She pocketed the gift and walked away down the alley. The man's wheezing laughter followed her. She headed toward Arthur's house, not more than a quarter-mile east. The gesture was nice, and there was a chance his story was true, but nice didn't keep you alive.

Remember that, Ming, Arthur had said when she first started guiding. *Not everyone is as noble as you, as the work we do for others. We must preserve ourselves first if we are to continue to help those in need. If that means we must become hard—*

"Then we become hard," Ming said. It made her so mad to know she'd screwed up near the border. Not because it almost killed her, but because she would have disappointed Arthur, let down patients that had yet to be saved. It also bothered her that this man, Max Elliot, had seen her weak.

Her building was little over a hundred feet away. There were three dwellings in the brick high rise. Arthur and she were in a two-bedroom on the ground floor. A blind man lived above them, and the top floor housed a woman with three young boys.

Ming straightened her suit and checked for blood stains; spat in her fingers and flattened errant hairs that had been pulled from her braid. Arthur had been mentioning the surface a lot in their recent conversations, and she didn't want him finding out about today's mistake. She finished composing herself and stepped into the home.

The sleep was fitful and when he woke, covered in sweat, Max still felt drained. As he went to the bathroom and splashed water on his face, he wondered if it would ever be possible for him not to feel tired. Simply knowing about this place was a burden that he assumed could never be lifted.

He washed the best he could in the minimalist bathroom and got back into his sweaty clothes. The garments were uncomfortable until he made it past the boarding house doors. Outside, the temperature was cool, and Max was thankful for that. It chilled him and helped to wake his senses.

Nothing had changed since he retired to the room. The City was still bathed in an aura of near dusk from the glowing obelisks, the streets still teemed with people, haggling over prices, performing, living. And as if she hadn't moved, Ming still held her position against the wall. Max scratched the stubble of his cheeks. "You sleep at all?"

"Like a baby," she said. "Thanks. I just returned the key."

There was something about her tone that made him doubt her, but he wasn't about to press the issue. "You're welcome. Ready to go?"

"I'm always ready. The question is, are you?" She pushed off the wall. "Like I said, the further west we go, the rougher the areas become."

"And how far is Lakzo's?"

"Deep. But not as far as Gehanna."

"How much extra do I owe you for taking this gig?"

"Nothing extra. Keep the same tour rates. But you pay me in advance for every stop. Now let's go find your daughter."

Ming turned quick, but Max thought he caught a softness invade her usual dark eyes before she whirled around and headed down the road.

As they walked, Max's mind drifted between thoughts of heroic rescues and nauseating defeat. He'd always been one to bounce back and forth between emotions, but since he'd taken this case, Max found himself drifting more frequent, and it was making it near impossible to stay on track.

"You okay?" Ming said, looking back.

Max had fallen behind without realizing it, and hustled to catch up. "Sorry, just lost in thought for a second there."

"This place will do that to a person. Let's stay close together." There was a graveness to her voice, and he couldn't tell if the comment was for his safety or hers.

After a few more blocks, Ming broke the silence. "Tell me about her."

Max looked over. "About who?"

"Your daughter."

"My daughter?" The memories of years seeped from Max's mind into his body, and his legs became heavy with their burden, slowing his pace further. "I'm coming to the realization that not everyone needs to have children."

"That's a good point," Ming said. "I do know a bit about having a family. One of the few things I remember from the surface. I remember it being beautiful and painful. Down here there's not much beauty to it though."

"Beautiful pain. That's a good description." A sudden laugh, more of an exaggerated snort, escaped his throat. "I was distraught when I found out we had a girl." A reflective chuckle this time. "Me, raising a girl. Worst nightmare. Let me investigate the Tongs

100

of Chinatown, get shot at, stabbed, but Christ, I didn't want to raise a girl.

"Guess I was scared." That was the first time Max had used that statement. Somehow it was not as difficult to say as he thought it would be. "My wife Eve wasn't, though. She was a rock. She handled everything while I dealt with my issues." He looked up at the massive rock ceiling above them and muttered. "I never handled them. Eve made sacrifices. I went to work."

Ming remained silent.

"I know how awful I must sound. I loved my daughter though. My wife too. I just… It took until Leigh Anne turned five years old before we finally started to do family things together."

"Better late than never," Ming said.

"She was slightly shorter than you. Big blue eyes. Only seen prettier blue eyes on her mother. She kept her hair long and liked putting it up in all types of buns and tails and wraps. She loved going to the beach—that's where I would usually take her when I found the opportunity. She liked reading and school.

"I just wish there had been more time. I was busy with work. Adult responsibilities. I assumed things would smooth out sooner rather than later. But there wasn't enough time to know. I can't even remember if I told them I loved them that morning before I left. How could I have known it was the last…"

"You couldn't know."

You couldn't know. Everyone makes mistakes. Surely your family knew you loved them. Max appreciated the condolences but they never seemed to reassure him. Trying to put his emotions into words always sounded stupid to him. Battling his past internally was easier than involving anyone, especially Ming. And maybe risking everything he had left to find Leigh Anne would finally right some of the wrongs in his mind.

Max didn't respond as they passed the landmark bench. The short-lived reprieve on his conscious from opening up about Leigh Anne wasn't enough to overcome the post self-loathing that was now creeping into his body. He avoided Ming's eyes. Whether it was there or not, he didn't want to see any sympathy for him. Because if she knew more about him, she would have no sympathy, only distain.

As they continued in silence, Max noticed the sky—could it

even be called that down here?—was darkening. Surroundings were still clearly visible, but the near dusk that he had become accustomed to shifted to a deeper shade, twilight almost. The streets seemed to narrow and the strange glowing obelisks were farther apart. Without his noticing until now, the boisterous crowds had thinned. There were few performers or vendors anymore. And the storefront barkers were more like wolves now, quietly stalking around the building, only approaching those nearest, those who seemed to be searching. The instruments and music had ended, replaced by the chorus of breaking glass, banging and coughing, and occasional yells from unseen sources.

Ming stopped. "Lakzo's is just around the next corner."

A high-pitched squeal punctuated her sentence. Max jumped, reaching for his gun and turning to the alley beside them. Hand on his holstered revolver, Max strained to see into the dim space between the buildings. His eyes quickly adjusted to the even lower light of the alley, and Max saw a familiar creature, the size of a small dog. Its eyes shone red. Jagged teeth jutted out from an elongated snout. Coarse black hair covered its body. Max shook at the sight, but Ming seemed unfazed.

"No problem, Mister Elliot. It's a feeder," she said. "City's full of them. Well, some parts."

"Right. I had the pleasure of seeing one earlier." Max saw that the feeder was not perched upon the ground. Its four-clawed feet appeared to be dug into a large dark form, and Max didn't need much light to know what the beast was standing on. He could smell the death. The decay.

Max took two steps deeper into the alley. The feeder did not flee. Instead, true to its name, it drove its snout down into the corpse. When it rose again, strips of dirty torn flesh hung from the beast's jaws. Two more steps, now just inside the alley, and Max could see the pool of blood congealing around the dead man lying face down. The feeder chewed feverishly on the cooling meat, swallowed and repeated its search, probing deep into the cadaver's back, pulling out fat, muscle, and nerve bundles.

Max released his grip of the gun and backed out of the alley. "Let's just do this and get the hell out of here."

"Agreed."

Lakzo's butcher shop—and the whole West End—was indeed less appealing than the East had been, but it didn't seem as dangerous as she'd made it sound.

Perhaps you're not deep enough yet.

Not that She'ol was anything to write home about, but still, the transformation had been noticeable. They stood side by side in front of the two-story building, the bricks the color of gray flecked stone instead of red flagstone. A large window had the faded signage of *Lakzo Meats* stenciled across it.

"Maybe you should come in with me," Max said.

"Nah. I'll be on the alert this time." In a flash Ming had a thin hooked blade in her hand, waving it in front of her face. "Just a little carelessness last time, being so close to the border and all. I let my guard down. Foolish."

The blade returned to its unseen hiding spot and Max went inside. The shop was icy and cured meat hung from the ceiling by twine. A glass counter displayed bowls of dark red meats that Max hoped were steaks and white and pink slabs resembling fish packed in crushed ice. Resemblances were the closest thing he could do to identify the products around him. They were dead animals, but he had no idea what kind. Or where they came from. He shuddered to think they raised feeders in the same manner humans raised cattle.

The Mara butcher—Lakzo, Max assumed—stood behind the glass counter, a bloody apron drawn around his thick belly. His clawed fingers clicked against the countertop hypnotically. Nostrils flared as Max approached, sniffing. They were always sniffing. As if they were trying to smell the sin and preempt what their customer might need.

"Yes?" it asked with the same soothing indifference all Mara had used with Max.

"I'm looking for a girl."

The butcher raised his hands, gesturing to the hanging goods. "The meats are labeled; choose your cut."

Max bit his lower lip to stay focused. "This one's still alive. She's pregnant...or was. Blonde hair, blue eyes. Twelve. I was told she was brought here a few weeks back."

Lakzo cocked his head, more sniffing, then: "Why would you come here, when you can find plenty of girls not currently suffering from the knife? At the brothel just around the corner, in fact."

For a split-second Max tasted success. He steeled himself to keep the shaking from overtaking his body. Once his voice steadied, he asked: "So she's here?"

"Indeed. But she's not well. Not well at all. Some fool human brought her. Thought he'd try his hand at *our* business for a while. Never a good idea."

And now I know Leigh Anne's kidnapper was human.

"I'd like to buy her from you."

"If she heals, I return her to the brothel. If she dies, I keep her."

It was time to dance, and Max was ready, no matter how vile the steps were.

"A while back, she was my first real taste of pussy. Healthy or not, I want to at least see her."

Lakzo's leathery skin cracked into a smile. "You humans and your love of young twat. It's too bad you have such an attachment to this piece of meat. You may see her. It won't do much good though. Unless girls heal on their own, they're no use to us. And she doesn't seem to be healing."

Max ignored the fury building up inside him as Lakzo moved from behind the counter. "Well, all the more reason I should take her off your hands."

"We'll see." He motioned Max toward the narrow staircase in the corner. "When we get ones like her, we keep them upstairs."

Max followed him up the rickety staircase and down a hallway. Blood-splattered floorboards lined the hall, creaking under their weight, and muffled moans of agony escaped through the paper-thin doors on either side. Each bloodstain hinted at a hurt girl. One like his daughter. Max ignored the coppery, sweaty smell of blood and sex, not wanting to think that Leigh Anne had been forced to contribute to it. All he focused on was the act of seeing her again.

They stopped at the last door and Lakzo retrieved a key. After the tumbler clicked into place, Lakzo swung the door open revealing Leigh Anne, sprawled out on a sheet-less mattress supported by a steel frame. A bloody towel filled with ice was nestled between her legs. She didn't turn when the door opened.

The creature leaned over and whispered a price in Max's ear, then said, "You have as long as it takes."

Max couldn't move his eyes from the pale, emaciated, and bloody body that was his only child.

The price was repeated, softly, and a large hand with sharp thick nails curling out from the fingertips came into view. Max opened his wallet and handed over some cash. He didn't know if it was the correct amount or not. He didn't care.

"Enjoy." The creature retreated down the hall.

Max stepped into the room and closed the door. His body was shaking as he fell to the floor beside the bed. "Leigh Anne." His voice was a whisper. "Leigh Anne."

Her head turned in slow clicks, and it felt like an eternity passed by the time her eyes met his. There was no sparkle there anymore. Just a cold, dead blue. She opened her mouth, her body trembled, but no words came forth.

"Oh, baby." He reached out, gently cupping her cheeks in his palms.

"Daddy?" Her eyes wide with confusion.

"It's me, baby, it's me." He wanted to smother her in hugs and kisses but settled for a light peck on the cheek instead. "I'm gonna get you outta here."

"I...I can't move."

Max looked down at her body. Thin, frail legs had replaced her strong ones, and the blood was thick on the towel between her thighs. "It'll be okay. I promise."

She coughed and struggled for air, her thin chest barely moved. "Hold me."

Max Elliot spent the next ten minutes in the filthy, squeaking bed, swaying back and forth with Leigh Anne soaked in blood and dirty water from the melted ice in his arms. He had no idea what to say. There was nothing that could fix the situation, nothing to erase her pain, nothing to heal her. Nothing that could undo his previous decisions. So he just held her and whispered over and over again about how much he loved her. How sorry he was that he had been gone that night.

Underneath his soothing whispers though, a rage built within him. He projected it at every faceless person and creature who allowed this underground hell to exist. And even more than the nameless sinners, he directed the hatred at himself. Because he *was* one of the reasons The City existed.

Max stopped rocking when he noticed that Leigh Anne's body was no longer trembling or expanding with breath. Whether she had been on the brink, or the brief assurance of her father's familiar presence allowed her to let go, Max had no idea. But she was gone, and tears dropped from his eyes as he looked down into her lifeless orbs. Death assured that her blue eyes would never sparkle again. Max sobbed quietly, biting holes into his lip as he laid his daughter out on the bed. He closed her eyes and used what ice was left to wash away the grime and blood from her face. He smoothed her dress. Kissed her forehead.

Max descended the staircase, his steps light, his face calm. Lakzo stood at his post, grinning. "I take it she has expired. Was postmortem coitus all you hoped for?"

Max threw back his trench coat and pulled the gun from its holster as he walked up to Lakzo. The creature threw out a clawed hand, driving his talons deep into Max's shoulder. The pain was immense, but it was not enough to deter Max. He fired two bullets into the creature's burly chest. Its blood, black and thick like oil, exploded over the already soiled apron. Lakzo staggered backward, his razor-sharp claws pulled from Max's flesh, and he discharged one last round—right between Lakzo's eyes. The Other's head shattered in a flurry of squishy black confetti.

Max holstered his gun. He stumbled out the door and into the arms of Ming.

"Mister Elliot! What the hell happened?"

Max struggled to stand up straight. "They killed her."

Ming looked up and down the street. "We gotta get out of

here." She grabbed his hand and pulled him away. Her grip felt good in Max's hand. He wanted to lie down. To drag Ming to the ground, curl up and sleep, knowing that they were simply holding hands.

"Stay awake," she yelled, jerking on his arm. Her voice and movements caused shooting pain to radiate down his arm. "He poisoned you with his claws. If you sleep now, you'll die."

What difference did it make? He focused on Ming and her dark hair as it bobbed through the streets.

"I know a place. Someone who can help you."

Max remembered stumbling along a few more blocks, his hand in hers. The streets seem to brighten, the crowds returned. Then, all was gone.

XIII

*W*ATCHING THE *SLOW-MOVING* Ferris wheel made Max *uncomfortable. Leigh Anne squeezed his hand tighter and without glancing down, he could tell that her eyes were growing wider with excitement.*

"Can we, Daddy? Please? Tiffany said it's amazing."

Max looked at his ten-year-old daughter. "I don't know, baby."

"Please? I'm not scared."

Eve giggled beside them. "Yeah, Daddy. She's not scared."

Max shot her a glance. "Oh, and I suppose you wanna go on that thing."

Another laugh. "No thanks. I definitely think that's a Daddy ride."

"You owe me," Max whispered in Eve's ear. He turned to Leigh Anne. "Okay, let's do this."

"Oh, thanks! You're the best."

Max survived the ride and Leigh Anne's smile made it worthwhile. The smile Eve gave him later that night made it even more worthwhile. She had her arms around his neck. She was whispering, but Max couldn't hear what she was saying. Then he watched Eve's face melt away. Dripping like morbid, bloody wax. Blackness and then there was sobbing in the dark. Leigh Anne was on the floor. She looked young, six maybe.

"Please, do something for her. Or take her to the bedroom, it's killing my head," Max said, massaging his temples.

"You're okay, baby," Eve said, rubbing Leigh Anne's bruised knee. She turned to Max. "Maybe if you hadn't been out so late last night, your head wouldn't be so easily bothered by your daughter."

Max glared at Leigh Anne's knee. The bruise was opening up. Blood seeped from the wound, soaking the carpet, filling the room, unending. Max got up from his chair, hot sand falling from his legs, which had been covered by his daughter as she played on the beach. Not blood, but sand as far as the eye could see. "Can you take me in the water, Daddy?"

"Sure." Max held out his hand to Eve. "How about all three of us take a dip?"

Knocking. Loud knocking, relentless. His head was pounding in pain with each rap.

The kitchen, no longer at the beach, surrounded him. "I'm gonna be out tonight and tomorrow."

"Oh," Eve said with more sadness than surprise. "Again?"

"Yes. Again. I'm working, Eve. I don't have the luxury of sitting around the house all day and night."

Darkness obscured his vision again. A woman was laughing in the emptiness of space. Then screaming. Leigh Anne was screaming. Then Max was screaming...

Then all was quiet, and Max joined the land of consciousness.

He rolled onto his side, head and body throbbed. His lips were parched and cracked. The details were still too fuzzy, much like the physical surroundings about him, but he knew Leigh Anne was gone. He closed his eyes to the nauseating pain and sadness, begging to be consumed by sleep again. If he could just escape back to the realm of dreams he could fix everything. Rearrange the memories and be better this time, correct his mistakes. Sleep was all it took.

Max was unsure if sleep did claim him again. Wasn't sure even where he was. Only that he had trouble focusing on anything beyond his wrecked body and sadness. The one thing that eventually broke the timeless stupor was a male voice.

"Welcome back."

It took all his energy for Max to lift his head. A slender man looked down at him. Close-set ears under brown hair in a side part. The greeting brought him back to reality and he reluctantly accepted the responsibilities that came with it.

"You're lucky to be alive." The tall man knelt, a glass of water in his hands. The sting of tears poked at the corners of Max's eyes as he watched the cold beads of condensation roll down the chilled glass. Max struggled to sit up on what he could now tell was a sofa.

"Here."

Max's shaky hands wrapped around the stranger's and together they brought the cold glass to his split lips. The man allowed only a small amount of liquid down Max's throat. Max swallowed and coughed, pressure mixing with the soothing coolness. He attempted more.

"Slow," the man cautioned.

The water flooded into the dehydrated pits of cracked flesh, and when his tongue was moist enough to speak, Max responded, "I don't feel very lucky."

"Charming. I can see why Ming helped you."

Her name further anchored him and the gruesome details of The City filled the missing gaps in his memory. "Ming? Is she all right?" Max tried to rise off the sofa, but the worn springs offered little firmness and he crumpled toward the ground. The glass tumbled across the wood floor, spilling the remaining water. The man crouched; his fingers, slender without being feminine, wrapped around Max's, and his hands were strong as they helped Max up until he was sitting upright on the couch.

"Easy there. She's fine. At the market picking up supplies."

Max's breathing slowed after the exertion and reassurance of Ming's safety. At least he hadn't allowed two young girls to die that day. Though it was a small consolation for the ache in his heart.

Max observed his surroundings; a long wall on his left was

covered in bookcases. At the opposite end of the room was a single desk littered with paper and leather-bound tomes. Large anatomical sketches of what looked like a brain and eye, drawn in minute accuracy and labeled, were tacked to the wall behind the desk. In the corner hung a skeleton, its head crooked and staring at Max with eyeless sockets.

"I'm a doctor."

Max looked down. He was in his undershirt, underwear, and socks. His skin was red and splotchy; several veins throughout his arms and legs were visible and pulsating thickly under his skin. Instead of their normal bluish hue, they coursed with what looked like infected, blackish-red blood. He remembered Ming's words: *he poisoned you with his claws.*

Looking back at the man, Max said, "Thank you for helping me." Though he had no idea what had transpired since his blackout. "Where am I? And who are you, to whom I owe so much?"

"My name is Arthur. And this is my home. Thank Ming, not me. She saved you." He stood and, like a relieved parent once they know that their child is all right, Arthur's tone changed. "What you owe me is an explanation as to why Ming is putting herself at risk to help you. Nobody kills a Mara. *They'll* be looking for you. What were you thinking?"

Max cast his eyes to the floor. His voice cracked while recounting the parts of the story he could remember. "When I pulled the trigger I wasn't thinking. All I saw was Leigh Anne's face."

Arthur left with the empty glass and returned with more water. "I am sorry for you. I truly am." He handed the cool glass to Max. "And I will help you regain your health, but in a day or so, you'll have to leave."

Max took a slow sip and nodded. "This is the kind of stuff they make you a slave for, huh?"

Arthur's lack of acknowledgement was all the confirmation Max needed. "I'm not a heartless man. But I made a promise to her sister that I would keep Ming safe. There's little chance you can elude them after what you've done. They will find you and—"

"You're up!" Ming entered from a door to his right, a wooden crate of supplies held again her chest. She put the box down, dusting off her jacket and trouser suit—which looked to be the same outfit as before—and Max was hoping that fact meant he hadn't been unconscious for long. She headed to the couch in her swift manner and for a split second, Max thought the young girl was going to hug him. She stopped before contacting him and offered her hand instead. "I got food. I'll make us all something to eat."

Arthur sighed. "I was just telling our patient that after treatment he'll need to leave."

Ming grabbed the box and headed to the kitchen, which was separated from his room with the desk and skeleton by a short half wall. "He just woke up. Can't this wait?"

Arthur left Max's side and followed her into the kitchen, his voice lowering to a volume Max could barely register. If Max possessed the strength, he'd dress and leave, but the mere act of finding his clothes seemed like it would drain him of any power he'd gained since waking.

Arthur threw up his hands and returned to the main room, hovering near the door. "I'll be leaving for the surface soon, and in preparation, I have some errands to run. But…we do need to discuss what's to be done. Rationally." He held up his index finger and he circled it in the air, encompassing them both. "This is not safe. Ming, I want you to think about what we discussed." With his point made, Arthur exited, much louder than when Ming entered.

Max looked diagonally across the room and over the half wall at Ming, embarrassed that not only was he in undergarments, but that his presence had caused a massive disruption between her and…

Who is Arthur? He looked and sounded American, so a blood relative was out. His closeness in age to Max made it unlikely that he was a friend or romantic interest. Whoever he was, it was clear that they shared a life together. When she'd emptied the crate, Ming looked up and found Max's gaze.

"It'll be okay." And for the first time, he saw Ming smile—genuine, like her sarcastic and cold exterior seemed to have thawed while he slumbered in his feverish coma.

Whereas the room with the couch and desk had been cluttered, the rest of the home was tidy. Past the kitchen was a bathroom and two bedrooms.

Dressing had been a struggle, but Max had refused Ming's help. His joints pulled and popped when he extended them to pull on his shirt and pants. He felt like a hatched bird stretching its wings for the first time, breaking through the stagnation of new life. Time seemed suspended as he dressed, dragging on, prolonging his excruciating burden.

It resumed normal speed once he took a seat in the kitchen and watched Ming make eggs. His stomach warned him to eat slow, but unlike with dressing, the energy exerted was more satisfying. When he was finished, she cleared the plates to the sink.

"I didn't realize how hungry I was. Thank you."

"I'm glad you liked it. I have one more dish for you." She brought a small plate to the oak icebox and removed something from a container inside. She returned to the table and placed it in front of him. Max looked down at what he could only describe as a whitish-gelatinous ball. Ming set a fork next to his hand.

"Dessert?"

"It's not dessert," Ming said. "It's medicine. The only reason you're still alive. Arthur didn't tell you?"

Max shook his head. "Just told me how lucky I was. And how I was endangering both of you. About that, I'm sorry. I—"

"The poison in their claws destroys your blood. There is only one thing that can cure the infection, if you get it in time: dumplings."

Max looked down at the egg-shaped ball. Its gelled surface undulated in the light. Sure as hell didn't look like any dumpling Max ever saw before. "That hospital ward," Max said.

"That's right. The dumplings will heal you. It is an expensive resource to The City…in more ways than one."

Arthur's frustration became more apparent to Max. "Tell Arthur I'll pay him. I'm not a charity case. I don't want him to act

113

ill toward you for helping me."

Ming dismissed him with a wave of her hand. "I told him you'd reimburse him. It's not that though. Money isn't a problem for Arthur. He's just worried. He's a surgeon. Or was. Well… it's a long story, I suppose. He always helps. He's just scared of what will happen if they find you with us."

"Is he…family…a friend?"

"He's my uncle. Sort of. My older sister raised me. When she got married to Arthur, he kind of adopted me too. After she passed away, I stayed with Arthur. Beyond her, he's the only family I ever really had."

Back on the streets, when she'd knifed her attacker in the crotch, Max couldn't see Ming as having this gentle side to her; her coldness had felt as eternal as The City's. "I'll make things up to Arthur."

Max looked down at his unorthodox medicine. Now that they'd stopped talking, the silence wrapped around him, constricting him from moving. The conversation to this point had kept him functional, kept his mind off the reason they were in this mess together. But it was also the one thing neither of them seemed to want to discuss.

"You've already had that stuff," Ming said as if knowing he still needed a distraction. "Arthur was injecting you with a liquid version while you were passed out. Now you have to eat it; the first three days are crucial. And today is still day three."

"Christ, I've been out for two days?"

"I recommend not looking at it. Two big bites."

Max sighed and picked up the ball, it was cool and squishy in his hands. His teeth sunk into the alien texture. Liquid and stringy, chewy strips flooded his mouth. He swallowed it down, feeling something dribble over his lips to his chin. He pushed the second half of the oval into his mouth. The taste was foul, and the consistency was what he imagined drinking a raw egg might be like. He tried to swallow it down without chewing. Grinding it up was only going to release the flavor further. He wiped his lips and chin, choking the mass down his esophagus.

He opened his eyes, not realizing he had shut them, and Ming was handing him a glass of water. He graciously accepted and drank two gulps in an effort to rid his mouth of the vile aftertaste.

"What the hell is that stuff?"

"It's the only reason Arthur bothers to live down here and deal with these monsters."

Ming cleaned and dried the dishes while explaining that Arthur had been a doctor in San Francisco when he met and married Ming's sister, Mingxia. Ming was only three at the time of the wedding and the age difference made her consider Arthur more of an uncle than brother-in-law. There was no mention of parents. Mingxia became ill by the time Ming was six. Arthur worked night and day to diagnose and help her. Nothing worked. He had become so desperate for help he would try anything.

Dumplings. It was a word whispered by back alley surgeons. A miracle cure.

"But nothing is without a price." Ming pointed to Max's branded hand. "He's marked now, same as you. Same as me." Ming held up her hand. Same Ouroboros, only hers was smaller and faded slightly. Max wondered how young Ming had been when she made the choice. "The worst part is that Arthur was not in time to save my sister. She passed away and we remained here.

"I was too young to remember much of the surface. They were the only family I had up there, and they were the only two I had down here. Pointless to move back."

Max wasn't so sure that was a valid point. But he remained silent. He looked at his own scarred hand. The flesh had completely healed since he succumbed to the Other's poison. The scabs had fallen off and he was left with raised skin of the one-eyed serpent devouring its own tail. This was his mark. For always.

"Arthur's life is taking care of me and still doing what he can to help people back on the surface. He's that miracle cure now for so many in the poorest parts of San Francisco. He takes them dumplings, never explains what they are or burdens anyone with the knowledge of this place. He charges only what they can reasonably afford—enough so we can live here and buy more."

"That's a selfless life. I'm impressed," Max said. "And what about your life, Ming?"

"I'm happy that he can help people like my sister. I do my part by being a guide, I take care of the house when he's gone. We're a team."

"But what do you want for your life?"

Ming finished drying the plates and sat back down at the table. "Now you sound like Arthur. He always wants me to go back to the surface; has offered a million times to live up there instead of down here."

"Of course he does. He wants you to find your calling like he has. You can't do that down here."

"Beyond us helping the sick, I just want to survive," Ming said. "One city is just as good as another."

"Living and surviving are different. Isn't there more you want?"

She sighed, stood up, walked to the couch, and sat down. "And what about you, huh? What is it you want?" She cast her eyes down, biting her bottom lip as if chastising herself for breaking the silent agreement to avoid the discussion.

Max stood, pushed in the kitchen chair, and headed over to join her.

"I'm sorry," Ming said.

"Don't be." Leigh Anne's face resurfaced and Max felt drugged as he sat on the opposite side of the couch. He teetered on the edge of the cushion contemplating the question that had numbed his senses, making him feel like he was balancing on the edge of a bottomless pit of depression and one more word could throw him into its unforgiving chasm. "I...I tend to only want things after I lose them."

"You can change that, you know? Mingxia use to say it's never too late to change."

Never too late...until you're dead. Hot tears welled in his eyes. Escape never lasted, and reality, like the tide, always came crashing back in.

Ming looked away sheepishly again.

"No, you're right," Max said. "What do I want?" Max couldn't even say for certain that he wanted to live. What was left to survive for? "I guess I want you and Arthur to be safe. Your purpose is to keep helping the sick. So I *want* to leave as soon as possible."

"I'm sorry. Don't think about this now. Focus on resting."

"Arthur is right. These creatures will think you're both accomplices in the murder."

"I don't think anyone saw us. We were out of there fast. Violence isn't new to the West End. By the time any other Maras found out what happened, we were long gone."

"No. They're like bloodhounds with those noses."

"I feel confident," Ming said.

"Well, I'm glad one of us is. Still, as soon as I can, I should go. I wasn't able to protect my daughter and I don't want to bring a similar fate to you or Arthur."

"Don't say that. You did all you could."

If only you knew, sweetheart. If only you knew.

XIV

McCLOUD WALKED TO his apartment from the market, his hands holding a paper bag of fresh produce, chicken meat, and broth. Most people he knew celebrated with dinner out or a night filled with drinks and live entertainment. But that wasn't really McCloud's style. He cooked all his own meals, had been doing it ever since his parents died, and he wasn't going to stop now.

The victory this morning had been minor, but McCloud knew he couldn't look at it as Harris just throwing him a bone. As with everything, it was an opportunity. The offer came earlier in the day, when a tired Harris had called on him.

After all the faith placed in Max, allowing him to be an unseen lead, forcing Johnston to remain in charge on paper only, Elliot had disappeared without a trace. At this point he'd been out of contact for a week. Harris's admission had given McCloud a second of hope that his skill and enthusiasm were going to land him the case, though the lieutenant quickly squashed those dreams.

"If he's gone AWOL, the mayor's office will want him

replaced with equal experience. You don't have that, McCloud, so Johnston's back on lead officially," Harris had explained. "The chief, the mayor, those men don't care about potential. Not yours or mine. They only want results. If *you* are lead and we don't make progress, it's the chief's fault for allowing you to run things, which makes it my fault for assigning you. *But* if Johnston is in charge, it's on the experienced head of Johnston."

McCloud had expected the copout. In his mind, he was already contacting Tom Proctor again, contemplating how he'd ask about getting his old job back. Or perhaps there was something else he could do for the juvenile system. Something away from the bureaucratic nonsense aspect of the job. While he understood the politics, he didn't agree with them. And he had no idea why he was being summoned only to be informed that again he had been overlooked for what he wanted; it was like Harris took sick pleasure in aggravating him.

Harris must have sensed his confusion. He massaged the purple bags under his eyes. "Listen to what I'm saying, McCloud. Even though the girl's homicide is out of my hands, I can technically give you a missing person's case...since you're a criminal investigator."

"Leigh Anne Elliot?" His voice had brightened assuming the mayor would approve due to his extensive work in the child services committee.

"No," Harris had said. "You're gonna find Max Elliot."

McCloud might not have been happy with the opportunity, but if Max was his open door into the files, then so be it. He'd allow himself to be an errand boy one more time.

Ahead of McCloud was a newsboy waving a paper in the air. "Unspeakable murders in Chinatown. Detective missing."

McCloud slowed. There was no way this kid had print on Elliot. It had to be something else. His building was just around the corner, but McCloud veered across the street to the boy instead. "Let me get a copy, please, son." McCloud fished a nickel from his pocket, doing his best to not seem impatient. "Keep the change."

The boy's eyes brightened at the tip. "Here you go, mister."

The bundle of newsprint went under his arm, and McCloud smiled. "Thank you."

As he ascended the apartment building steps, McCloud's pace hastened. Inside, he left the groceries out on the counter, unable to delay his anticipation anymore even for something as minor as storing the food. He opened the paper and laid it out across the dining table.

The first phrases of the article were surreal. Never before had McCloud been at a crime scene that had made front page news. There was a picture of the housing complex just outside of Chinatown, and the journalist laid out a good chunk of details, painting a story of barbaric torture. As McCloud read on, his fascination morphed to frustration as he realized that Harris had neglected to share all the new details that were in black and white print for all the world to see.

Marian Bell was the third and youngest child of a carpenter. Her older sisters had left her for barely a minute when the child went missing. The parents were co-owners in a successful construction business; they were upper middle class through and through. Americans. Good Americans. This poor young girl was the only victim who could be identified in the triple homicide. According to the article, the other children at the scene had been "fatally injured beyond recognition".

In their morning meeting, the lieutenant had alluded to the media storm they knew was on the horizon once the girls were identified. But he failed to let McCloud know that it was no longer something lurking in the near future. It was here.

And that wasn't where the story ended either. McCloud flipped open the paper to continue. Harris's timing for McCloud's new missing person assignment suddenly became clearer. Someone had leaked info to the press about Max. The journalist did not name the source, but they revealed that Max Elliot's family was murdered in much the same way as Marian Bell. And that subsequently Elliot was given lead in the bizarre murder. The article criticized the decision as amateur, stating that putting a vulnerable detective on such a personal case ought to have embarrassed the department. It went on to assume that since receiving the case, Max had met a similar fate and that's why he'd been missing.

McCloud's blood ran cold when he passed over the moniker for the killer. *The Chinatown Surgeon.*

Someone had snitched and the paper published the truth, then chose a name to inspire terror. And Chinatown was a great name to drop, even if the bodies weren't found quite within city limits.

McCloud read a bit more and then folded the paper. He returned to the produce, a sardonic smile on his face while preparing a dinner of chicken soup. The Mayor had to be outraged, but McCloud doubted that his wrath came down on Harris for putting Max on the case. He would be mad that it backfired and that the press got hold of the truth instead of the cover story from Johnston.

Broth boiled and McCloud cut vegetables. The mindless tasks were relaxing and he reminded himself it didn't matter that Harris's generosity hadn't been prompted by McCloud's determination and grit. Turns out that Harris needed to save face by locating Elliot before the detective did something more to jeopardize the case now that he was completely rouge…or dead. Either way, McCloud had his chance to shine. And he couldn't waste it, regardless of Harris's ulterior motives.

When dinner was finished and dishes cleaned, McCloud returned to his reading chair. Ignoring the bookshelf filled with dusty spines of teacher textbooks, children's fables, and a few classics by Dickens and Shakespeare, McCloud consulted the thick file on Max Elliot. Harris was giving him two days before he had to return the documents.

McCloud left the folder unopened on his lap and closed his eyes. An image of Max Elliot formed behind his tired eyelids. It was easy to see him as a detective, but McCloud had to see him as a man. A father. A husband.

Remember, Tom Proctor's voice echoed from somewhere down the hall of years. *When we work with children, one must separate the child from the delinquent behavior. The behavior is the problem, not the kid. We work to understand their motives.*

And what were Elliot's motives? Who was he? McCloud questioned if he and Max had similarities in how they worked a case. How they lived. How they measured success.

Without the influence of the files yet, McCloud gave the sarcastic, drug–addled detective the benefit of the doubt, imagining, perhaps falsely, scenarios that had given Max the reputation he'd earned as an "accomplished detective". Clearly, others saw him in this light for a reason. And if McCloud was going to find him, he had to understand him. As strange as it seemed, envisioning the thirty-six-year-old detective as a student proved helpful.

Max wasn't a bad kid. He'd made bad decisions. Now it was time to find out why. McCloud opened his eyes and the folder.

Max spent each hour that crept by regaining his mobility and trying not to think about Leigh Anne. He paced the living room, working the kinks out of his legs. He perused through the stacks of anatomy texts and patient diagnosis, but the content was too dry to read in his current state. A momentary excitement built in him when he found a few historical works, Plato and other Greek philosophers, books he hadn't considered in ages, but as a young man they had thrilled him, taught him how to question and think critically. But when the printed word was in front of his face he found the strain to be too much on his eyes. On one shelf, he saw a mantle clock among the rows of books. Its hands read two o'clock, and Max wondered if it was the time in the real world and not in this subterranean hell.

He napped in between his travels around the home, but the sleep was short and interrupted. He didn't like the places his unconscious mind travelled to and the limited outcomes his nightmares offered for his future. Ming spent her time working on the house and preparing future non-perishable meals and ones that could be saved in the ice chest. She also spent time in her room, reaffirming their silent pact to not acknowledge Leigh Anne's death. Though Ming did not neglect checking on his status.

"How do you feel?" she asked noticing he was awake again.

"Surprisingly well," Max lied, sitting up from the couch. "I can feel my energy coming back, it's just taking its damn sweet time."

"Good," she said. "I have a few more things to prepare for the surface trip. Then we can talk more…if you want."

Max had a feeling he knew what type of talk she was

suggesting, and he still had no desire. He wanted only to forget. He'd convinced himself his focus should remain on health so he could get out of their hair. True, he could have slipped away from the home at any time, but he knew Ming was attached to him for some reason. If he disappeared without warning or left in anger, he'd hurt her. And he wanted to avoid that if possible. He had a recent, uncharacteristic desire to express respect in his future decision making. "When's this surface trip?"

Ming looked at the clock. "Within the next twenty-four hours."

"And does it have anything to do with what Arthur told you to consider before he left?"

Ming frowned. "He's found someone we can live with up there. He wants me to move there tomorrow with what I can carry. And then he'll join me."

"But I showed up."

"It's not you. I don't wanna live there. And I told him that. There's nothing up there for me."

Hearing the same feelings he battled voiced by this sixteen-year-old girl was an odd experience. Max believed every word when he'd said there was nothing back home for him. But the same phrase of despair, no matter how true it was, uttered by someone so young and kind as Ming was heartbreaking. If life had shown him anything since his night of adultery, it was that he did have feelings. He'd always had them as a child, but as he aged, something happened. He'd been around the dregs of society so much he was accustomed to it, and each day he embraced his own loss of humanity. His job became enforcing laws and investigating murders, *not* preventing crimes and protecting. There was a huge difference, even though he told himself that punishing criminals was a deterrent to others. And along the path he switched from experiencing emotions to preventing them and suppressing them away. Max didn't want to think that Ming could have as little hope as him for a future somewhere else.

"What if you try?"

"I said I'd try, but it wasn't supposed to be for another week. I wanted to prepare myself. He's moving it up because he's worried that they're looking for you."

"All the more reason for you to go."

"If the Mara wanted us, they'd have found us by now," Ming said. "I told Arthur we'd keep the original plan. If he's so willing, he can take everything up and I'll follow next week."

Max wanted to argue, but she was a kid. It was time he acted like an adult. And he was going to start tonight.

Arthur came home while Ming was plating the chicken and noodles she'd cooked for dinner. "Looks delicious." He pecked her on the cheek, then put his stuff down on the couch. Max received a nod.

"Hello, Arthur."

"How are you feeling?"

"Pretty good, all things considering."

From his discarded items on the couch, Arthur picked up his medical bag and walked over to Max's seat in the kitchen.

"Food's just about ready, Arthur. Can't this wait?"

"Mr. Elliot?" Arthur pulled his stethoscope from the bag.

"By all means. I appreciate the check-up."

Arthur looked back at Ming. "I'll only take a few minutes."

Ming huffed and brought over utensils and cloth napkins.

"Pulse is strong and steady," Arthur said, releasing Max's wrist. He examined the veins in his arms and legs. "The dosage with this meal will probably be your last. I don't wish to hex you, but I think you're past the danger zone."

"That's what I like to hear, doc," Max said. "I think I need to get going as soon as possible."

"To the surface?" Arthur returned the stethoscope to his black bag.

"I think so. We could go separately of course."

Arthur smiled. "Together is fine."

"I'm not going tomorrow." Ming set the plates against the table with too much force and the water cups rattled. "I told you that."

"Fine. Stay here," Arthur said. His tone was calm and he gave Max a knowing look, pleased with Max that regardless of Ming's decision, Max would be nowhere near her.

Arthur pointed at the mantle clock. "That's the time in Chinatown." The hands were positioned at six o'clock. "I keep track of the days based on the surface so I know what season I'm coming up in. It's early evening now. I'll take you to the exit in eight hours, and you'll reach the streets around mid-morning."

"I suppose you're getting what you want." Ming pushed noodles around her plate.

"You allowed me to see my daughter one last time. Got me moving so I didn't feel like a complete failure. Now I just want you to be safe."

"You also said you have nothing on the surface. You're like us. We should all stick together. You can help us. Arthur—" she turned to her uncle "—he can help us. He's a police officer. That's gotta come in handy—"

"I need to go, Ming. My staying here is too dangerous."

Her eyes filled with anger and he couldn't tell why. What use did she see in him helping her and Arthur?

"Might as well head down to Gehanna instead of the surface," she said.

"Ming!" Arthur chastised her.

"What? He'll wind up there anyway, I'm sure."

Max ignored the comment, and they ate the rest of the meal in silence, everyone seeming to mull over their own demons. When they were done, Ming cleared the table. It seemed that she went out of her way to create as much noise possible with the plates. Afterward, she murmured a goodnight and headed to her room.

"Don't worry about her," Arthur said when she'd gone. "Your departure will allow her to remain here until the original day she had anticipated leaving. She'll be ready by then. Thank you for understanding."

"I'm not sure why she can't see the problems with the three of us staying together," Max said.

"She might have spent her teenage years in a subterranean-nightmare city, but adolescent emotions still rule her, no matter how old she may appear." Arthur stood up and took a dumpling from the icebox. He got a fork and placed Max's final dose of medicine on the table.

"I wish she was still cold and leery of me. Better yet, she

should have let me die."

"She said you were forthright with her. That you tried to save her when she was accosted. And most importantly, you were the first person she'd met—other than me—who was in The City to help someone besides themselves."

Max let the words sink in as he looked at the plate of jellied medicine.

"It's your last dose. Don't let it sit long."

"Thanks," he said, breathing hard. "Here goes." He pinched his nose shut and bit into the ball of medicinal nutrients. *This is helping me*, Max told himself when slick, jelly-like strands stuck to his throat, accumulating in many swallows to detach them from his esophageal lining and a near loss of control of his gag reflex. "What the hell are those dumplings, anyway?"

"You do not want to know." Arthur stood up. "Take my bed tonight. It's preferable to the couch, and you need all the rest you can get. Remember, six o'clock."

"I can't take your bed, Arthur."

"Nonsense. I've had great sleep recently. One night on the couch will be no inconvenience." He pointed down the hall to the bedroom door.

"You're a good man, Arthur."

"And apparently, so are you. Ming would not be acting this way otherwise."

"She said the Mara would have come by now if they knew. She right?"

"Ming isn't using logic well right now. But on this point, she makes a valid claim. However, the Mara are patient. Biding time is not beyond them if it serves a purpose." Arthur led Max to the bedroom and turned on the light. The bed was small and the room was bare save for two more crates of books and medical equipment. "I'll see you at six," Arthur said from the doorway.

Max sat on the bed, then looked back at Arthur. "Come on, let me in on the dumpling secret."

"I told you not to ask." But Arthur seemed to consider, then took a deep breath. "I discovered the medicinal properties of the Mara's special dumplings when trying to save my wife. I was too late for her though. The product itself disgusts and revolts me. Their production is not a practice I condone. But it happens here all the same, whether I disagree with it or not. Most exploit the medicinal properties out of greed and a desire to prolong a wicked life. I try to make sense of the madness by using it to help worthy people beat cruel and unfair diseases." Arthur pointed at Max's hand. "Your burn, completely healed; your blood, rid of all toxins. In a day or two, your skin will shimmer as it never has before and should you have had any asymptomatic illnesses hiding in recesses of your body, those will be gone too.

"The Others have found a way to synthesize these effects using the beginnings of life. There's no delicate way to put it, so I'll just say it. They use embryos, plucked at the specified moment and put through a process secret to all but the Mara. Many have tried to duplicate it and failed."

Max's stomach roiled. He had slurped down a treated fetus. His head spun with revolting images and possibilities. The worst of all being that he had possibly ingested the remains of his daughter's aborted amniotic sac. His uvula quivered and food rose again. Max steadied his breathing and willed the nausea away.

"Try not to think about it," Arthur said. "That's what I do. As a doctor, this dangerous procedure goes against my nature. But if the Others continue the barbaric practice, I'd like to think I've at least brought something positive out it. That I've cured some good souls in the process. Worthy souls who wouldn't have had a chance otherwise. Like you."

"Well, maybe not like me," Max said.

"Ming thinks you're one of the worthy ones."

The reassurance felt good despite Max's inability to accept it as truth. In addition to the temporary assuage to his mental state, it also calmed the storm of bile that was battling to vacate his stomach...but not by much.

"Goodnight." Arthur closed the door and Max heard him return to the couch.

His dreams were nightmares. Gigantic Maras ripped fetuses from young mothers, then handed the slimy, quivering sacs to power-hungry denizens of The City. Drug addicts healed up their bodies just enough to prolong their lives for the next fix. Criminals, harmed in heists, healed their wounds and strengthened for the next job. Evil old men bit down on the chewy slop, amniotic fluids splashing across their laughing faces. Cackles ringing out as they cheated death, extending their wicked life of debauchery and inflicting pain on others without the threat of a punishment in the afterlife.

It was a miserable sleep, and Max woke with a scream building in his chest, sweaty sheets stuck to his body, and unsatisfying answers chewing at his nerves as to why he was worth the dumplings and not Leigh Anne.

The house was quiet and the heavy shades kept it dark. Trying to make as little noise as possible, Max left Arthur's bedroom and went to the hallway bathroom. He had no idea what hour it was, but he didn't want to disturb anyone if it wasn't close to rising time yet.

He washed his face and spent too long looking at himself in the mirror. He should have been worn and haggard. He was not, and it was another reminder of the suffering someone else went through so he could be mended by the dumplings.

Ming thinks you're one of the worthy ones.

I hope she's right.

Leaving the bathroom, Max saw a dark shadow on the couch. It looked as if Arthur was sitting on the cushions staring at the wall. But the movement of the dark form was all wrong. Suddenly, the whole room felt wrong. The shape was swaying, and a ragged sound emitted from the darkness of the heavily-curtained room. If the man was sleeping, it was not a peaceful rest.

Max took a few steps forward. "Arthur?"

The shadow twitched further. Then the sound became a moan, pleading almost.

"Arthur, is that you?" Volume came from deep in Max's chest and exploded into his voice. He didn't care about waking Ming. Something had happened. Max took a few steps closer to the couch, slowly, letting his eyes adjust to the darkness. It was Arthur all right, and he was bound with rope.

Max darted to the bedroom, retrieved his gun from the holster hanging on a chair. With the cocked pistol in one hand, he crept along the hallway, drawing two window shades as he went. Artificial light spilled into the house.

Arthur's voice was frantic now, high-pitched and indecipherable. When Max was satisfied that they were alone, he raced over to Arthur and laid the gun down, mortified by the sight, unsure of the best way to proceed.

Arthur's eyes were red and puffy. His lips had been sewn shut with fishing line. He had torn the flesh when he tried to open his mouth to get Max's attention and blood was seeping from the stretched wounds, and still his mouth remained tightly shut. His body and arms were wrapped in thick ropes. Only his legs and neck were free, though his neck was not unscathed. A piece of paper had been affixed above his Adam's apple. More fishing line—through a hole on either side of the paper—went through the skin on both sides of his neck. Unlike the stitching on his lips, the holes in his neck were massive. Looking down, Max could not see evidence of the needle used, but he had an idea. The wound was big enough to fit a small finger through...or a claw. A sheet of paper hung from Arthur's bleeding neck.

"Stay calm. I'm going to get a scalpel from your kit. Cut you loose. Okay?"

Arthur's lolling head steadied for a moment and he gave two strong nods, before a daze seemed to reclaim his eyes and drop his head in swaying rolls again.

Max grabbed the medical bag that was still on the kitchen counter and a butcher knife. He cut away the rope bindings with the knife, then opened the medical kit and removed a scalpel. "Keep still."

Max cut the note from his neck and put the paper on the kitchen table. "You should be the one to cut through the line in your mouth. You're a doctor, you'll do better than me."

This time Arthur shook his head.

Max knew there was no easy way to do this; the pain would be immense. He rested the back of Arthur's skull against the sofa, then placed his palm flat against Arthur's forehead to prevent the man from moving as much as possible. Gentle as he could, Max began sawing through the most accessible stitches in the front. He felt two give way, a rush of air whistling through the freed section of lips. Fresh tears streamed from the corners of Arthur's eyes.

The tug of skin below the scalpel was sickening to Max.

Max dropped the scalpel into the bag, blood seeping into the fabric from the dripping blade. He pulled out a set of surgical scissors. With a few front stitches gone, there was enough room to get the scissors in, and the scissors would be less painful…he hoped. A few quick snips and Arthur yawned wide, groaning, spitting out blood and tiny pieces of flesh.

With Arthur safe for the moment, Max looked back at the bedrooms. "Ming!"

"Gone." The word was labored and weak.

"What?" Max hovered close above his lips, barely able to hear through Arthur's mask of pain and confusion.

"I don't have much time. They used a talon on me."

"I'll get the dumplings from the icebox." Max stood. "Ming!"

Arthur put a feeble hand around his arm. "They took them all…except one… Fed it to me…" Arthur sucked in heavy, coughing on the air and blood, lungs seeming to work overtime to combat the lethargy setting into his organs. "It was just enough to keep me conscious while they sewed me up."

Max closed his eyes. "I'm so goddamned sorry," he breathed. "I'll get help. I'll find more dumplings."

"No time. Been hours."

Max looked to the clock on the wall, shocked to see it'd been six hours since they had said goodnight.

"The note." Arthur looked up at him with saucers of glossy pain.

Max grabbed the paper note from the table. Read it silently.

"Ming's alive." He looked up from the paper. "Captured, but alive."

Tears mixed with blood as small vessels in Arthur's eyes split from the mounting pressure of the poison. Trails of gore ran from his eyes to his bobbing Adam's apple and pooled in the V-shaped depression of his neck.

"Find Ming." He coughed, spit blood. "Save Ming."

"I will." Max clasped Arthur's hand. "I swear I will."

"I'm ready to see my wife again." Arthur's eyes closed.

Max held his hand until Arthur's death rattle gasps for air stopped.

Shaking, Max stood, wiped sweat from his brow and fell into

one of the kitchen chairs. He looked at the note, Arthur's blood drying on the edges of the paper. The print was scratchy and small, but quite legible.

THIS MAN DIED FOR YOUR CRIME. THE GIRL WILL WORK FOR US UNTIL THE END. SHE WILL BEG FOR DEATH. EVERY DAY YOU WILL KNOW THAT SHE IS ALIVE AND SUFFERING BECAUSE OF YOU.
THAT IS YOUR PUNISHMENT.

Max looked at his pistol lying next to Arthur's corpse. Eve was dead. Leigh Anne and Arthur too. Ming gone forever.

She will beg for death.

Max had managed to let down everyone who had ever cared for him. He wanted to mash the revolver into his mouth and pull the trigger. It would be so easy, and then all the pain would be gone.

You did all you could. Ming's sweet voice filled his ears.

"No...I didn't," he told the silent room. His eyes burned with regret. Max dropped his head to the table and cried. Choking on his sobs.

Somewhere in The City, Ming cried too.

PART II

1

WHEN HIS PULSE finally slowed, and his swollen eyes had no more water left to shed into the hairs of his unshaved cheeks, Max fell asleep on the floor.

He woke on a beach, the sands white and hot beneath him. He sat up and surveyed the land, expecting to see Leigh Anne nearby, but found only blue skies and endless dunes. Max struggled to his feet and looked behind him—the same gorgeous but barren landscape greeted him. There was no ocean, no people, not even his daughter, who he was sure he was destined to find here.

There came a rumble in the distance and the mounds of sand shifted beneath his feet. Stabilizing himself, Max watched dark clouds swarm, closing in a circle until the last patch of clear blue sky disappeared above his head. The ground shook again, and this time he fell against the soft sand. He tried to get up, but he couldn't find purchase, gravity pulling him down, dragging the grains of sand down too, down into some kind of abyss. Max scrambled up a dune on his hands and knees as more of the ground was swallowed up into a hole that was forming in the middle of the beach, but he couldn't escape the drawing force. He rolled onto his back and looked down to see a mechanical mouth in the hole, gears and steam belching amidst iron teeth. A mutant hybrid from the industrial assembly lines that opened and closed devouring sand into its maw. The steel jaws opened and shut rhythmically, waiting for Max to tumble.

The rains came next, pelting him with cold hard drops. The heaven's tears turned out to be his savior though. The water hardened the ground enough for his feet to dig in, and Max was able to claw himself up, away from the mouth, up and up until he collided with the sky. Dazed, he placed his hand in front of him and felt cool glass, streaking with rain and condensation. He was surrounded by glass.

"It's okay." Her voice came from outside the hourglass. Soft and sweet as it had been when she was alive. "You can save her. There's still time, Daddy. Save her."

Max woke with a hollowness in his chest and extremities. An emptiness that dulled his body but thankfully not his head. Ideas swirled within his mind like the storm clouds from his dream. Above all else, a desire to act formed, to take a final stand, to run through the streets, killing them all, burning down the West End one rat-infested building at a time until he found Ming.

But that wouldn't save her.

If he really cared about Ming, about Leigh Anne, then brute force was not the way. But if he planned, if he calculated multiple outcomes, then Max had a chance. He contemplated the predicament and a fit of hysterical laughter threatened as he accepted the irony of this new dilemma, how close it mirrored his decision that October night that now seemed so long ago. Another missing girl, another long shot, and lots of pain ahead.

This time Max would make the right decision, and win or lose, it was going to be his last case.

Max paced through Arthur's house. He looked over books and artwork, trying to feel Arthur's passion in his anatomy sketches, sat in Ming's room to envision how she felt each day leaving for guide work. He closed his eyes, asked the walls where to start, then roamed over the living room bookcases again. But he found no new insights. Lacking even the faintest idea of how to begin this new journey pushed him toward the crushing vacuum of hopelessness.

No, it wasn't hopelessness; it was being realistic. The flame of action that his dream initiated began to dwindle. He should have known from the get go that this was asinine. Even back when he'd allowed Harris and McCloud to drag him into this. Max had to have always known the futility, even if only subconsciously. Ninety percent of the time a detective knows, deep down, how each case will play out. That's why he'd chosen the vices of Chinatown after Eve and Leigh Anne, to avoid the failure that he knew was inevitable. If he'd just stayed there then he could have limited the death toll to his own family; instead he'd destroyed Ming's too.

Max struggled to breathe against the surmounting pressure in his chest. He should be back in Ku's opium den right now—all these problems would go up in smoke. Everything would—

Then his attention was caught by something on top of Arthur's bookcase. He saw Leigh Anne's hands. Adolescent fingers wrapped around a box as if presenting it to him. It was a *Himitsu-Bako*. And he could almost hear her voice urging him to solve it.

As quick as they'd appeared, the hands vanished. Max closed his eyes, imagining her presence up on the bookshelf, not wanting to lose the thought of her being nearby. Never had he seen images of Leigh Anne while sober; at least he didn't think. Perhaps though....

He thought back to when McCloud first came for him at Ku's. Yes, he'd imagined her hands around the puzzle box just before lighting up. But this time, rather than sadness and regret, the sight of her hands seemed to alleviate some of the pain, dissipated a minutia of the growing pressure in his lungs.

Max opened his eyes and even though the visual was gone, he felt a surge electrify his body. As he picked up the shoebox-sized *Himitsu-Bako* and sat down on the floor, he wondered if he could use her presence for motivation instead of punishment. Unlike before, Leigh Anne wasn't missing. She wasn't trapped in some demon's brothel. He'd found her and she was free and perhaps she chose to show him the puzzle box.

Closing his eyes, Max turned the box over in his hands, savoring the strength he imagined he pulled from the wood having been touched by Leigh Anne's ethereal presence. He suddenly wasn't thinking about the lucky discovery of the box or about the energy; he was just breathing.

His mind drifted over the current situation, turning it over in numerous directions along with the painted wood. Eventually his concentration centered on his first experience with such as puzzle. He had been at his grandfather's house, manipulating a similar box repeatedly in his ten-year-old hands, when Max had announced: "It can't be opened."

The newspaper crinkled as his grandfather had lowered it from his face and studied Max. The old man leaned forward in his armchair. "Are you sure?"

"Of course. There are no clasps or hinges or...anything."

"Didn't I tell you it was a puzzle?"

"Yeah, but we've done puzzles before, and they're never like this. How can you even get inside?" Max knew his grandfather hated when people complained, but he was stumped.

His grandfather folded the paper and stood from the armchair. He approached Max's spot on the carpet, and with an exaggerated groan lowered himself to the floor next to the boy.

"Things are not always what they seem." Taking the cube in his hands, Max's grandfather slid a finger gently along one edge. Before Max could process the move, the seemingly flawless corner twisted.

"How did—"

"Try."

The cube was handed back and Max had gotten to work without a word. He felt the second corner twist in his fingers. Within the box something popped, ever so gently, but Max could still register the movement on the pads on his fingers. He turned the contraption over to find that a small rectangle of wood had released from the center of the wall side. He glided the piece gently out and it was like magic: the wooden cube was coming undone in his mind's eye and he was planning three moves ahead.

When the puzzle was finally solved, Max had released an

inner chamber that held a single gold coin.

"There are many puzzle boxes. Almost as many as there are mysteries in life. This one was pretty simple, with the right help of course. Would you like to try a harder one?"

"Yes," Max had said, without hesitation.

"Harder ones will take longer. Much longer."

"That's okay." Max smiled. "I want to solve them on my own."

His grandpa smiled back. "Good. Just remember that nothing worthwhile is ever easy."

His grandfather got up from the floor, several groans this time, and headed to the closet. He retrieved a much larger *Himitsu-Bako*. This one was painted in a collage of flowers, vines, rivers, and all manner of jungle scenes.

He paused before giving it to Max. "But what if there's no money inside this one, or in others? Would you still enjoy it?"

"Of course! I just want to solve it. On my own this time."

"Then here you go."

It was a nice memory to hold on to while he worked, and the first Max had that didn't remind him of what a rotten person he'd become.

Max spent the next four hours in Arthur's home thinking and carefully manipulating the box. Sliding pieces back and forth. Pressing corners and panels. He kept his mind preoccupied with The City, replaying conversations with Shin Sho, Charlie, and the butcher, while his hands moved to their own rhythm. He thought about the murders back home and the powdered drug known *as sǐ fěn* while the memory in his fingers played out across the lacquered wood.

The moves became easier and he solved the box repeatedly, committing to memory the order that clicked opened the compartments. Max's thoughts clicked into place too. Yes, saving Ming would be his end goal, though he was sure the path to her would branch in ways that were still unforeseeable. As long as he didn't get sidetracked for too long and every decision was made keeping sight on that final goal, Max would be okay. Because the hard part was not successful implementation of the plan. The hard part was remaining free from the stranglehold of inner demons.

Max brought Arthur's body into the bathtub and cleaned him as best he could. The blood was gone, but the body had turned a hint of blue from the poison. Veins darkened by whatever toxin was stored in the Mara's claws ran thick and visible all over his body. When Arthur was dry, Max wrapped him in a sheet and laid him in bed.

Max then located a large, durable cloth knapsack and filled it with some of Arthur's finer clothes and the medical supplies he found around the house. The clock, silverware, and various other items he found while rooting through the packed crates—crates that Arthur should have been bringing to the surface right now— also went into the bag. Possessions that should have started Arthur and Ming's new life together would complete Max's mission. If it looked valuable, it went into the knapsack.

Max took a bath, then checked Arthur's clothes. The pants and arm sleeves were too long, so Max just put his same suit back on. Once he was dressed, Max folded the Mara's letter and placed it in his inside coat pocket. Before leaving the house, Max made sure he had his gun and all the remaining money. He taped a kitchen knife on the inseam of his right leg. He slung the bloated knapsack over his shoulder and before he walked out the door, he pocketed the small photo of Ming off Arthur's dresser.

It took Max a while to find a pawn shop, lots of trial and error since he didn't have a guide, but he managed, and after he left, he was a little richer and had an idea of where he could secure some help for navigation through the West End of The City. The kind of help that would mind their own business and simply take him where he wanted to go, no questions asked. The pawn shop owner told him to search the Nest, a pub and hangout for freelancers, work-for-hire types.

He didn't allow himself to feel bad over selling the belongings. Arthur was dead, and to get Ming back he would need as much money as possible. This had been just one of the choices needed to reinforce the goal of her return. But just like the box, it was a process of moves. A long process. And some moves were not possible prior to other moves being committed first.

Since leaving Arthur and Ming's house, Max had a feeling he was being watched. Initially, he had played it up to paranoia, but now, two blocks from the pawn shop, he was positive. Spinning on his heel, Max heard a young man call out from fifteen feet away. "Hey, mister."

Max glared at the approaching stranger, tensing up, not knowing what to expect. The young man got the hint and slowed his speed. He raised both hands and stopped just a few feet from Max. "Sorry to bother you, mister. No harm intended. I saw you come out from Doc's place awhile back. I tried to get your attention earlier but no luck."

Now that he was standing closer, he looked more like a kid than a man. Nineteen at the oldest, Max guessed. And he didn't seem to pose much threat, compared to what Max had already seen down here.

Then again, things aren't always what they seem.

"Yeah." Max shrugged and started walking away.

"Boy, not one for small talk, are ya?" The teenager hustled alongside and kept pace with Max. "I was just curious if you knew where Doc and Ming are."

"You know Ming?" Max slowed his pace.

"Well sure I know Ming." He laughed. "Why, we joke with each other all the time to stay away from the other one's guiding prospects." Another grin. "Shoot, we the only good guides in the whole damn area...sir."

Max stopped walking. "Arthur...uh, Doc, he went up to the surface." Max tried to relax, to allow the fakeness to leave his voice, to employ the very tricks he was trained to detect in a lying suspect. "Ming went with him, I think. They were both gone before I woke."

"Oh." The boy looked sheepishly at the ground. "Wish she had told me."

"Look...."

"Zeke." The boy reached out a hand. "Name's Zeke."

Max ignored his offer to shake, leaving Zeke to withdraw his hand, ashamed. "Look, Zeke, you seem like a nice guy. Wish I could be of more help to you. I was down on my luck and Arthur gave me a place to sleep this week. Good Samaritan. That's all I know about him. Is there anything I can do for you? Because I have things to attend to."

The boy remained silent and tentative for a moment before answering. "Well, I don't suppose you need a guide?"

"No thanks, kid."

"I'm just as good as Ming." He raised his hand in a pledge. "I swear."

"It's not you, kid, it's me." Max walked away.

Zeke hurried after him. "I'm telling ya, I could be a great asset to ya. Especially if the West End's in your future. I know those places like the back of my hand."

Max stopped, ready to play up his insanity to scare the kid off. "Fine. You wanna help? I need to find Gehanna."

"Boy, you want the deep West. Why you wanna go there for?"

"Because Zeke, I want to watch a sixteen-year-old slave be kicked and beat within inches of death." Max didn't blink, didn't breathe, just stared at the guide.

"Oh." Zeke gave a weak smile, but he wasn't taking the cue to shove off.

"How about I pay you what I paid Ming, but all you have to do is give me directions."

"Now you're talking." The chipper, go-getting tone was back in his voice. "Go two blocks north. When you get to the street sign marked with a single triangle, head west. That street will lead you right to the fires of Gehanna."

Max took out two bills. "Thanks"

Before he could take two steps, the boy said, "If you've never been, you may wanna take a detour to a few shows or clubs at least."

"And why should I do that?" With the way Ming had acted about it, he couldn't afford to ignore any piece of information about this legendary place. He could filter out the sensationalism later.

"Not sayin' you're new or nothing, but if you are, well, most men think they want what Gehanna has, but they find out they can't really stomach it. Most of the clubs here and in the East aren't slave shows."

"So I've heard," Max said.

"Well it's different when people ask to be in a show, ya know? Like I once met a woman who wanted to die. So they signed her up at a club to be in a show with someone who wanted to be a murderer." Zeke shrugged. "They fulfilled their dreams while The City watched."

"Jesus," Max said.

"See, watching someone who wants to die in She'ol ain't quite the same as watching a slave die in Gehanna."

"Still, I saw death games at the casino. I can handle Gehanna."

"With all due respect, mister, it ain't the same. Even the casino is different. Those slaves get a fighting chance—though slim. They sign up for the games, and those that live are given a freedom decree by the Others."

Max thought of the One Bullet game, and how happy the winning human had been.

"There's no escaping Gehanna for a slave," Zeke said. "And those deaths…it's different."

Perhaps there was merit to what the kid said. Max had fled the casino, which if the stories were to be believed, was tame in comparison to what he would find in this black heart of the West End. If he lost his composure in Gehanna, what would happen?

"I could take you to a few places prior…sorta like a warm up to the real thing."

"No." Max shook his head and took out another bill. He couldn't risk some innocent kid taking him around again. "But you can give me the names and directions for me to start the warm-up on my own."

II

AFTER MCCLOUD'S INITIAL surprise and slight annoyance
that his missing person was Max Elliot, it dawned on him that it
didn't matter. In his mind, McCloud was still working for those
little girls. For the abducted Leigh Anne. For his sister Janice, who
was never far from his thoughts. And when McCloud's visit to
Max's residence had been fruitless and no one in the area knew
anything about the detective's whereabouts, he didn't let himself
dwell on the unfair fact that yet again he'd received a case which
no normal police officer could solve. Max was a loose cannon,
and he'd actively try to stay hidden if he wanted...assuming he
wasn't dead as the papers suggested.

Instead, to stay motivated, McCloud envisioned Janice and
her love of sketching. Messy squiggles—a masterpiece in her five-
year-old mind. It built his confidence again as he stepped onto the
landing and headed to the apartment of Charlie Willis. If he
couldn't find Max, then he'd locate all his associates.

He knocked on Willis's second-story apartment door and
looked around; he couldn't believe that the brownstone hadn't

been condemned since the quake.

Ten seconds passed. Twenty.

Three more knocks.

McCloud put his ear to the thin wood. He thought he could hear someone inside.

"Charlie?" He paused, listening. "I'm a friend of Max Elliot's. Can you speak with me briefly?"

After a minute of continued silence, McCloud looked at the door handle. His mind told him to leave, but his body commanded his hand to the knob instead.

"Charlie?" He reached out and took hold of the doorknob.

The seconds crept by with the knob in McCloud's palm, his breathing louder than anything else he could hear. This time the voice in McCloud's head was screaming at him to turn around now. But again, his body had other plans. He applied pressure to the knob and, ever so slow, twisted his wrist. To his surprise, it met with no resistance.

McCloud held the knob in that position, cylinder ready to plunge back into the latch housing the moment he let go. His breath was caught too, and the consequences of his impending action played through his head: Police misconduct, inadmissible evidence. But there were no other leads. The case would go cold within a day of receiving it if he didn't discover something useful soon. He had to succeed at all costs this time.

Do you like my picture? Janice held up the paper. *It's us! See there's you and—*

Each second was a precious moment wasted. He couldn't save the other girls, but as long as he didn't hesitate, maybe he could prevent the Chinatown Surgeon from snuffing out another young life.

McCloud pushed and the door swung inward. He pulled back from the opening in case of an attack. "Charlie Willis, this is John McCloud with the San Francisco Police Department. I am just here to talk with you."

Silence.

"I'm coming in." McCloud reappeared in the doorway and cautiously slipped into the apartment.

It was dim, and while he waited for his eyes to adjust, he listened to the sound of ragged breathing. This time it was not his own. The room brightened as his eyes adjusted and he could see the outline of someone.

"Sir?" McCloud said.

As he approached, the outline materialized as a man sprawled on the couch. His body smelled of sweat and his hair was matted to his flushed forehead. An unkempt beard sprouted across his face. The man wiggled and stretched, seeming to work aches out of his joints, grimacing at the effort.

The man's eyelids fluttered open. "Charlie? Is that you?" He rubbed his face with a shaky hand, then his mouth dropped. "Whoa, who are you?" He struggled to sit up.

The man looked sick but not from fever or flu. McCloud had seen someone in a similar condition once. When he first joined the force, he arrested a man for being so intoxicated that he was berating customers in a local pub. The department cooled him off in a cell overnight. By the morning, though, the man was clammy and shaking. He needed whiskey. *Just a finger*, the man had begged. *I'll die if I don't have a sip. I know it.*

"Relax," McCloud said. "I'm not here to hurt you. Seems we have something in common. I'm looking for Charlie, too."

The man finally made it to a sitting position, his breathing heavier than before. "Charlie ain't here. You have to come back."

"That's okay." McCloud used a calming voice. "I think you can help me. And, maybe I can help you. What's your name?"

The man swallowed and looked around the room as if someone else was ready to jump out and surprise him. "I don't need help. Charlie should be back in the next few days. Ain't my place to do business when he's gone."

"Relax. This isn't about *business*." McCloud shut the door and walked over to an armchair. He was moving on sheer instinct, channeling some reckless soul, unconcerned for police protocol. He pointed to the chair. "May I?"

The man looked at him with wide eyes.

McCloud took the silence for approval and sat down. He took off his hat and his gaze went to the messy table in front of them— burnt matches, ash and crumbs littered the surface, barely visible in the low light—then he placed the hat on his knee. A pouch similar to the one Harris gave McCloud sat on the edge of the table's corner. It was inside out and coated in a white sheen, like it had held something powdery in the recent past.

Gotcha.

"I'm just here for a few questions. And I pay handsomely for the answers." From his jacket pocket, McCloud removed the pouch Harris had given him and took a gamble. "Interested?" He opened the drawstring, spread the opening, and extended it to the man.

The man's eyes grew wider, and not with fear or confusion. They grew with hunger.

Definitely gotcha.

"Who are you?"

"Does it matter? You seem to be dry, and I don't know any other places where you can find this stuff." McCloud felt like he was channeling Elliot.

"You're a friend of Charlie's, right?" The man pushed damp hair off his forehead. Scratched at his sunken cheeks and took a deep breath.

"Yes. I'm a friend." McCloud risked the lie. "Jonny Jones." In that moment, McCloud became the fictional name. Because McCloud had never done this before, never given false pretenses in the past. But maybe some guy named Jones could.

"I'm Barnes," he stuttered. "C-Chris Barnes." He bobbed his head over and over, stuck in nervous-tick loop. "Now let's have a taste. I gotta get my head straight."

"Not yet," McCloud said.

"Come on! Just a pinch. It'll even me out."

McCloud tensed. Perhaps he'd pushed the role too far. Thick cords popped from Barnes's neck and a vein in his forehead ticked with his enraged pulse.

If you're willing to play the role at all, you got be willing to go all out.

"No, *you* come on!" McCloud countered. "You've palled around with Charlie long enough to understand how this works. I get answers first."

Barnes glared at him. "What do you want to know?"

McCloud leaned closer. "Who's been running around town carving up flesh and stealing bones?"

Charlie pocketed the last of the cash from the table in front of him.

"You've had quite a run of good fortune," hissed the creature sitting across from him.

"Right place, right time, I suppose."

"Mmm. Perhaps." A wickedness passed into the Mara's eyes. "The first time, dare I say, was pure luck. This second time is an unbelievable coincidence. But, if there's a third…" The creature's lips turned into an expression somewhere between a grin and a snarl.

"There ain't gonna be a third time." Charlie knew the Mara could smell his fear. Hell, they had probably figured out everything by now. But it shouldn't matter. He'd given them what they wanted. They would probably let him walk away intact.

"Then our business is done…permanently." It raised scaly flesh above its eyes. "Yes?"

"Right." Charlie nodded. "Thanks."

Charlie stood, and, using every ounce of strength he had, turned his vulnerable back to head for the door. Even though it was five steps away his knees shook with fear. His stomach clenched with the thought that at any minute he'd be attacked from behind. Here he was, turning over bounties to save his ass and then trusting *their* word for his safety.

He was two steps from the door, and there was still no indication of an attack. Charlie's hand turned the knob now. His heart thumped in his throat. And finally, when he was in the hallway, he could breathe a little better.

When he was out on the cobblestone streets, Charlie looked up at the rock cavern ceiling and breathed deeply. Everything was coming together and it was almost over. Soon he'd be free to make a fresh start.

Within five minutes, Barnes was near tears. A grown man weeping. To think that someone could be so in thrall by a powder. It was unreal.

"I don't know." Barnes rocked back and forth on the couch. "I don't know. I don't know. I don't know."

"Sure you do," McCloud said, soothing him with soft, measured speech. It was similar to encouraging one of the juvies. Only he would have never lied to kids. But to Chris Barnes, McCloud could care less. "Just like you know why I found this baggie at the scene of the murders."

Barnes wasn't even forming words at this point. Just moans of resistance while shaking his head.

"A name. All I need is a name."

"I can't," he breathed, barely audible. He looked McCloud in the eyes and the detective saw a moment of clarity in the junkie's face. The fever of the drug was replaced with fear. A wild, frothing fear.

"What are you afraid of?"

"I…" Barnes looked down at the baggie. "I guess… I can tell you about one of them."

"One of what?"

"One of the murders, dammit! But only if you give me a taste."

"As soon as I get what I want," McCloud said.

"Charlie." And with a guttural yell, the walls of resistance crumbled to McCloud's desire. "Charlie! All right? Charlie," Barnes sputtered past clammy lips. "It was all Charlie's idea. I had nothing to do with it. Him and Poppens. All them. I just made deliveries around town. I swear."

"Charlie?" McCloud said.

"Yeah, now give me a pinch."

"But why? How?"

"Look, you asked for a name, I gave you a name!" Barnes started to rock a bit, his leg shook, and the springs of the worn cushions groaned.

McCloud hesitated. It'd been one thing to manipulate Barnes's weakness. But now McCloud was about to distribute an unknown and potentially dangerous drug to a civilian.

Barnes's eyes were wild; his cracked lips were plumping with saliva at his excitement. He seemed ready to lunge at a moment's notice. Realizing that to back out now meant there would be a physical altercation, McCloud uncinched the bag. Without taking his eyes off Barnes, he reached in and pinched the powder between his thumb and index finger. He sprinkled the drug into the pipe on the table and leaned back.

Barnes snatched up the pipe, bringing it close to his chest, guarding his treasure from a double cross. He then lit a match and sucked deeply.

McCloud leaned further back in disgust. Barnes exhaled and thick smoke rose to dance within the shadowy room, creating a deep haze of gloom. A sickly-sweet aroma overpowered McCloud and he covered his mouth and nose with his hand.

When the bowl was spent, Barnes melted into the couch, a vacant smile on his face. Then the man began humming. The notes were choppy and off key. In the dark, they took on an eerie quality. Barnes's head rolled from side to side. His song falling and rising in volume.

"Barnes?"

What are you doing? The voice of reason that had been buried by his need to win was tunneling up from the depths. *You gave him that drug and if he dies, it's on your hands.*

"Barnes?"

The man's head raised, the smile of an imbecile plastered across his face. "Oh, so close to visiting them. So very close. But this is okay. Really. Anything beats the emptiness."

"You can hear me?"

Barnes nodded. "I can't hear them though. Usually they are calling me...must be a weak batch..."

"Barnes!" McCloud snapped his fingers and Barnes focused for a moment, then tapered back into a dizzy stupor. "Why did Charlie kill Jeffrey Poppens? And what were those three girls doing chained up in that complex?"

"Charlie didn't kill Jeff...or the girls." Barnes's head lolled and he leaned back. "Oh, I've missed this feeling."

"You said you were giving me one of the murderers. If..." McCloud let the words sink in for a minute.

"That's the last of it," Charlie said, handing over most of the cash he had received from the Mara to Tommy, a member of the Suey Sing Tong. He had enough left to survive until he found a legitimate job. If he found a job. But that was a problem for another time. Now was the time for closing this chapter with the criminal organization. Forever. "We're through, right?"

"Indeed, Mr. Willis. Your debt paid in full," the man said.

And then some, ya bastard. But Charlie wrapped a cool exterior over his burning rage.

Tommy smiled. Charlie sickened at how similar this smile was to the one flashed when Charlie owed a thousand dollars and Tommy was sent to threaten his sister.

You wouldn't want anything bad to happen to her. Would you? And he smiled after those words left his lips. A cruel, smug smile.

"You come back anytime," Tommy said.

"Don't count on it. I'm outta the game."

Tommy chuckled. "That's what they all say."

"Barnes." McCloud tentatively reached out and shook the man by the shoulder. "Barnes, you okay?"

The man remained unresponsive. The only sign of life was intermittent twitches that seized his body.

McCloud shook a bit harder. Barnes's head flopped to one side. But he didn't wake.

"Damnit," McCloud muttered and stood up. He ran sweaty fingers through his short hair, paced the floor. He walked back to Barnes and leaned forward. Bracing himself using one hand on the back of the couch, McCloud brought his ear as close as he dared to Barnes's face. Hot breath tickled the tiny hairs of his lobe.

Barnes was breathing at least; shallow, but it was something.

McCloud regained control of his pulse with deep breaths in through his nose and out through his mouth, repeating to himself that Barnes would be fine. That he had not inadvertently caused a drug death. He closed his eyes and thought of Max again. How would Max handle this situation? It was getting easier to understand the widowed detective.

A repose came over McCloud's heart and lungs, his guilt receded and he eyed the unconscious man. Barnes was a user. If it hadn't come from McCloud, it would have been opium or booze or heroin from someone else. McCloud had an obligation to help victims, past and future. If gaining the knowledge to save his community from the Chinatown Surgeon meant hanging Barnes out to dry, so be it. This was his one big chance. A high-profile case. He doubted anyone would protest if he bent a few rules of proper procedure, especially if it meant taking a madman off the street...or finding Max.

With that rationalization, instead of a search warrant, McCloud walked into the kitchen. He braced himself for dirty dishes and moldy food. Something that matched the personal decay of Chris Barnes, though he found the kitchen very much in order. McCloud moved to the far end of the living room to a bookcase on the wall.

Beside the bookcase was a wooden desk with a closed rolling top. He put his hand on the curved top. He'd be a fool not to go through the house.

McCloud pushed back the roll top; the thin, intricate wood disappeared, clattering to its resting place inside the desk. He froze, looking behind him, worried that the sound may have stirred Barnes. But the man remained catatonic on the couch, eyes open and glossy, mesmerized by whatever they saw in the world beyond.

McCloud returned to the desk, inspecting stationery, quills, ink bottles, and random odds and ends. McCloud opened the center desk drawer and found a bundle of enveloped letters tied with string. He picked them up and slid two out of the loose packing. They were to Charlie Willis, but the address was the state prison and the attention was to the warden, as it was with all inmate mail. He turned the envelope over, noting that it had been previously opened. He placed the bundle of letters on the desktop and took out his notepad. McCloud copied down the name and return address: Brittny Willis.

Reading the letter may have yielded more pertinent information, but that was still a piece of privacy he wasn't ready to breach. Not yet anyway.

Back at the station, McCloud left the name Brittny Willis with Harris's secretary, Tina. All he said was he needed any information they had, if any, on this woman as soon as possible. Tina promised to alert McCloud as soon as she had more details on Brittny—specifically as to the accuracy of the return mailing address. He also asked to have any files on Chris Barnes brought to him when possible. McCloud neglected to leave Harris an official update though. Perhaps he *was* unconsciously taking cues from Max. As detestable as the man seemed, McCloud was learning secrecy was a good way to get results.

After returning to his desk McCloud reopened the file on Charlie Willis. When he had first received the manila folder, he'd given it only a cursory glance. Willis was a two-bit criminal. Had his hands in a lot of pies, but he didn't seem to be a major player. He was a rat, and rats have a way of getting into the hardest places. Whenever he got arrested, or when he wanted to avoid it, he would snitch on those dark nooks and crannies of society that he worked so hard to penetrate. It also seemed that Max Elliot was his favorite go-to detective.

However, second time through the documents, McCloud ran into a glaring contradiction on page five. He looked it over twice, flipped the page to see if a similar incident ever reoccurred, then rechecked. He spoke aloud: "Sentencing Date: March 9th, 1909; Term: 6 months; Conviction: Narcotics, ten pounds of opium; Arresting officer: Max Elliot." Even saying the words did not clarify his confusion. "What the hell, Max? Who arrests their personal snitch?"

Below the logged-in evidence was Max Elliot's signature.

There were no trial transcripts to view. Sentencing had been carried out behind closed doors in an arbitration hearing.

It had to be one of the first major arrests on the Smoking Opium Exclusion Act, even though they'd been cracking down since the late 1880s. This was a new enemy, and he felt San Francisco was ground zero for the drug war that had been launched. He could see it happening already. Cocaine was being used in numerous elixirs and governmental agencies were seeing the hospitalization reports; it was just a matter of time until that was criminalized too. And if the snowball effect was to continue, a crackdown on even more drugs was not only likely to occur, it would be an unwinnable war.

Another big reason McCloud wanted to move away from criminal investigation. It might have sounded morbid, but there was a victim and a perpetrator in a homicide case. Simple enough. Find the murderer, put him away, get justice. But who was the victim when someone was taking a drug? You can help them, but why put them in prison, watch them morph into the craving creature that McCloud had found on the couch? They'd become a fiend wearing the skin of a human, just like Barnes. And if they did beat the addiction while imprisoned, they were still confined to the company of crooks. How could someone change when the environment they were placed in was exactly the type of lifestyle they were trying to rid themselves of?

McCloud closed the file and opened his mind to a hundred more questions.

McCloud decided to walk home. The trolley or hansom cabs would have been faster, but he needed to think and the night air was helpful at stirring up his insight. As he walked, McCloud turned theory after theory over in his mind. Theories like department cover-ups that backfired all the way to Max himself being involved in the drug world. Max disappeared as a hero. But McCloud hadn't found a hero in that opium den. Maybe Max didn't just go there to forget what happened; perhaps Max was allowed to go in that direction so that he would be forgotten.

While McCloud's thoughts wandered elsewhere, he turned at the lamppost for Crestfall, then automatically sidestepped the pothole on his left. Now that there had been multiple murders and with such young victims, there was a greater outcry. Now the police department had to act.

And Max was nowhere to be found.

McCloud reached his building and took the steps slowly. He looked up and down the street before letting himself into the structure.

"Your lead is dead." It was McCloud's first interaction the following day.

"Excuse me?" McCloud looked up from his desk of notes and pictures from various crime scenes.

Tina unfolded the sheet of paper with McCloud's handwriting on it. "Brittny Willis. She's dead. As in no longer alive." Tina smiled, but McCloud thought it was a terrible time to be joking.

"When did it happen?"

"Dead and buried seven months ago. I confirmed the last known address as the one you supplied." She started to walk away. "Homicide victim. Unsolved. Find the file downstairs if you want more."

"Yeah. Thanks." McCloud picked up the paper he'd written her name on. "Dead," he mumbled.

He crumpled the paper and threw it in the receptacle next to his desk. After rummaging through the file, he learned that Brittny Willis wasn't just a homicide victim. She had been killed last year.

Last year Charlie Willis was given a six-month jail term due to Max Elliot. McCloud counted out the months on his fingers. Brittny would have been murdered sometime while Charlie was in jail. He grabbed up the folder on Eve's murder. Six months ago, shortly after Brittny, Max's wife was killed. And Charlie was not in jail during the murder and abduction. Now Max Elliot goes missing.

McCloud wanted to jump to a conclusion, but he knew he couldn't. He needed more details. And he wasn't sure how to get them.

As if from infinite intelligence, a new idea occurred. Charlie's sister was dead, so perhaps he was now in possession of her residence. Maybe he split his time between the sister's and the apartment he shared with the druggie Barnes. McCloud grabbed his coat and headed toward the doors. On the street, he checked the address and picked up his pace.

III

ZEKE HAD GIVEN him three places to try. At least it was a better starting point than randomly walking into buildings, and it got the kid off his back. Directions to Peek-a-Boos denoted it as the closest, and Zeke's description of the concept was bizarre enough to prompt Max there first.

Peek-a-Boos looked like another hotel. But the Mara behind the podium did not dress like his East End brethren. He was shirtless, pectorals and stomach chiseled with tight muscle. Leather pants and boots covered his lower half.

"Welcome. Sit. Shouldn't be more than fifteen minutes." He gestured to a waiting area and Max took a seat across from a man writing in a notebook.

The other occupants of the room included a Spanish-looking man with a thin moustache and strong jawline dressed in vibrant-colored robes; to his right was a brutish man with greasy, thin hair past his ears, though his girth had more to do with fat than muscle. Then there were the two young women, one in an eggshell straight-front corset, at her waist a very short petite coat, and the other was dressed in a frilly negligee and cream stockings. Both wore lace-up boots. They had similar features and looked frail, and the way they held hands, scooted their chairs closer, and how they wrapped around one another's necks and ears to whisper secrets made it hard to tell if they were sisters or something more.

Max closed his eyes to the people around him. He didn't acknowledge them. He felt a sense of superiority, like his reason for admittance was more noble than theirs. Noble or not, he certainly didn't feel the same as he had at Arthur's when he had felt Leigh Anne's intervention and presence. It was just as well that she wasn't watching over him anymore. Her—essence? Spirit?—memory didn't deserve to be exposed to a place like this. And Max avoided further scrutiny on what his daughter had become; that was a dangerous road to start down and could only compromise his mental state. Instead he focused on his new cause, picturing Ming, smiling, happy—well, as happy as a pessimistic teenage girl can be. In the safety of Arthur's sanctuary, she was happy. Ming had achieved a mental balance that Max never could. She worked with the scum of The City. But she left it in the streets and shared love with Arthur, getting satisfaction from helping others. Max would need to attain that level of balance if he wanted to succeed.

Then he thought of Eve the night he met her. It had been at a museum. Max loved history—arguably the biggest puzzle ever. And back then he never missed a good history exhibit. She'd been near the plaque showing a picture and description of the Great Wall of China. She looked beautiful that day. Her hair wasn't quite blonde, but the lightest color of orange he'd ever seen. And she was one of the most beautiful women he'd ever seen too. After he started courting her, there was no way he'd believe anyone that said in ten years she'd resent Max…or that he'd be indifferent to the fact.

Things fall apart sometimes.

"Sir?"

Max opened his eyes to the shirtless Mara towering over him. "Ready?"

"Yes."

Max stood up and the Mara led him to a winding steel staircase. "You know the rules?"

"Not exactly."

They started up the metal steps. "Listen carefully. I hate to repeat myself. I'll start you on the top floor. Each floor has two rooms. If a red light is over the door, someone's in there. Don't bother them. Go to a different one or wait a few feet away. If the light is green, open the door, step inside and close the door."

Max nodded.

"Stay and watch for as long as you want in any room. Use the stairs in the middle of the landing to descend to level two, then to the ground floor again, and follow the arrows to exit in the back. Got it?"

"I think."

They took another turn in their ascent and the Mara laughed. "Been awhile since I've given those instructions. We tend to have a lot of repeat customers."

If it hadn't been for the exposed, massive chest of scales and haunting facial features, talking to this Mara was akin to any regular joe in the bar. The conditions might have been gloomy, but this guy's personality painted him as a jovial proprietor that didn't sell anything less than savory. For a moment, Max wondered if Zeke had lied to him.

They stopped at a door.

"Once you're in, the only way out is the inside stairs. You can walk straight down if you like, you can skip rooms or spend hours. Some rooms fill and empty about every twenty minutes on average. Other rooms have perpetual guests. They're numbered if you want to keep track." He stuck a key in the lock.

As always, Max had questions. But there was no point in asking. He doubted any answer would prepare him for the next adventure.

The lock clicked and the door opened to a dimly lit lobby. Max could just make out the opening of a stairwell in the middle. There were two doors; one on the east and one on the west. The east door had a large I painted on it. The west: II. The roman numerals were painted in white. Max stepped forward and as soon as he was clear, the door was pulled shut behind him. The lock engaged with the finality of a slammed coffin lid.

Max shuffled forward, the bare floorboards creaking under his tentative steps. He moved to the west and a blast of crying came from the east as door I opened and a man exited. He threw the door shut behind him and the sobbing was silenced. The man glanced up, caught Max's curious gaze for a moment, then jerked his head low and descended the stairs.

Max looked back to door II and approached. He placed his hand on the cool brass knob. Now was the time to show why Harris had wanted him back on the force. He had to become the case. He'd failed at the casino. He couldn't afford to falter again.

"Come on," he whispered, closing his eyes. He could follow the Mara's rules, pretend to enjoy himself—

Can't pretend here. You have to absorb it. Be it. Just like Ming became The City during the time she was a guide.

Yes, he could do that too. Ming had Arthur and the will to continue her purpose of helping the sick to stabilize herself after long hours in The City. Max would need to learn to balance himself daily with his new purpose of saving her…and perhaps, if he was lucky, Leigh Anne would return and aid in centering him as well.

He opened the door and stared into a deeper blackness than the main hall. Within the void there was a single, face-sized circle of light at eye level. And through the circle, a candescent red glow emanated. Max stepped inside and closed the door. He could hear music, something classical. He put his hands out, finding there was another wall in front of him. Apparently, the circle had been cut out of this wall—a hole for him to look through.

Curiosity overcame him and Max leaned into the hole, his forehead coming to rest against cool glass. A window. And through the window was the *actual* room—the scene. In essence, he was standing in a cubbyhole-sized room *inside* of a larger room. Max pressed against the glass, its surface fogging a bit. The light came from red-tinted lamps in the back of the room. In front of the lamps was a table with phonograph on it, a rare nickel-plated horn reflecting the red glow.

The needle scratched and a quartet sang.

> *By the light of the silvery moon,*
> *I want to spoon…*

In the center of the room a naked man hung suspended from

the ceiling. Ropes of linked chain metal tethered his arms, legs, and several spots on his back, keeping him stomach down as if he was flying through the air. The chains were connected by steel hooks that were pierced through the man's calves and forearms, with the bulk of his weigh supported by the six chains in his back. He wore a thin leather harness that must have helped with hip support. The straps came around the inner thighs of his crotch keeping his balls and cock in a firm chokehold, the pooling blood making the man's penis stiffer than any normal erection.

Your silvery beams will bring love dreams,
We'll be cuddling soon,
By the light of the moon.

Max watched in disbelief as a woman danced with slow, sweeping gyrations to the music around the man, who hung at about her neck level. Black stockings clung to her legs, which looked more muscular beneath the fabric than most women he'd seen. The stockings clipped to a matching garter belt; her sex was unclothed but covered in a thatch of soft, dark curls. She was topless except for a corset that showcased an impressive set of breasts. Her nipples were hard and red with excitement.

She slid her fingertips ever so gently over the man's back. Then she crouched under him, and with long nails, brushed the tips up and down his naked body, causing him to shiver. She sat under the human canopy and produced a long dagger. With as much grace and ease as put forth previously by her fingernails, she slid the point of the dagger down his chest. When she pulled it away, a few drops of blood beaded in the path left behind. She twirled the tip of the blade into the skin around his nipple. The man winced, biting his lower lip when she eased the knife deeper. She licked at the blood and then brought her crimson-stained lips to his. The woman drove her bloody kiss deep into the man's throat.

With bloody kisses sealing their lips, Max gasped as she jabbed the knife further, then retract it just as fast. The man stiffened; the woman pulled away from his lips and placed the knife down. The man's face flushed. Max watched him roll his eyes downward, trying to see past his chest to his love handles.

The woman sat under the incision she'd made. She licked her finger and slipped it into the wound, pushing its entire length up inside with slow circular adjustments, basking in the blood that fell upon her.

The man grunted in pain, his body shook. Then she pulled out her finger, and the man shuddered with relief. She blew on the cut, eliciting more reactions from the man, moans and trembling that Max couldn't identify as pleasure or pain.

The woman stood up, her body splattered in dark red. She went to a sink and got some supplies. When she returned to the man, Max was sure she was disinfecting and dressing the cut. After leaving his left side bandaged in gauze, she returned to her spot under the man. Her attention shifted to his swollen cock. She tapped at his rod with her long nails. Max could feel pinpricks of electricity surging through his own shaft, could almost feel the terrified excitement growing on the man's face.

Wham.

She slapped his cock backward. The man lost his breath, stomach clenching. She slapped him three more times in quick succession and he looked as if he would vomit, spittle dripping from his lips. Max cringed at the sympathy pains he felt twisting in his own gut. The woman knelt again and took the man's scrotal flesh into her mouth. She started to gnaw on his balls. That's when Max walked out and closed the door.

He looked across the main hall to the east door. The light above was red again, so Max moved with caution down the stairs.

The next floor contained two green-lit rooms. He looked down the remaining stairs. One more level and he would be at the ground and a hundred feet from the exit. He didn't have to stay.

Really, was Zeke right? If you can't bear this, how are you gonna get Ming back? So some man gets his tallywhacker beaten. So what?

Max headed to the east room. Opened the door into the small cubby hole. Closed the door and moved right up to the window with the fire of motivation reignited. The same kind of red filter from the last room bathed this one in a familiar grainy glow.

A woman in a black Amish cape dress sat on a rocking chair reading from a stack of papers. To his surprise, the circular, cut-out window of this room had no glass. Instead, thin wire meshing covered the hole. Her words were garbled, flowing and alive, but lacking coherence. A dialogue of rapture, speaking in tongues; the creaking of the rocking chair, created a haunting undertone to the coded message.

Max leaned forward, pressing his damp forehead against the metal. She turned the page, a stream of unconscious feelings translated in a string of words. These rooms were a glimpse into people's lives, someone's desires. Max had paid to be a voyeuristic fly on a hotel room wall.

She flipped to another page, though there was no way she was actually reading that fast. Another page flipped. And another.

The woman froze, then looked up and smiled. "I'm glad you're here."

Max's heart sped up, but his body froze.

She stood and approached the window, then leaned into the mesh.

Max pulled back. "I—"

"We're going to write a story together." Her voice was breathy and hopeful. "The whole City will know your name."

Max leaned in again, staring at her wide green eyes and the small creases on her mocha skin. She had a wide jaw, and her face was thin.

"I can't," Max said. "I have to find someone."

"This will help find them," she said. "Let me show you how I write." She lit a cigarette between chipped nail polish fingers, but the smoke rising past her curly brown hair wasn't tobacco. She took a puff and held it up to the mesh. "Smoke and then tell me the story."

"No."

"Smoke, smoke." She blew the poisonous air at him, filling the small cubby. Max remained hypnotized by her lifeless eyes. "Please stay with me," she said.

Finally breaking the spell, Max fumbled with the handle, almost forgetting to close the door once he was back on the main floor. A man stood a few feet away, waiting to go inside as Max caught his breath. He stared through Max, silent.

Max straightened and stepped aside. "Enjoy." He turned and walked to the stairs, again leaving the second room unexplored. He descended to the ground floor with a series of disjointed laughs. Not because something was humorous but because there was nothing else Max could think to do. And he desperately needed to do something. So he laughed. And it was easy to keep laughing when his head felt like an airy cushion; it made the staircase sway a bit as he stepped off it and then entered into the east room on the ground floor.

He stopped laughing when he peered through the circle in that room and saw a man in bog boots and overalls mopping the wood beneath an operating table with two stirrups on one end. Max's head felt fuzzy and his eyes drooped as he watched the mop head slosh through puddles creating a pinkish-colored water. He leaned against the glass, stared into the bucket of brackish water, and in its cleansing waters, thought of the smoking woman. He'd allowed her to drug him with whatever that smoke was; stood still for it.

There was more laughter and Max wasn't sure if it was him. His mind seemed to separate from his body. With forced effort, he touched his hand to his chest, then lips, the flesh felt foreign. No, he wasn't the one laughing, though his heart was drumming loudly against his breastplate. Max pulled back from the room being cleaned and looked around the dark cubby.

The light was green when you walked in here. Wasn't it?

He gazed into the grainy blackness, imagined he heard breathing, that the laughing was someone whom Max had accidentally walked in on.

Max looked back to the window. The man was still mopping, mechanical in his movements. But he wasn't laughing either. He was sour looking and his eyes were as dead as a Mara's.

The laugher faded into a bubbling noise and Max looked down at the bucket. The round metal sides were breathing, swelling in and out, sloshing about the bloody contents inside. The man rinsed the chunk-coated mop in the churning water one last time. Then he picked up the supplies and left through a back exit. Before the door closed, something fell out of the bucket and landed on the floor with a squishy slap.

No, it can't be.

A raw uterus slid toward Max. Possessed fallopian-tube arms reached out, gripped the floor, and scooted the uterus closer. The womb's vaginal entrance opened in a fleshy smile.

Trying not to scream, Max bolted from the room. "It's the drug. That's all." He slapped his face and swung his arms in wide circles, to awaken his senses. *Just focus on the arrows, find the exit.* Before he knew it, Max was back on the street, but the drug kept him paranoid and anxious.

It'll pass, it'll pass. Just breathe.

Why the hell did I freeze, let her blow that stuff in my face?

"Hey, mister."

"Shit!" It was Zeke. "Don't sneak up on people."

"Sorry 'bout that."

The scare had shocked some of the drug out of his system and for that Max was thankful, though he wondered if the clarity would last. "What the hell are you doing here?"

"Just keeping an eye on a prospect while I look for other clients."

It seemed strange, but Max's mind was flying too high to know if he was overreacting. A dangerous thought flashed: he'd let that woman fill the cubby with smoke on purpose. It slipped away and lethargy filled its absence.

Sleep...

"No!" Max shouted, waking himself out of the trance he'd spiraled back into without realizing it.

Zeke looked a bit concerned. "Sir?"

"Sorry... I mean, how many are there?"

"How many what...sir?"

"How many clubs are there in the West End that run slave shows?"

"Lots of 'em, I reckon. Maybe twenty-five or so. And past the fires of Gehanna, they have the Seven Stone Clubs. I'm guessing you didn't care for the peep show all that much?"

"There's too many..."

"Too many, sir?"

Max gazed upon the vast city before him. Twenty-five locations, countless shows and performers and stages and rooms at each one. Impossible odds.

"I...I need a place to rest a while. Just...to think."

Zeke pointed at a purple sign in the distance. "*Sĭ fĕn* is the best way to unwind."

Max followed Zeke's outstretched finger and found his legs

propelling him forward. The royal purple sign was a beacon that cut through the dusky light, calling to Max. Around him The City sprawled out, veins of vice branching out in every direction. Each holding a slim chance of being Ming's prison, because there was no guarantee she was even here, or in Gehanna for that matter. There was no one to interrogate, no clues. He closed his eyes, but he didn't hear or feel his daughter's reassuring guidance.

The case is over. There's nothing left.

Zeke didn't follow the man. Guy had gotten himself messed up in the peep show. Maybe taken some drug in there, though he couldn't tell what. The assured tone the man had spoken with earlier was gone. And a trip to a *sǐ* den would be the closer; something to make sure he was down long enough for Zeke to collect.

Ahead, Max stopped at the building and looked at the purple sign. "Come on, man. Get your ass in there," Zeke whispered to the silhouette in the distance.

Max looked back, but Zeke ignored him. Held his breathe. "Come on."

Max turned back to the door and went inside.

Zeke waited another ten minutes after Max entered, not wanting to risk the guy getting cold feet. When he felt confident that Max was committed to the *sǐ fěn* ride, Zeke hurried away.

IV

THE BUILDING WAS one of the older ones in the area. It had remained somewhat intact through the quake, but the disaster had taken a large toll on the eight-story housing tenement. The subsequent repairs were more than likely not up to the new building codes. It was part of a government program, and the city didn't have the money to put into refurbishing ghettos. There were more important buildings to restore in the eyes of the governor, though even the nice areas of San Francisco were being built up *too* fast. McCloud believed they were sacrificing planning and soundness for speed.

Rather than dwell on the city's affairs, McCloud entered and headed up the stairs. He exited onto the third-story landing and saw a woman in front of an apartment, fumbling to produce her keys.

"Excuse me, ma'am," McCloud said.

The woman found her key and jabbed it into the lock.

"Do you happen to know Brittny—"

The woman didn't even look up as she threw herself into the

room and slammed the door shut. He walked past her room. The chipped paint smelled of fear and the hallway was lined in peeling wallpaper. Two doors down, he saw the number he was looking for: 308, inlayed on a splintered and poorly-painted surface.

He knocked four times and stepped away from the door. After three seconds, McCloud was conscious of the tightness in his muscles, the electricity building in his feet, ready to snap him into action.

Five seconds.

He realized he was holding his breath; he let a bit out in relief.

Ten seconds.

He let the rest of the air out and relaxed a degree. "Brittny Willis. My name is John McCloud. I'm with the San Francisco PD. You are not in any trouble. I just want to talk with you."

He knocked again, then waited.

"Not the best way to be let in." A voice from behind.

McCloud whirled around. Hand snapping to his holster. A thin woman in her thirties stood in her doorway on the opposite side of the hall. "My God, ma'am. Don't sneak up on people, please."

The woman chuckled. "Shouting that you're a cop is dangerous was all I was trying to say. This ain't a very trusting building."

The electricity had dispersed and McCloud straightened his jacket and adjusted his belt, allowing the calm to replace the storm. "I'm looking for Brittny Willis. You know her?"

"Did."

"Did?" McCloud pretended.

"Some cop just like you came knocking. Asked me a bunch a' questions, then told me they'd found Brittny in an alley. Broken neck." The woman shook her head and sighed. "Cop said be careful, then left. That was all the respect she got."

"I'm sorry to hear that, ma'am."

"It's the no-good brother's fault. I'm sure of it. Snakey one, he is."

"Does he stay here? Perhaps the department can be convinced to take renewed interest in solving Brittny 's case if I can offer up a fresh angle like the brother."

She glared at him with a critical eye. "I see him staying here every now and again. He's rotten. You should haul him away next time he shows up. Ask him whatever you want while he's in jail."

"Yeah, I may just do that." McCloud looked back at the door to 308. He thought about how he had disregarded procedure and barged in on Chris Barnes. He turned back to the neighbor. "My name is John McCloud. I'll be checking in every so often. If you happen see the brother, Charlie, please note the times he shows up. I'd appreciate it."

"How much you appreciate it?"

"A lot." He extended his hand to shake, a bill folded in his palm.

When her hand felt the cash, she smiled. "Oh, sure, officer. I can do that."

"Thank you," McCloud said. "I'll check in with you from time to time."

He'd never paid for information before. But it didn't feel as dirty as he thought it would.

"Oh yes, very good." The Mara grinned, leading Max down a hallway. "You will love it."

The complimentary glass of *mogjiŭ* they gave him on arrival had settled into every fiber of his body, mixing with whatever effects of the previous drug remained, and Max felt like he was floating down the hall after the creature. The doors on either side blurred slightly, and he noted that most places in The City looked identical. Always one hallway connecting to another, lined with room after room, like a hotel…or a prison.

The Mara unlocked a door on the right with an iron key and presented the room. "Sir, if you'll have a seat inside, get comfortable, your hostess will arrive shortly."

Max walked in, returning a drunkard's smile to the Mara's sharp, yellow hospitality. If he had any reservations left, they melted away when he saw the Ming-style bed with plenty of silk embroidered pillows. It beckoned to him with delicious, slothful memories from the dens of San Francisco. Max took a seat on the mattress; at least his prison cell would be familiar and welcoming.

With another creepy chuckle, the Mara left, closing the door behind him.

Max relaxed into the pillows and closed his eyes, enjoying the sensations of the *mogjiŭ*, focusing on the absence of all pain.

There was a soft knock at the door. "Sir?" A short, thin woman entered the room. Her hair was straight and shiny black. Max placed her age as late twenties, thirty tops. She wore a floral patterned maxi dress, the top loose fitting of Tang dynasty women. She held an opium pipe, not unlike the ones he was used to back home. She moved at a measured pace, avoiding eye contact with Max.

"First time?" Her voice was prim and proper; she took great care in placing each tool of her trade on the desk table near the corner. From the pipe to the match, everything had a specific order.

"Yes. What can I expect?"

She turned to the sound of his voice. Blind pupils, no more defined than cloudy swirls of green, surprised Max, but he said nothing.

"*Sĭ fĕn* is unexpected." She opened a small jewelry box, and using a miniature wooden spoon, measured out an even dose of the powder inside. "It can take you places, show you things. It is essence of others, of human existence. Has power for so many things…just depend on person."

Max watched as she emptied the spoon into the pipe, her sightless eyes on him, her fingers never missing a move.

"For some it can open new worlds, give insight." She smiled slyly. "But often, it leaves more questions than answers and closes insight." She presented a tightly packed pipe and an oil lamp. "You know how to use this?"

"Yes."

"I will leave now. You will be safe here." She measured her steps back to the door, then turned to face him again. "I return later to check on you. Though I will not disturb you while using. After this first journey, you may stay as long as you want and I will continue to visit as needed."

The woman bowed and left the room, followed by the click of the lock. Max's eyes shifted from the pipe to the door handle. There was no inside lock. This time, he was trapped. Alarm didn't

flood his body though; he was still floating. He closed his eyes
one last time, checking if he could find the strength he had back
at Arthur's, allowing a pause in the downward spiral for signs of
Leigh Anne to reemerge.

Nothing.

In the absence of her grace, his thoughts conjured up Ming in
one of those peep show rooms. Tied up, cut, humiliated, and
disfigured as amusement for perverts. But it wasn't enough to
motivate him to walk away and find sobriety. The fact that the
place he'd attended was only one of countless actually gave him
more of a push to continue his collision course with the infamous
sĭ fĕn. After all, Ming could be anywhere in the whole city. Rules
didn't seem to apply. It just depended on how badly they wanted
to hurt her, what kind of humiliation was the best punishment. All
the money and determination he had left meant nothing in the face
of such daunting odds. Even if he did find her, what if it ended the
same as with Leigh Anne? Did he really want to experience that?

No. He wanted to sleep, pain-free and long.

He vaporized the *sĭ fĕn* and inhaled. The smoke tightened in
his chest and the pressure was familiar as an old friend. He held
the smoke in his lungs for as long as possible, reveling in the
aching tissue with the knowledge that once he exhaled, the
mystery would be revealed. When his oxygen supply had
dwindled to a fierce burning in his chest, Max let the smoke out
in a thick cloud that hung in the air longer than any smoke he'd
previously seen, before dispersing into nothingness.

The euphoria built in his feet first. He could feel its tingling
grip slide up the microscopic vessels of his legs. Branching out,
the numbing sensation crawled up through his torso and into his
other appendages, culminating with flushed cheeks as it seeped
into Max's face. His eyelids grew heavy and his cheeks felt like
loose jowls.

Max was sure his eyes were still closed. And yet he saw the
room around him...or did he just sense the room?

He focused on the impression and at some point became aware
of a distinct sound, a low hum of murmurs. In that moment, it
seemed that Max could never recall a time when he had known
life without the vibrating whispers in the tiny room. The inaudible
voices felt natural.

Max focused on the chatter, trying to pinpoint individual pitches. It was impossible, though. The voices intensified until the room seemed to come alive and pulse with a beautiful and haunting mesh of various speech that wove together and blanketed him. Even though the volume had increased, the words were no more intelligible. The language was foreign to him. If it was a language at all. Maybe it was just humming; it was impossible to tell.

All he knew was the words soothed him. And if there was a meaning he could ascribe to the sound patterns, it was that whoever—or whatever—was speaking needed Max's presence. It wanted him to stay.

The wall in front of him shook. Not like an earthquake, though. He knew what those felt like. Had lived through the worst of them. This was something else, more akin to the ripple of a pond's surface after a tossed rock.

Then the room filled with a new noise: the crinkling of paper but magnified a hundred times. The crackling sound of parchment scratched at his ears until there was an audible *pop*. The room stopped vibrating and fell away as if it were sections of panels being unzipped one at a time. The loosed pieces disappeared into nothingness and Max was nowhere.

Images flashed through his mind or in front of him. He caught only glimpses before they were gone. The images never registered fully, but there was always an emotional response that stayed in his body and was compounded with the next set of feelings invoked by the following image. Fear. Love. Pain. Joy. He was a child, then a young man. He thought of women. Intense lust. Of friends. A road of pain. But the pain was littered with patches of pure ecstasy. It was like he was living someone else's memories. Experiencing a stranger's life. The ultimate form of voyeurism. It was perfect; Max didn't even have to be himself anymore.

When the movie reel of the unique life ended, Max could finally make out his location. He was in a cave of some sort. It was unclear how the rock dwelling was illuminated, but it was. Glowing with an uncanny light. Pointed rocks jutted up from the ground while others dripped down from the ceiling. Seemingly frozen structures, they fought to connect—teeth coming together in a giant rock maw, waiting to swallow him forever.

He could hear the sounds of babbling water. A small stream perhaps was rushing by; the gravel at his feet was covered in the smallest of puddles. A cat padded up to him through the glistening wet rocks and stopped a few feet away. Its fur was alive with color. Red, green, yellow, blue, all the colors of a rainbow were splashed across its coat. The colors were hyper bright, alive as if pulsating and shifting across the cat's body.

Its eye's glowed red and its small mouth opened. The cat began to sing. Max could sense an urgency in the cat. He wanted Max to speak to him. He wanted Max to communicate. But Max couldn't think of how. He focused on the feline, who was now nodding its head. Max opened his mouth and sound flooded out. He could understand, and he spoke in tongues. He was in the land of the dead. There was much here to see and to do. The cat would show him. The swirling, colorful cat would show him everything.

Come back. There is so much to show you.

The panels of the room began boxing up, reforming their structure, covering up the cave. The wooden siding locked into place with loud booms. The room assembled around him and still the pounding continued, only now the knocking was gentle, and suddenly Max was conscious. Hazy and a bit confused, but he was awake. He heard a soft voice. "Mister?"

Max groaned and looked up, the ceiling blurred then refocused. Slowly, the sensation of bedding registered against his body and he realized he was laying on a mattress.

"Mister," the female voice said.

Max turned his head at the sound of the lock clicking. The door opened and the hostess from earlier poked her head inside. Seeing her face again helped give Max a slight foothold in reality. He still felt very lightheaded.

The woman closed the door behind her. "Sir, you have a visitor. The man said it was urgent, I thought I would ask." Somehow her blind eyes were guilty for disturbing him.

"A visitor?" Max's voice cracked and the final syllable got caught in his throat, raising to nothing more than a high-pitched squeak.

The hostess found the glass pitcher of ice water and filled up the cup on the nightstand beside Max's bed. She held the cup in his vicinity and Max received it with shaky hands. The woman laid her soft hands around his, keeping them steady as he guided the drink to his lips.

"Slowly," she said.

The water cooled the cracks in his lips. The moisture loosened his throat, soaking into the dry patches like rain in a barren desert.

The woman smiled and returned the cup to a small puddle of condensation that had formed by the sweating pitcher on the nightstand.

"Thank you." His voice already stronger. Besides the dehydration, he wasn't in pain. He was just…fuzzy. Like a film of cheesecloth covered his vision. "I have a visitor?"

"He said his name was Mr. Willis."

"Charlie," he whispered.

"Said it was of dire urgency, but we can send him away if you do not wish company. And if you think this person will bother you, we can have a—"

"No. Send him in, please." Max took another sip of water, this time on his own. The woman left and he fought the haze, trying to formulate some coherent questions on why Charlie had—

"Max." The door was open again and Charlie was in the room. "Finally." Charlie headed to the table and took a seat.

Max placed the cup back on the nightstand. "Charlie." It was half question, half statement. Seeing him there, in his less than immaculate suit and weasel-like thinning hair…it seemed to be a dream.

"Yeah, Max, it's me." Sympathy in his pained face. "How…how are you?"

"Where have you been?" The words echoed in his ears and he wasn't sure how loud he had spoken them. Max struggled to sit up higher on the bed, fighting the lethargy of the drug still wrapping itself around his muscles. "You left me." He finally sat up against the wall, hands planted on the bed, fully extended, helping to keep his support. "What happened to our plan?"

"Look, I didn't mean for this to happen. I'd been waiting for you, I was." Charlie held up his palm as if taking an oath. "I got pinched by Tommy. I owed money to the Suey Sings. They traverse down here. Bad luck we ran into each other. They almost killed me."

"I know the feeling."

"You gotta believe me."

"How did you find me?"

"Once I got free, I looked for you in the nearby brothels. I finally decided to throw out some feelers. I've been asking guides for anyone fitting your description." Charlie leaned forward. "Max, I spent hours each day for the past week talking with people. I can't believe I found you. Glad you're okay."

"Why wouldn't I be?"

"Well, in case you didn't notice, this place can be a bit much. Some people fall hard. I'm hoping you haven't spent all your time in this *sĭ fĕn* house."

"I haven't." Max took the cup and finished the rest of the water. "I got a lot accomplished."

"Good," Charlie said. "Let's get you outta here and back up to the surface. We'll rest, then double our efforts and come back. Stronger than before."

"Return?" Max had thrown in the towel when he stepped foot in this room. Why was Charlie trying to fuck up his plans again?

"You said you'd do anythin' for your daughter, right? If you have information on her whereabouts or the abductors, then we gotta get you rested first."

Max felt a bit of his resentment toward the man fade. Charlie had no way of knowing what was going on. He thought "accomplished" meant leads in his daughter's case. Max couldn't bring himself to tell Charlie that Leigh Anne was dead. "Guess it wouldn't be a bad idea to regroup."

"Of course not. Whatever's been going on here has been for a while. Another few days won't hurt nothin'."

Anger and relief battled for Max's attention. He had been so close to it all being over, so damn close. "Fine," Max said. "How do we get outof here?"

"There may be only one way in, but there are a few exits. Let's go."

Max's body felt like rubbery appendages floating in water,

almost like he glided out of the room and across the streets. Following Charlie's lead required massive concentration and energy. Eventually the buildings thinned, and the cobblestone roads led to dirty unpaved paths.

"So," Charlie said, as they walked, "Ya feel better now that you seen this place?"

"I don't think 'better' is the right word. But...at least I-I..." Emotion seemed to be the only thing cutting through the *sǐ fěn* hangover, and he might as well say it now. "I know what happened to Leigh Anne."

"You found her?" Charlie didn't seem as surprised as Max expected him to be at the admission.

I didn't tell him yet, did I?

Maybe I did.

Max stumbled and stopped to gather his bearings. They were no longer surrounded by The City; the area was now large boulders and much lower ceilings, jagged like the ground where Max presumed the Mara somehow dug through the earth. There was a clear path though, cutting through the rocks, slowly ascending upward. Max noticed people. Not massive lines, but a small trickle of groups here and there, winding their way up the switchback path and disappearing into the rocks above.

"Yeah. I found her. She...she's gone now." *Physically and spiritually.* Max's eyes burned with the threat of tears. But Max couldn't allow himself to grieve in front of Charlie. "What matters is I got to see her. She...she knew it was me. We—" Max slipped as they climbed.

"Careful," Charlie said, grabbing Max's elbow and steadying him. "*Fěn* packs a punch. Effects last for hours."

Max composed himself and moved forward again.

"Sorry 'bout your daughter. Least you got to see her. Sure that meant a lot." Charlie turned his head back to Max. Was he scowling?

No, it's the drug.

But his words did come out harsh, didn't they?

Up ahead was a Mara standing at a point where the makeshift path disappeared into an archway of wet rock.

"Just added security for the migration back and forth." Charlie's voice sounded normal again.

"God, I've got to sit down. This stuff is playing games with my head."

"We're close. There's a lift soon, and above that a bar. Sort of a halfway house. Good cover. We can rest there."

"That would be great."

"Don't focus on the act of movin'. Talk with me and just let your legs go. If you focus on the climbin', it's gonna wear you out quicker. So...you went to the den after finding out about your daughter?"

"Sort of...made a few other stops, met some other people." Even in his compromised mental state Max knew it was best not to mention Ming. They entered the cave and the colder temperature helped make his legs numb to the exertion.

"I would've smoked *fěn* too. I sorta lost it when Brittny died. You remember Brittny, right?"

It was like Charlie hadn't heard him at all. Then Max noticed that the crowds had thinned considerably. The cave passageways were narrow, moist and dark. Oil lamps lit the path and every once in a while, he caught the shadow of a person or persons ahead of them.

"Uh, Brittny. I—"

"She was my sister."

"Yeah, that's right." But he only half-remembered the sister he'd met once or twice.

They moved in silence for what felt like hours. Time distorted while Max tried to recall something about the woman.

The money! Max gave cash to Charlie to help his sister when he went to prison.

Then, Max was pulling up short to avoid running into Charlie. The narrow rock walls had opened and he was waiting by five other travelers—all silent, looking at the ground—and two Mara who stood in front of a grimy lift door, thick and green with patina. Decades of decay seemed to drip from layers covering the old iron.

"I...I do remember your sister, now. She—"

"We'll talk about it up top," Charlie said.

Max stood, focusing on breathing, willing the fog to clear from his mind. What the hell had he experienced in that room? They were like memories, but not his own. Someone else's dreams, life, and yet—

The earth trembled and a grinding whine could be heard in the distance. The sound grew, echoing in the small rocky chamber until the clang of metal on metal halted the crescendo. The Mara unlatched the door and opened the lift. Charlie, Max, and the five other men quietly boarded.

With another shaky start, the gears ground again and the metal cage ascended into darkness. The world below blotted out, and Max wished the whole City would pass out of his mind too. Just like a nightmare hangover. The magnificent cat of colors, Cheyenne, the West End slums, and Peek-a-Boos. All of it. Just erased.

The lift stopped, jostling the men around. The door screeched open and the passengers poured out onto a wooden floor. The world of San Francisco, the real world, slapped Max's face, bringing him once again into the present. The crashing of a billiards game came from the corner, beer drinking and card games dominated the tables packed into whatever establishment they had entered. There was even a piano playing and drunken singing as accompaniment.

"Come on," Charlie, said, leading Max to an empty table.

Max sat down, dropping his head into his hands. "This is not much better for my headache."

Charlie left him and walked to the bar. He returned with two drinks. "Club soda." He pushed one glass in front of Max. "Here, take this." He held up a white pill.

"What is it?"

"Should stop that headache."

That was enough for Max. He placed the pill in his dry mouth and washed it down with the entire glass of club soda. He repressed a burp from the carbonation. "Back there…I was saying, I do remember your sister. This stuff is playing hell on my memory." Max offered a wan smile. "Sorry to hear about her passing. What happened?"

"You remember when they locked me up? How I told you I couldn't do six months? That I *needed* to be out, *needed* to make money."

Max winced. He felt worse now about the whole incident than he had at the time. "Yeah. I remember giving you what cash I could spare."

"Tommy and the Suey Sing Tong—the one I ran into down there." He pointed at the ground. "I owed them a lot of money."

Max swallowed hard, his throat was dry. "Charlie, I—"

"The Tongs can't do much to a jailbird. But they can do somethin' to his family."

Max focused on Charlie's eyes, the best he could. The pill hadn't worked yet, because the world was still hazy and painful. But perfect vision or not, the expression in Charlie's stare was easy to read: Anger.

"I gave them everythin' I had. But it wasn't enough. They killed my sister while I was locked up. And do you remember why I was locked up?"

Max felt his body start to fall. He slammed his palms on the wooden table to help keep himself upright. He looked around, but the pub festivities continued. No patrons were watching them. Max tried to say something, but he couldn't form the words.

"Because of *you*. Because when they raided the pad you were too fuckin' yellow to admit you were there buying a little for yourself. You pulled that undercover detective bullshit." Charlie's eyes narrowed and his words seethed with venom. "You should have been locked up with me."

"Chaw…chaw…Chaw-we..." But Max's lips wouldn't work. They refused to speak the name his mind was shouting.

"The Suey Sing Tong let me live. Told me that was part of the punishment. Sound *familiar*?"

Max needed to scream but his mouth was gone. His limbs were gone.

"And after they broke her neck, they still wanted their money. In fact, it wasn't until today that I repaid every last cent." Revenge-like daggers sparked in Charlie's eyes. "You know how I made all that money back? All those gambling and drug debts?"

And then Max was crashing into the table.

"Don't worry." He heard Charlie's voice in his ear and arms gripping him, then a shoulder and body supporting him. "You shouldn't drink so much." And then he was moving, half-dragged but unable to put up any resistance. "Not to worry. I'll get you home safely."

V

Max's eyes flicked open from a dreamless sleep. His surroundings focused—bare room, dirty off-white walls and ceiling. That's when the pain in his skull materialized. Dull and achy, gnawing on the back of his eye sockets. Max went to sit up, but a force yanked him down and his head whipped back. Pain travelled his spine and kicked the sides of his stomach. He tested the waters a second time, using more ease, and again found himself restrained. Max's aching head was overshadowed by a racing pulse, and panic seized his muscles. Someone had tied him down.

With slow struggles against his bindings, Max observed more details, including the rough fabric under him. He twisted more and noted that he was on a table. The surrounding room was barren except for a metal stand and tray in the corner. The objects were a little too distant to be identified.

"Welcome back."

Max raised his head, and the sight of Charlie made him sicker.

"What'd you do to me, you bastard?" As Max lowered his

aching head, he glimpsed the coarse brown rope that covered his chest, hips, and legs in three points of bondage.

"What did *I* do?" Charlie pointed a finger at his chest which was covered by a thick smock over a black dress shirt. He resembled the man who had been cleaning up the bloody floor in Peek-a-Boos. "That any way to treat someone who brought you a gift?" Charlie held up a cool glass of water. He made his way over to Max, lifted and cradled his head. Max thought about resisting. But as soon as the cool water ebbed past his cracked lips, all ideas of fighting were gone.

"There ya go." Charlie eased his head back to the covered table. "I want you to be awake for this...my crowning moment."

"You drugged me."

"Nothin' gets past you, detective." Charlie sneered and moved to a farther corner, near the metal tray. "Do you remember where we left our conversation?"

"Jesus, Charlie, I just...my head is—"

"Take your time." He smiled, wicked and patient.

Max closed his eyes and concentrated. He sighed, his dry throat catching and cracking. "We...we were discussing your sister's passing."

"Her murder!" Charlie slammed his hand down on the tray eliciting a metallic jump from the objects on top. "She had nothin' to do with my debts to the Suey Sing. But they took her anyway. And it's your fault."

"Charlie, I didn't do anything to your sister. I—"

"You coulda gotten me off. You threw me under the bus to save yourself." With a screech, the metal stand was pushed closer to Max's table. "We both knew there weren't no undercover investigation. You were in the wrong place at the wrong time buying drugs."

The kicking returned to Max's stomach, causing painful spasms, then releasing into bowel–loosening nausea that made him want to vomit. He had missed all the clues. They were right there and he'd been blinded to the big picture.

"If you fessed up or even just said I was a part a' your undercover operation, I'd have been free. I'd have worked to make the money to pay back Tommy Sing. And my sister would still be alive." The table was pushed closer still, screeching across the floor like knives on a plate. "Ya get it now?"

The table was close enough to see medical instruments on top. Gleaming in polished steel, Max could almost feel the sting of their surgical precision. "Yeah. I get it."

"Perhaps," Charlie said. "But I wanna make sure you know every detail." Charlie looked down at the surgical tools. "Jeff Poppens knew the secrets to sǐ fěn. Said he'd teach me. We'd go into business together. But we'd have to be really careful; I'd never met a human with that knowledge. How could I say no? I'd been to The City. I knew what a rush the stuff was. Hell, if I hadn't dragged you off, you would have made more trips to that den…or never left.

"See, the powder doesn't come from a plant." Charlie picked up a long flay knife. "It's human bones. If they want to be nice, they kill the person first. If they want to be cruel or prove a point…they let the pain drive the person insane. Let the pain of being skinned alive *kill* them." Charlie dangled the blade above Max's right eye. "Which option do you think I chose for your wife?"

It was like waiting for a punch you knew was coming; didn't stop the pain.

"Don't bother telling me how innocent Eve was and how she didn't have nothin' to do with our problems," Charlie said. "I know all 'bout it! My sister was innocent too! That night was *your* fuck up. Not mine." He jabbed the knife downward, taunting Max. "And you chose to pay the price by sacrificing me. You got to go home to your wife. Your kid. While I rotted in a cell. And of course, 'your hands were tied,' there weren't nothin' you could do but offer to give me a few bucks until I could get back on my feet.

"Well now you really are tied, Max. And payback's here. I waited a long time for this. It's genius really… Your wife was our first batch of product, and we made a lot of money. Once the seed had been planted, our customers wanted more."

"Fuck you."

"Jeff found the bodies. We experimented. Trying to find differences in the highs obtained from male and female bones, in young and old, Negros, whites and Asians, all of it." Charlie chuckled. "Things started to get out of control. I mean, we were careful. Only one crime was ever found—your house…but I let that one get discovered on purpose." A sick twinkle of satisfaction flickered in his eyes.

"Two," Max barked. "You forget about Jeffrey's house? It was a slaughter. Or did you let us find that one too?"

"No. The Mara left those bodies because they don't care. They leave no traces that can tie back to them."

"They left the powder."

"No, they didn't. I did." Charlie smiled and some of the air went out of Max. "Destroyin' your family wasn't enough. I wanted more. At the same time, our buyers were talking too much. And word got out about our *sǐ fěn* business. There's no way to reason with the Mara. Once those things knew there was a human making *sǐ fěn*, I had only one chance to save my ass. So I acted first. I went to The City and told some chemists that I knew the human traitor to their secret: Jeff. I was off the hook. And once I knew they'd handled him, I planted that leather pouch. Was the only chance to give the cops a clue…only way to get you back in the game. Wasn't sure it'd work, but here you are." Charlie laughed.

"Why would the Mara believe anything you say?"

"'Cause not long ago, I delivered them a pregnant teen, free of charge…she was also free of fight."

Bile pushed against the back of his teeth and swallowing it down made him sicker. "Son of a bitch." Max strained upward and glared at Charlie.

"After we killed Eve, we took Leigh Anne with us. I mean, she fought at first. But after a few rounds with me and Jeff, it left her. The dope and *fěn* helped too. The Mara got a young girl to use as they saw fit. And use her they did. Heard she wound up at a butcher's shop—"

"You knew all along."

"'Course. I'm a snitch. I *exist* to know. And my final payment to the Suey Sing came from the Mara when I snitched on your whereabouts after you killed Lakzo."

"What?"

"I watched you. Followed, kept my own contacts tailin' ya. You shot Lakzo and fled with some child guide. The Mara had no leads. I changed all that, gave 'em some info for a price. The bounty was just enough to clear the last of my debts with the

Sings. And now I have you."

The bindings hadn't loosened from his struggles, and Max knew he was going to die. Not only die, but go through the same torture as his wife. The only consolation being his demise would be ironic penance for his mistakes.

Charlie returned the blade to the tray and grabbed a pair of bone scissors. "Gotta lose the clothes." He cut up the side of Max's pants leg. The blades maneuvered around the ropes and continued through the thick waistband and up his shirt.

"Once we cut all this away, you're gonna be impressed with the procedure. I've perfected it. I bet I can take your skin all in one piece—"

The room shook. Pounding resonated.

"San Francisco Police Department! The building is surrounded."

"Well, I guess you'll have to settle for a quick kill instead!" Max spat. "Best laid schemes of mice and men."

Charlie looked at the door which was buckling in the frame. He swiveled back to Max. "No, we can't end it like this. You'll come after me, won't you?"

"Until my last breath."

Charlie grinned. "I expect nothing less."

The knife slashed downward and Max closed his eyes, ready for the end. But nothing happened. He opened his eyes to the sound of the window rising and footsteps landing on the fire escape. He turned his head sideways and saw the flay knife stuck through the tarp and into the wood, its thin blade now bent from the hardened composition of the table.

The front door splintered off its hinges and swung inward. John McCloud filled the opening, revolver drawn and twisting from side to side.

"He's gone out the window!" Max shouted.

McCloud hurried past him and peered out. "He's gone." John turned to Max and holstered his gun.

"How the hell did you find me?"

McCloud walked over and pulled the bent knife out of the table. "It's a long story." He tugged at the ropes binding Max's chest, then applied the knife.

"Can't be as long as mine," Max said. "Trust me."

"Once again, Harris tasked me with finding you." McCloud cut more of the bonds. "I figured if narcotics were around, you'd probably try to push your old contacts for info. While looking for Charlie, I found letters from Brittny Willis, this address. I've been checking in each night on my way home from the station. I had a hunch.... And tonight, it paid off. I saw Charlie dragging you up the front stairs. Good timing, huh?"

"Amazing timing."

The last of the ropes fell from Max's body. "There," McCloud said, tossing the blade aside.

Max sat up slow, testing his limbs, trying to work the numbness out of his body and calm his heart rate.

When he felt somewhat composed, Max extended his hand. "Thank you, McCloud."

"You're welcome." He clasped Max's hand. "Now, I told you my side, so please, what the hell is going on?"

"I owe you that. But...I need a place to stay. I can't recoup at my house, they'll look for me there. They don't know you, though."

"*Who* will look for you?"

"Uh... Charlie," Max said. "I can explain better tonight."

"Look if you don't want to explain things, that's fine. I'll get you over to the station. They can provide any protection you might need."

"John." Max looked deep into his eyes, trying to make him understand. "I will tell you. But I can't go to the station. Just trust me on this. I simply can't answer the hundreds of questions they'll have. *But* I'm willing to share the truth with you."

"Dammit!" McCloud looked at the open window. "Fine. You have one night with me. But that's all."

"Agreed. Just get me outta here."

An hour and a half later, Max had bathed and was changing in a spare room at McCloud's apartment. All he had left was his trench coat. The pants and shirt had been shredded by Charlie's scissors. While testing out a box of John's old clothes for something that somewhat fit, Max noticed the only decorations in the room: two framed photos and a certificate. The first photo was of a girl, perhaps fourteen, in a white, plain dress. The second was the same girl, several years younger, standing beside an older teen. Max laced up his shoes, noting the structure of the teen's face, easily seeing how the bones could transform years later into McCloud's current mug. He examined the certificate before leaving.

When he came out to the living room, he sat across from the young detective. John had a glass of brandy in his hand. The alcohol looked good, but Max wasn't sure he should ask for any yet.

"Thanks for the clothes."

McCloud waved him off. "That's the least of my concerns."

"Okay, then let's talk shop. You've been with the department for three years?"

McCloud's face screwed up into a mask of confusion and frustration. "Max, I just pulled you off the chopping block—literally. You've been missing for weeks. You owe me answers."

"Fair enough." Max leaned forward. "I need you to meet me halfway though. I need to know I can trust the guy I'm sharing this info with. I just want to know more about you."

"You first." McCloud glared from above the lip of his glass as he took a sip of the booze.

Max sighed. "I found out the powder is called *sĭ fĕn*."

"What is it?"

"It's a very ancient concoction and one few people know about. When he got out of prison, Charlie and Jeffrey Poppens teamed up to manufacture it."

"This whole thing revolves around Charlie, doesn't it?"

"Yeah."

"I tracked down his cohort, Barnes," McCloud said. "I think I have some vital information for you, but I'm not sure I made the right connection. If I have, it's bad. It's…it's about your family."

Max held up his hand. "I know the connection already. But can I get one of those before I spill the story?" He pointed at the brandy. "I think a drink might make talking about this easier."

John poured a highball and brought it to Max.

"Thanks." Max took a long sip. "So, three years on the force?"

"Yeah."

"I noticed the degree in the bedroom. You were going to be a teacher?"

"It was my first passion. I know university is where the money and prestige are at, but I was always good with adolescents." A sad note of regret played in his words.

"What school did you teach at?"

"I never quite made it through my internship."

"Why?"

"Life got in the way." McCloud stared down into his glass.

"Always does," Max said. "Didn't you work with the juvies before investigation?"

"This is not really the time to discuss my attempts at fixing the problems of the social services sector." McCloud finished his drink.

"Fine." Max raised his hands. "This whole thing was about retribution for locking Charlie up. He killed my wife." Alcohol created such a nice veil when talking about unpleasant things; Max lifted his glass. "May I have another?"

John filled it up and returned to the chair, passing the drink over. "Murdering your wife seems a bit excessive revenge for six months." McCloud's knowing, young eyes studied him. "What did you really do?"

Max sipped the liquor, his gums already feeling the numbing bite of the previous drink. "Charlie was in debt to the Suey Sing. He couldn't pay back the money while he was locked up and so they killed his sister. He blames me for her death. He got me back that October night in Eden Plaza." Max downed the second drink, hoping to keep his emotions subdued. "A wife's life for a sister's."

"And what about Leigh Anne?"

Max shook his head. "She's gone."

McCloud looked like he was about to ask more, then stopped. "Did something go south between Charlie and Poppens? I got the feeling that Charlie wasn't responsible for the massacre of the little girls or his partner."

Max's eyes moved to the mantelpiece where he found another picture of the young girl. "My turn. Who's she?"

McCloud followed Max's gaze. "She was my sister."

"I'm sorry."

"Me too," McCloud said. "The detectives wasted time. If they had moved on the details I gave them..." His voice started to quiver with anger.

"You can't know—"

"Time is always man's greatest adversary. They failed to act."

Passion burned in McCloud's eyes. Max didn't see him as the same investigator that had dragged him from Ku's opium den anymore. In fact, Max's perception of just about everything had transformed since that time. And the changes kept coming despite his efforts to slip back into a drugged state of uncaring. "Remember what they did with the Juvenile Court over in Cook County at the turn of the century?"

"What's that to do with anything?"

Max ignored him. "I read about a lot of changes."

"Yeah, yeah. I read them too. Like finally realizing the motive of the juvenile court is to provide rehabilitation and protective supervision for youth."

Max nodded. "Their way of doing things is spreading. I think you'd be good working with the juvies again."

"Been there, done that. Even followed the JPI, world's first child guidance clinic, *and* Mrs. Ethel Dummer. But legislation is the only way to enact sustainable change. And laws are hard to get passed. I changed my focus to criminal investigation and now homicide." McCloud's stare turned hard. "My turn. What happened between Charlie and Poppens?"

"Charlie was sort of responsible for Poppens's death. One of the Tongs found out that they were producing the *sǐ fěn*. And far as the *fěn* goes, only the Tongs supply it, and it's heavily regulated." Max felt it best to leave out details like the drug is sold by demented creatures who live underground in a topsy-turvy flipside world of reality. "Charlie knew the Tong was on to him, so he fled and sold out Poppens as the supplier. The Tong—most likely the Suey Sing—took out Jeffrey. They assume the supplier is off the street, so Charlie is home free."

"Then you show up."

"Yep, and he gets a chance to fill me in on the master plan, then kill me too...*if* you hadn't arrived."

"One more question. What were they doing to those girls?

Why…why skin them? Why was he going to skin you? I mean…my God, it's madness. Murder is one thing. Vengeance and hate. But…what we saw…"

Max gestured to the photo frame. "What happened?"

McCloud emptied his glass. "It's a long story."

"The answer you're asking is longer and I'm not even sure you'll believe me."

McCloud returned to the liquor shelf and poured another generous serving, staring into the numbing elixir. "This stuff is getting easier to drink."

"Careful," Max cautioned. "Soon it becomes hard *not* to drink."

"This doesn't seem like your style, Max. You know, caring about other people's past. I mean unless you can use it to your advantage."

It didn't sting as bad as it could have. "I…I want to trust you—"

"Why?" Ice clinked in McCloud's near empty glass. "Why do you care?"

Another scheme was developing in Max's head. The constant drugs either depressed him into quitting or gave him courage that plans could work out despite ridiculous odds. "I—"

"How about *your* past? Specifically, the time period when you were partners with Lieutenant Harris."

"He mentioned that?"

"No, Harris doesn't mention anything. It's in your file." McCloud nodded. "That's right, Max. You were my damn case. And I solved it! I'm only sticking my neck out and keeping you here because *you* swear it's the right thing." McCloud poured himself another glass, his words slurring. "I'm being looked over for promotions because of you, and yet I'm still trying to help. And you want me to prove myself."

Max closed his eyes. This truth hurt a lot worse than the last one. "If you have my file then everything's in there."

"I wanna know about the Digger case. It was the last one you ever worked with Harris. And afterward, it seems like everything changed."

Max looked off to the edge of the room. "He would bury his victims in pine wood boxes. They were lucky if they had three days' worth of oxygen. Dehydration may have claimed them before suffocation."

"I remember the headlines."

"We found his hideout in an abandoned industrial warehouse, but everything went to hell when we engaged."

"And you both testified later that Cullen Smith, also known as the Digger, attacked you. Defending your life, Harris shot the man, resulting in his death."

"And the death of his last three victims—their burial locations died with him."

"Oh," McCloud said. "Files didn't mention that."

"No, I bet they didn't," Max said. "Sure you don't wanna go back to the juveniles? Leave all this shit behind?"

"The kids are just as much heartbreak."

"Different kind perhaps."

"Enough." McCloud threw up his hands. "I get it: no one wants me on homicide. That's not relevant at the moment. The case is what matters. Now, let's say I believe all this. Where does it leave us?"

"Stealing the bones was part of the process," Max said. He needed McCloud now, and despite the bizarreness of the story, he was gonna give him the truth. It was the only way.

"What?"

"It's why they skinned them," Max said. "To…to help make the powder. Charlie told me they'd killed more, but had been so careful, the skin and organs hadn't been found. Charlie said we would have never found the remains of the three girls if…if the Suey Sing hadn't been tipped off and killed Poppens for encroaching on their business."

"You're right. I don't believe you." McCloud's head swayed, probably too much booze. "How can that be true? Human bones? Ground up to make drugs?"

"You got another reason someone would kill a human that way?"

John leaned back and sighed.

"The hardest part is over. We put out a warrant for Charlie Willis's arrest. I heard his confession, and you'll get a similar story from his accomplice, Chris Barnes. Other than that, it's over. We'll have police looking for him on every corner."

"What about the Tongs who killed the girls?"

"That's what it's like working homicide. A hundred and one cases. Add these to the caseload. Hundreds of nameless faces. Some will get justice, if that's what you call it. And some won't."

"We can investigate—"

"No. We can't. No one is going to talk with you about the Tongs of Chinatown. They're too scared. The girls will be black and white images on our desk. Stacked in piles with the rest and forgotten over the years." Max stood up and walked over to the mantle. "And all those black and white faces become memories of things that could have been different. Reminders of failure." He looked back at McCloud. "That's what you are signing up for if you become a homicide detective in San Fran. Is that what she wanted?" He pointed to the photograph.

McCloud's eyes took on a glossy swirl from the alcohol. "I raised my sister after our parents died overseas. When I was selected for university...I wasn't around as much."

Max returned to his seat, face softened.

"The day I took my final exam was the day she went missing."

"I'm sorry, John."

"Me too." He hung his head. "A lot more could have been done for my sister, but guys like Harris sit on their goddamn hands. They fail to act fast enough."

"Everyone has their reasons."

"Yeah? What's his?"

Max looked at his dossier on the kitchen table. "Harris made a mistake that night with Cullen Smith. He shouldn't have shot him. We could have gotten those buried box locations."

"But your life was in danger."

"Maybe. Maybe not. But Harris rushed that decision. And it's plagued him since. Now he weighs everything."

McCloud's head lolling was dramatic now. Max wondered what unformed thoughts were gathering behind those inebriated eyes.

"It's not important. Tomorrow I'll write a report on what happened and I'll turn it in to Harris...along with this." Max pulled out his badge from an inside pocket. "And I won't be coming back this time. Harris can do whatever he wants with the info."

"Which more than likely will be nothing," McCloud said. "He—"

"He'll handle Charlie and keep an eye on the Tongs, which is what he has to do. Because at this stage, the cons of a police war in Chinatown are not worth it. Criminal investigators don't spend as much time in Chinatown because those people don't report petty stuff. Murder sometimes isn't reported either, but we get called in on the big stuff. Now, you have some things to think about. And, if I may, I'd like to retire. The couch is fine with me."

"There's not that much for me to think about, Max." McCloud stood up, staggering. "I'm going to do what has to be done. At any cost. All I've learned from you is to run away when something gets hard. Good night." John left the room, heading for his own bedroom.

"You ever think you should have stayed with teaching?"

John stopped, turned, and looked back into the room. "I decided I could save more kids on the force than in the classroom. Kids like Janice."

"Fair enough. Maybe it's not that no one wants you in homicide. Maybe you belong fighting for those kids instead." The vibration of his words seemed to hang in the air. "Something to think about."

Darkness claimed the light. "Goodnight, Max."

VI

JOHN MCCLOUD AWOKE three hours later than he had anticipated. His head hurt from the brandy and his mouth was dry. Memories of the previous night were limited. He recalled the animosity. Being told to give up on a battle.

John made his way to the kitchen to prepare breakfast. He moved at his own hungover pace. There was no need to rush. He'd be walking into the station with Max and the identity of Charlie Willis as the murderer.

John stopped as he passed by the living room. The couch was empty.

"Max!"

There was no answer. John entered the kitchen and found it empty too. Only a note on the table remained as a trace of his visitor.

> *McCloud,*
> *Thank you for yesterday. I will forever be in your debt.*
> *Janice was lucky to have a brother like you. Best of luck and*

I hope to see you around.
   - Max

John was out the door within fifteen minutes of reading the note. He rushed to the station, a sixth sense telling him Max was already there. That he would share all the developments with Harris and take all the credit. Max Elliot, selfish as always. McCloud had done the work; he'd saved the stubborn detective. He should be there to share in giving over the news.

The station was in a buzz when he arrived. McCloud ignored the bustle and made a beeline for Harris's office. He heard the lieutenant's voice from the open door. "And send someone over to McCloud's. We don't want anything to—John!"

McCloud nodded from the open doorway. An officer he didn't know stood in front of the Lieutenant's desk. "Well scratch those orders," Harris said to the man. "Get the rest of the A-shift out there looking for Charlie Willis. Bring that son of a bitch in."

"Yes, sir." The officer nodded to McCloud as he left.

Harris was beyond grinning. His face was beaming, and the swollen bags of sleep deprivation under his eyes were smoothing out. "McCloud, my boy. How the hell are you?" He walked around the desk and stuck out his hand. John grasped it and Harris pulled him close. He patted McCloud's forearm and then shoulder, almost comfortingly, like a grandfather to a young boy. "Max told us what happened. Wanted to make sure this nut didn't put you on his list and show up at your home while you were recouping."

"Th-thank you, sir. I'm fine though. Just sluggish. Yesterday took a lot out of me."

"More than just yesterday," he said, a hint of compassion. "You've been on surveillance for...ah, who cares. You did it. You saved Max's ass and now we know exactly what's going on. When we catch this guy, the mayor'll want to see you."

The mayor?

"Sir? I don't quite follow. Charlie is still out there. Besides, I thought Johnston was the public head."

"Since that story broke, people have a lot of questions. As you said, Max never pushed, but the public will. They're angry; they want action. Now we can counter when they demand what we're doing. Excuse me, *you'll* be answering the questions...*Homicide detective*." Harris beamed.

Well, wonders never cease. Max had strolled in this morning and given me all the credit. And Harris is like a new man. Three girls carved worse than the prostitutes of Whitechapel—this is going to be a big case. And I'm leading the charge.

Max had never been so happy to be home. But he kept his vigilance despite his relief, checking the front lock twice and then wedging an armchair under the doorknob. He didn't think Charlie would come for him now. He could have easily stabbed Max as he fled, but vengeance born of true hatred couldn't be rushed. It might take years before Charlie surfaced for him again.

Secured inside, Max disrobed and crawled into bed. Luckily, exhaustion surpassed his mind's musing over how his life had changed forever, and sleep snatched him moments after lying down.

Max rested for much longer than he planned.

When he finally rose shortly before noon, he ate and then took down his three favorite puzzle boxes from the closet. It had been a long time since he last held the polished wood in his hands. So much had happened, and he needed to relax so he could evaluate his current situation.

Max picked the box that he recalled as being the easiest to solve of the three and turned the puzzle over a few times in his hands, taking the time to admire the intricate patterns that adorned its side.

For the next hour, Max familiarized himself with the old stress relievers, solving each box numerous times. Committing the moves to memory so he could fluidly move through the sequence with his eyes closed. Each slide, twist, and click drew out more of his apprehension, allowed him to uncloud his thoughts.

He mused over Leigh Anne and his grief-stricken dream and sober hallucination. Unlike many officers who relied on religion to get through this line of work, Max always found belief in a supreme power quite difficult. Not that The City had changed his mind; however, if creatures more evil than humans existed, then perhaps there was a slim chance that something equally as powerful as the Mara but on the side of justice also resided in this crazy world.

Plus, it was nice to think that Leigh Anne and Eve were in a better place.

But even if the afterlife was all a lie and his family wasn't looking down on him, and all that awaited in death was the cold embrace of nothingness...so what? It didn't mean he shouldn't comply with Leigh Anne's final wish to save Ming—even if it had been just a hopeful hallucination. Max had felt good giving McCloud credit for the case; that emotion wasn't imagined. And if he found Ming, the sense of accomplishment would be a thousand times greater.

There was no escaping death, and Max saw very limited options for himself. If he died rescuing Ming, then at least he'd have beaten his final fear without shame. But without the sense of purpose that pursuing Ming provided, he'd inevitably return to the slow, self-destructive spiral McCloud had found him in; and that death no longer seemed as appealing.

VII

"**Mayor McCarthy**, I present you Lieutenant Harris and Detective McCloud." The mayoral aide nodded to the men.

"Ah, thank you, Clancy." The mayor stood, smile plastered on his face. "Gentlemen, welcome, welcome," he said, coming from around his desk. The aide departed as the tall official held out his hand. "Harris, always a pleasure." He turned to John. "And Detective McCloud. This is an honor."

The mayor's enthusiastic grip wrapped around John's hand. "The honor is mine," McCloud said.

"Please, sit…sit."

John glanced around at the mahogany finish across the room—desk, floor, and bookcase—as he sat beside Harris and in front of the mayor.

"I'll be speaking at a press conference tomorrow and I'd like both of you to join me. But before we discuss that, let's hear the newest developments in the case. I believe you have a suspect?"

Harris cleared his throat and looked at John.

McCloud felt like he'd shrunk in the chair. The smell of wood polish around him hurt his head as the mayor turned his eyes on the department's newest homicide detective. "Well, we...we do." McCloud fumbled to retrieve the case folder from his attaché. "We've implicated Charles Willis in the murder of Eve Elliot." John finally got the mugshot of Willis on the table.

The drop of the mayor's smile was almost imperceptible. "*And*...how about the ten-year-old female victim from Broadway, Marian Bell? Or the other two girls?"

"Well, based on the nature of the crime, we are under the belief that Willis perpetrated those crimes as well." John wished he had more hard evidence, but Max hadn't spoken a word about the Tongs to Harris. At least according to the lieutenant.

"And how strong is this belief?"

"We have a first-hand confession to Detective Elliot from Willis himself," Harris said.

"Elliot, huh?"

"We also just picked up an accomplice of Willis's who should prove quite helpful," McCloud said.

"But we don't have Willis?" the mayor said.

"We will," McCloud said.

"Okay," the mayor said, "ignoring the conviction sticking for now—I'm sure it will—how do we find Willis and what do you need from me?"

VIII

THE REST OF the day and the one following were those of preparation for the path he'd chosen. Max needed a few tricks up his sleeve before he returned to The City.

While he worked, he felt a few cravings for the *fěn*. Especially after he unpacked the closet; shifting through old boxes had depleted his energy. He was shocked at how fast he tired. He just wanted to relax and listen to the cat sing away his aches with its foreign, purring language that Max had not fully understood and yet, at the same time, somehow comprehended. He wanted to tango with the memories of the dead. Absorb someone else and live their life.

The cravings were strong but not insurmountable. To elude their grasping hooks, Max constantly reminded himself of Ming's sacrifice for him and his dream.

There's still time, Daddy.

When he was done with his tasks, he took a sheet of paper and sat down at the kitchen table, a *Himitsu-Bako* resting beside his hand. He picked up a pen, gave it a shake, and pressed the metal nib to the paper, beginning a note. Today he was putting more faith in another person than he ever had before.

But if there's nothing left to lose, why not try something new.

After he signed the bottom, he folded the letter, stuffed it in an envelope and went to the bed to retrieve his suit coat. Max slipped the letter into the inner breast pocket and felt the stiff paper of something already inside. He pulled out the black business card.

We have no-limit black shows in Gehanna.

Max took a moment to study the card with more intent than before. A large triangle was embossed on the backing of the card, and beneath it seven cryptic seals consisting of mathematical lines and spirals mingling with crosses and geometrical shapes, symmetrical in some seals, and a type of ordered chaos in others. Max slipped the card back into the pocket and hung it in the closet for tomorrow.

He raised his palm, studying the ouroboros. After a quick breakfast, he would return to Goodfellow. From there, he would make his way back to The City and then to Ming's house, where he would leave the letter in a safe spot. After that, Max would find Ming or die trying.

He'd made the right choice back in The City; Leigh Anne had told him there was still time to save Ming and he believed it, regardless of her absence now. Her soul was at rest somewhere and it was doubtful he would see her again. And if Max desired the same peace for himself then he must complete the task. And he couldn't have reached this conclusion if he hadn't had his faith tested—capture by Charlie and then rescue by McCloud had been necessary moves in the puzzle.

Just before he fell asleep, he whispered to the empty room. "Hold on, Ming."

THE CITY

PART III

1

"**D**O YOU WANT to die?" a man shouted from atop a large wooden crate.

Max slowed and looked up at the soapbox. The man was staring at him with deep black eyes.

"Of course you don't," the man answered his own question. A few onlookers had gathered around the orator in front of the business the man was advertising. The dark, piercing pupils broke from him and Max breathed relief.

The man on the crate wagged his finger at the audience. "You can't help but wonder though…"

Thick clouds of tobacco and steam billowed up from the gathered crowd, but the barker didn't seem to mind. He smiled, shifting slowly on the platform. "And now…now, you will get your chance to experience the dead. Step inside, let their darkness embrace you. Dance with them and share their secrets."

Max pulled his coat tighter and walked away. The City seemed colder this time, but it no longer felt foreign. The carnival atmosphere was like a discarded lover: the terrain was familiar, but its company was unwanted.

As he headed west, Max thought of the cat he had met in the land of the dead during his own *sĭ fĕn* experience, its vibrant fur alive with possibilities. Max wanted to share in those secrets again, but he shook off the idea. That was an illusionary death only, and he had a much more important job. This time, he would not lose sight of it.

Max was able to find the hospital ward with ease.

Dumplings and skin puppets.

He contemplated buying a couple of dumplings for the road and inquiring what the puppets were, but he didn't want to get sidetracked. Past the hospital, Max retraced his steps, making sure to detour around the butcher shop. It took a bit longer to find Peek-A-Boos, but not much. Then he saw the street sign with the triangle emblem.

Follow that road straight to the fires of Gehanna.

Max paused, lingering in a trance on the street sign, forcing every fiber in his body to believe he would find Ming there. Not just hope for it, but to have unwavering faith. His prayer was broken by a man in a bowler hat.

"You, sir!" The man pointed a long black cane at Max from the opposite side of the street. "I have just what you need."

Max looked across the street at the impressive brick building. Its design was close to a miniature version of the hospital at the border.

"You won't find skin puppets like mine in Gehanna."

Max slowed to a stop, reminding himself that the path to Ming would branch in ways he couldn't yet foresee. Maybe there *was* time for a pit stop. "What's a skin puppet?"

"Sir, this is you're lucky day. You do not want to stroll into Gehanna without knowing a thing or two about puppets. Come here."

The man waved him over, and Max crossed the street. Drawing closer, he saw that a black eye patch covered the man's right eye.

"Come in, come in. Name's Henry. I guarantee you'll be so pleased, you'll tell all your friends. Tell 'em all to ask for Henry." He held the door open.

Max looked up at the three-story building, then turned to the man's good eye. "What's a skin puppet?" he asked again.

"That is best answered by seeing." The man touched a finger to his good eye and grinned, his patchy beard pulling back to reveal a missing canine and incisor.

Max stepped past him; cologne mixed with body odor and smoke seeped off the man. Inside, the lobby was cold and sterile. Instead of white washed walls, they were gray and weathered. There was a large desk near the far wall, and behind it, shelves of think ledgers filling the entire wall. A Mara dozed in the desk's chair, leaning back, booted feet on the desk, loose trousers and half-buttoned collar shirt. The creature raised his head as Henry took Max past him and to a set of stairs. They nodded to each other, and the disinterested reptile closed its eyes again.

"Gehanna is a zoo. Most of their puppets'll be third-rounders. Beat to a pulp. We're the best in the West." Henry took the first steps upward.

Max followed him to the second story. They passed through a door and stood in a single corridor. The hint of antiseptic lingered in the air. Both walls were lined with rooms, thick white doors with circular window cutouts—more prisons. Two gurneys and a wheelchair lined the wall space.

"So what sets you apart from the competition?"

Henry walked to the first door on his left—his cane seemed to be more for stage presence than his health—and tapped the circular window at the top of the door. "Take a look."

Max looked at Henry, then at the window. All he could think about was his experience at Peek-a-Boos. Max took a step closer; paranoia tickled his feet, ready to send him running. He looked back at Henry; the man was motionless, grinning, waiting. Max held his face to the double-paned window. Through the wire-enforced glass, he could see a padded cell like the kind he remembered from visiting prisoners in Agnews Insane Asylum before the quake. But this cell appeared to be unoccupied.

Thwack!

A grimy hand slapped the glass, smearing its surface, and Max staggered backward. "Holy shit!"

Henry erupted in raspy laughter.

Max glared at the man's rheumy eye.

"What luck!" He brought a calloused, tobacco-stained hand to his chest. "But really, go look. It can't get out."

"*It?*" Max said, still not ready to return to the window.

"That is a skin puppet. Though there are many other terms for them…far less flattering."

Max inched back to the glass in tentative degrees. He peered in and saw the back of what looked like a man. He was clothed in a loose white gown over pajama pants. But something was wrong about the way the man held himself. His movements were strained, strenuous and jerky. As if sensing Max's presence, the man slowly turned around. And when Max saw the man's face, he understood why Henry used the term *it*.

The man took a few shambling steps forward and Max noted the mottled skin of his face. The same dark, raw patches covered his exposed arms. A red-yellow puss seeped from the open wounds, staining the front of his gown. Similar stains spotted the legs of his pajama bottoms. As the man came closer, more horrifying features grew in clarity. When *it* was close enough for Max to see the dead, dilated eyes, Max left the door.

"What's he sick with?"

Henry shrugged. "Death."

"He's sick, not dead."

Henry moved to the window. "Alive but dead. A puppet of decaying skin, moving to an unknown marionette." The man gestured with his cane as if he were still on the street, playing to the crowd. "Animated flesh only. There's nothing else in there." The decaying man pressed up against the glass, smearing his gore across the circular window. Henry seemed transfixed. "Look at those eyes. Tell me I'm wrong."

Max stepped closer. He gazed through the smudged window, watching the skin puppet lurk around the cell.

"I tease though. That's a third-rounder, like most you find in Gehanna. He's just for practice. But it was a good laugh." Henry cocked his head down the hallway. "We have all levels of puppets." He started down the corridor and Max followed as the man gestured into one room then the next. "Look at this one. She hasn't decayed a bit." Pause. "And this fellow's had some work done to his body. But he's still in near top condition." Pause. Henry focused his good eye on Max. "You name the age, gender, and I can get it."

Max circled around in the hallway, surrounded by windows looking into suspended lives. "I don't understand what it is you're selling."

"Not everyone wants to be involved with the masses and public displays in Gehanna. We understand that. You can buy your very own skin puppet from us. Take 'em to your personal room or home, or rent them in their cells by the hour. You tell me what you want and I can arrange the perfect match."

"But in this state, dead, what would I use them for?"

"Anything you want." Henry's grin was one-sided, wrinkling the skin around his right eye. "Anything you can't bring yourself to do to a *living* human...yet."

"Yet?"

"To break your bones, as they say. Practice on the real thing so when the time comes, you know what to do. Restraint is often a skill learned with experience. Newbies often lose their tops their first time with a slave or fellow performer. Go too far. Or maybe they just need to let off some stress. That's what third-rounders are for—they've been through the gauntlet. Just tell me what you want. Torture. Sex. Unending companionship."

"Sex?"

"Well, not with someone like old number one down there." Henry walked a few feet, jabbing his cane toward door number six. "But this one's a beauty."

The woman in room six sat cross-legged on the floor, rocking back and forth in her gown. She didn't have the disfigurements of number one. Instead her face was smooth with plump cheeks, her short hair curled and set. Max even detected makeup around her eyes.

"I could get you a prophylactic if you wanted someone like her."

The woman stared off, hypnotized—or lobotomized—by something only she could see.

"Is it contagious?" Max couldn't imagine someone wanting to have sex with a person that seemed comatose.

"Contagious? Yes...no. It's not transferred through the air. That much we know. Beyond that..." He shrugged. "I've learned there are no hard rules regarding the puppets. Sometimes they bite or scratch you; I'd say that half of those people get sick. Two days tops and their body functions fail. The other half of the people get better."

"Do the bite victims die?"

"For a day or two usually. Then they wake. But their body is still dead. They don't talk or eat—though if you force them to eat, they last longer." Henry thumped his cane on the ground. "But no. You're not interested in coitus, are you? You want to relieve some stress. You need to know you have *it* in you." That glossy eye, swirling with curiosity roved over Max, and he felt Henry had a bit of the Mara magic in him, smelling out his client's true desire.

And he was right. Max did need to know. He'd never killed anyone before. Lakzo didn't count. He was a Mara. To get Ming back, there was a chance he'd need to know he could hurt someone, kill someone, that was human. But did these *things* deserve to die?

Henry must have seen the contemplation in Max's eyes. "I believe that when a person dies, their essence leaves…goes somewhere else," Henry said. "We have no medicine to raise the dead, but the Mara have ways to heal the physical body. They've gotten so good at it with the dumplings that I think we could keep a body alive for decades after they *should* have died. But souls have a life span that all our techniques just can't alter. And when a soul leaves, that's it. The person we knew is gone forever. I think these dead puppets are just people who abused the dumplings too much, for too long," Henry said.

"The body won't quite die even though the soul is gone?"

"Exactly," Henry said. "At least, that's my theory. But what do I know?"

A puzzle piece clicked.

"Henry, you've given me a fantastic idea. And for that I thank you."

Max didn't purchase a puppet, but he did leave Henry with a large tip. Another important move had been made and he couldn't have done it without Henry. From the beginning, Max had wondered how he would be able to pay for Ming. The Mara were not going to settle with cash alone. And violence seemed inevitable. But now, perhaps there was an alternative he could employ. It was always good to have options.

Max found a boarding room back in the East End, near where

THE CITY

Ming had found him. It was time to plan the grand finale.

II

JOHN MCLOUD POKED into his drink. The amber, diluted by the melted ice, stared back at him with its numbing indifference. The watery booze was becoming his best friend after the long uneventful hours at work. He finished a bottle that, until today, had gone a year without much use. Now, it helped with the grainy photos of death.

He'd received four more cases since being promoted to homicide. None were making progress. The three butchered girls had become legend. But Willis was nowhere to be found. Even with all the mayor's connections and added manpower, there was no trace of him. Chris Barnes had been of little help and once he sobered up in jail—a week of misery that landed him in the prison infirmary—he was released with nothing to tie him to the investigation. Unlike the Whitechapel crimes of Jack the Ripper, there were no letters, no hoaxes and so far, not another murder.

Though the drink hindered him more than it helped, McCloud was able to come up with a plan to keep an eye on the Willis case while still pursuing his new victims. He would employ the same technique he used with the juveniles. When he wanted to know if they were keeping true to their word, he didn't wait for another delinquent report to come in or worry that when similar misdemeanors occurred that it was his suspected child. Instead, McCloud tailed them once they were released from the courts. He'd watch their movements and if their habits started to revert, he'd swoop in before damage was done.

Barnes was his last remaining clue. He'd foul up again. Criminals always did. Adult criminals. The kids had a chance though. If you worked with them enough, you could change their cycles, but it took a lot of time and effort.

Taking a sip of the alcohol, he wondered if a time would come when he stopped having diluted booze. When he was so quick to drink that the ice didn't even have a chance to melt. It scared him. Then it angered him that Max may have been right. And not just about the drinking. In just this short time, he was losing faith that homicide was any different than criminal investigation.

Before retiring to bed, he thought about the young men he had worked with in juvenile services. He wondered if they'd grown up to be like Barnes and Willis. At the time he'd worked there, he felt like he'd given those boys hope. But talking with the mother of Marian Bell didn't give him hope for her family's future. All she wanted was justice for her daughter's memory.

But there wasn't as much justice involved as he'd originally thought. It was becoming painfully clear that when a person is killed, that was it; they're gone. You can call it whatever you like, but the living who pursue the murderer do so for vengeance. That's what he really was. McCloud was a soldier hired for retribution. And the man who confuses vengeance with justice might as well dig two graves: one for the enemy and one for himself.

The alcohol also got him thinking that perhaps his own motives were nothing but misplaced vengeance and anger from Janice's death. McCloud shook his head. Not wanting to go down that path, he crawled into the empty confines of his bed and let sleep claim him.

III

ZEKE PACED BACK and forth, looking for the tell-tale signs of a newbie: wide eyes and neck arched, confusion etched into their furrowed brows as they gawked at The City for the first time. That's when he swooped in for the sale.

But there was nothing today.

He passed his building again and looked down the alley. The south side of the building usually ran higher visitor traffic, but that also meant there were more guides to compete with. Though at this stage he needed a sale so bad that he was not above chasing away some of the younger guides. Three hours was more than enough to waste in one place. He stepped into the darkness of the alley.

Zeke avoided a puddle as he made his way down the alley, then saw a dark form huddled against the wall, just ahead on his right side. He slowed. His hand moved inside his jacket, his fingers slid into the brass knuckles, and the weight of the knife against his lower leg became noticeable.

It was probably just an addict nursing a hangover, but Zeke

stayed alert. His body tensed as his right foot came within a few feet of the form. Zeke prepared to run past it when something struck his left leg from behind. He was so distracted by the form at his right leg that he didn't expect his left to be swept out from underneath him.

Zeke yelled as his tailbone hit the stone ground. He was quick though, swinging his right leg around, hoping to strike the attacker. His leg hit nothing but air, and he rolled to his hands and knees. Before he could stand, Zeke was struck on the back and fell to the ground. He rolled, reaching under his pants hem, and grabbed the blade strapped near his ankle.

Zeke struck out as he rolled and the steel sunk into something. His assailant yelled and whatever weapon the man had wielded clamored to the ground. Zeke jumped to his feet, ready to get the upper hand. He lunged—blade out—at the form that had fallen against the brick building. His back seized in pain though, causing Zeke to stagger, giving the shadow just enough time to dodge. Zeke's blade struck the brick. He swore and the knife fell from his hand.

Zeke tried to turn and throw a punch, but he was tackled. He felt a moment of piercing pain drive into his head...then nothingness.

Zeke opened his eyes. His head ached, and the room was blurry.

"Rise and shine."

Zeke jumped at the voice and felt resistance against his body. A face hovered over him. The features seemed familiar, but Zeke's head was too fuzzy to identify the man.

"Zeke, right?"

Zeke tried to swallow, but his throat was dry and the action hurt. The inability to sit up panicked him and the fear heightened his alertness despite the pain. He realized that he was tied and more than likely on some sort of tabletop. He struggled again but didn't feel any give in the ropes.

"What the hell you want, mister?" Zeke said, his voice cracking.

"Answers." The man walked out of view.

Zeke strained his head, but was unable to keep his sight on the man. From what Zeke could see, the room was bare and unfamiliar. "I don't know anything. I take people where they want to go. I don't ask questions."

"Sure you do," the man said, reappearing on Zeke's left side this time. "You asked about Ming and Doc, remember?"

Shit! It was the guy he located for Charlie. "How did you find me? What do you want from me?"

"It took three days of staking out areas to find you. Then I tailed you for two more before I felt confident to strike." He paused. "And what I want is Charlie."

"Who?"

"Zeke, I know you sold me out to Charlie Willis. But my problem isn't with you. In fact, I'm ready to let you go. I just need to know where to find him."

"He was asking for someone fitting your description, so I mentioned I seen you. That's it...nothing else. I didn't rat you out!"

"You know what I like about this place?" The man—Max, Zeke thought his name was—acted like he hadn't heard him. "People mind their business. I carried you over my shoulder for a block to this boarding house. No one said a word. And I'm betting that if they heard you scream...no one would do a thing."

Zeke knew he could gain the upper hand if he kept his cool and sounded confident. This guy didn't know the area. "Then I got nothing to worry about. The street takes care of me, mister. And if people saw me dragged away, you're right: they wouldn't say a word to you. They'd get the Clove Street Boys instead."

"Clove Street Boys, huh?" Max smiled. "You make that up based on the Clover Street post down the way?"

"They'll kill to get me back, they will."

Zeke felt the muzzle of a gun press against his temple. "Even if you were telling the truth—which I doubt—it doesn't matter to me. Because if anyone does bust in here, I'll blow your brains out before they even know what's happened." He pulled the gun away and brought a knife into view. "Now, you tell me where Charlie is and I cut the ropes. Don't tell me, and I cut off a finger."

"I don't know where he is!"

Zeke felt the man clamp down on his hand, driving his wrist against the tabletop. A blade thunked and he heard it sink into the wood followed by piercing pain that transversed the length of his arm. Zeke's ears throbbed and he howled. Some type of fabric was stuffed into his mouth, but he couldn't stop screaming. The gag sunk farther into his throat. Water trickled down and he fought to swallow it. Air didn't want to come through the wet gag and the whole time his hand felt raw and exposed; every nerve seemed to by firing.

Max put his finger to his lips. "Yelling only makes it worse. You'll suffocate."

The words finalized the panic sinking into his mind and Zeke struggled to slow his breathing. His eyes filled with hot tears, but he calmed himself. He relaxed his hand as best he could, though he could feel hot sticky wetness pooling under his palm.

Oh, God. Zeke trembled. But he couldn't look down at his hand. Despite the fiery spasms that engulfed his entire hand, Zeke knew his thumb was gone. Knew that if he looked, he'd find a giant cleaver sitting where his thumb should have connected to his palm.

The man reached out and removed the cloth. Zeke sucked in air, lungs burning with each gasp. "If you scream again, the gag goes back."

Zeke coughed, trying to force the water out of his aching lungs. His chest burned and it took a couple of minutes for him to steady himself.

"Now I'll ask you again: Where is Charlie?"

"I don't know!"

The man leaned in, sure enough pulling a cleaver from the wood and raising it over his head.

"Wait! Wait, oh, God, just wait." Zeke tried to calm the bubbles welling in his throat. "H-he was staying at the R-Red Dragon Inn last I saw him."

"Give me more."

"I-I mean, he came around a bit. Never seemed to need a guide, just paid to know what was going on in the area. To have eyes and ears when he wanted them. It's been going on for a while." Zeke stopped to catch his breathe. "Usually boards at the Red Dragon Inn when he's here. But I ain't seen him in a while."

The man put the knife down. "See? That wasn't so hard."

"Let me go, mister."

"If you try to come after me, stop me, or you contact Charlie, or if I find out you lied to me, I'll kill everyone you know and burn you to death."

A new type of fear gripped Zeke. Deep in Max's eyes, Zeke saw a black fire of rage and knew he wasn't lying.

"Understand?"

"Yes."

The man cut the ropes and left.

IV

Two WEEKS LATER, Max still felt good as he sat inside the pub sipping on a pint of *mogjiŭ*. Over the days, he danced on the line of sobriety, a slight buzz here and there, but never falling off the wagon or losing his mental facilities. Power was his new main high. He'd got exactly what he wanted from Zeke through having a stronger will. He hadn't hesitated with his threat; he'd chopped off that kid's thumb. If only he could do that in San Fran; crime would be greatly reduced.

Max had rented a room at the Red Dragon Inn after the info he'd received from Zeke. There was no reason for the kid to falsify anything. Max knew he'd scared him worse than anyone ever had. When Zeke had been lying there helpless, Max had contemplated killing the teen. Just hacking away at his neck. Who needed a puppet when he could break his bones with Zeke, someone that deserved it? But he had quelled the dangerous desire blossoming inside himself and let the young man live because Max believed that Zeke hadn't known what Charlie's ulterior motive was for finding him.

The big puzzle had nearly revealed itself in his mind's eye, so now he spent the days in shifts. He slept for five hours if he was lucky, then travelled deeper and deeper each day into the West End. Watching shows. Eliminating places Ming wasn't. Understanding the people and the creatures. Growing ever closer to Gehanna. Then he'd spend a few hours at this bar just watching the inn. Max was running low on time though. At this rate, he'd reach Gehanna in two more days of exploring. And if he didn't have his prize by then, he'd be forced to revert to his original plan.

Today, through a grime-streaked window in the pub across the street, he watched the Red Dragon Inn. An hour passed and little activity transpired around the place. By his count, he'd only slept seven hours in the past day and a half. But he was too close to waste time sleeping. He had healed his shoulder where he'd been stabbed with a few visits to the hospital ward for dumplings. The ends justified the means. And momentum had a way of blocking everything else out, giving him eyes that only saw victory. He just hoped the lack of sleep and tunnel vision wouldn't make him too careless…or too callous.

Not possible to be too callous here.

Max finished his drink, slapped his cheeks, and headed out the pub door. He needed to get his blood circulating and the best way was mapping the interior of the Red Dragon Inn again and again. He took thirty minutes pacing over familiar routes, committing the floor layout to flawless accuracy in his memory. There was only one other guest he encountered, and they both ignored each other as they passed.

This stakeout is a longshot, the voice of doubt chided for the first time after its long slumber.

Max let himself into his room but ignored the voice. He thought about John McCloud watching Brittny Willis's building. Not knowing when or if Charlie would ever show up.

If McCloud can dedicate his time, then I can give it a few more days.

That night, the relaxing act of cooking had not quelled

McCloud's agitation. Now, he was in bed, staring into the blackness of his eyelids but not feeling tired. If he wasn't thinking about the Marion Bell case, he was recalling scenes of equal depravity in his mind's eye. Constant death was taking him to a higher level of stress than he had anticipated. All crime was upsetting to a degree, but seeing the murders, the creative ways humans picked to destroy each other was painful to a man's very core, his essence.

When he'd punished his conscious enough with gore, he switched over to the meetings with the mayor and media. Proctor had once told him that the press were parasites. If it bleeds, it leads. He'd never noticed it before. But recently, sensationalized tragedy was all McCloud saw.

Then there was Max. Where was he now? He'd disappeared again, but this time nobody gave it a second thought. If Max was as intimately tied to Charlie as the story implied, was it a coincidence that both men were MIA? Max still knew way more than he'd let on.

McCloud got up, lit a candle, and opened the files for Max and Cullen Smith on the bed. He read through the details a third time. He felt like an archeologist slowly uncovering pieces of evidence, statements; bones of a long dead animal. McCloud used his imagination to add flesh and blood to the skeleton of the Digger case and the backstory between Harris and Max.

Then McCloud lied down and closed his eyes. He saw a much younger looking Harris the night he and Max encountered the Digger. Harris stood taller, his skin taut and vibrant. This was a time in Harris's life just before the weight of the world crushed him.

Something changed the night Harris shot Cullen Smith. Despite losing the Digger's last four victims—three women and one man—Harris saw promotions shortly after, while Max seemed to fade away from the department. The report alleged that the suspect was attacking Detective Elliot, threatening his life when Harris drew his revolver and shot to save his partner. McCloud found it difficult to believe the physically smaller Digger attacked Elliot. To read the report, the two were grappling in close quarters. It sounded too dangerous to shoot; how could he guarantee Max's safety?

It may have been a dream or his imagination as he tittered on the edge of sleep. But in his mind, McCloud saw the partners slinking through the warehouse. The Digger surprised them. They surprised each other was more accurate. Harris fired the gun off reflex and that was all she wrote for Cullen Smith.

Then McCloud opened his eyes, the only clear memory being the gunshot. As for the rest, there was nothing more than a fragmented dream to go on, but he had the impression that Max had taken the fall for his partner's mistake. Faked the danger his life was supposedly in, and allowed Harris to not be brought up on misconduct charges. Even if McCloud's reasoning was off, there was more to the story than what was in the files. If there was truth in Max's sacrifice, the tense relationship between him and Harris made a lot more sense.

"I'll find you again," McCloud said. And when he did, he'd expose the underlying cause of that night with Harris, he'd find out what was going on with the Chinatown Surgeon, and if Charlie *was* the same guy. Because there was still so much that didn't make sense. Unlike the mayor and Harris, McCloud was not satisfied with waiting to find Charlie. And Max knew more than he was saying—he was the keystone to everything.

V

Max MADE IT two more days before he felt his last shred of patience start to fray.

Scanning the crowd filing through the doors of the inn, the faces were blurred and Max felt anxious. He knew this was the last day. If he waited any longer, the loss of motivation and doubtful voice that was speaking more often to him would be too great to overcome, and Max would find a *sǐ fěn* pipe in his hand. He'd give it one more hour and then call it quits, grab some sleep and head to Gehanna. The—

Down the street he saw the off-white gambler's hat, bobbing above the crowd. Shock and unbelievable relief course through him.

No…is it? Max dropped some coins on the table to cover the bill and dashed into the street, ducking into the alley with enough time to confirm the greasy mustache and gaunt cheeks of Charlie. The waiting game had consumed everything, and when Max finally convinced himself to believe his eyes, Charlie was already ascending the four steps to the inn. Max pushed off from the brick wall and slipped inside the Red Dragon about three seconds after Charlie.

There would be no extended surveillance this time. Max would strike now. Charlie's capture was all that mattered.

Ahead of him, Charlie took the steps to the second-floor rooms quick. Max moved slow to avoid detection. Charlie reached the landing as two men hustled past him and down the steps. They were griping about something that Max couldn't quite understand, but he used the distraction to bolt up the remaining stairs unheard. Charlie was just ahead, putting a key to the lock of a room on the right. Max leaned into another doorframe, not wanting Charlie to see him, counting how many rooms down he was.

A woman's scream ripped out from somewhere on the floor. Charlie went rigid and looked the opposite way down the hall. Luck was on Max's side for once. Before the shriek ended, Max committed himself to action, crossing the hallway in three bounds and coming down on the back of Charlie's skull with a piece of rebar. Charlie fell into the door and Max snagged the key. The woman continued to cry out in short bursts from a nearby room.

Max reminded himself that the woman wasn't his problem. He looked at Charlie, thankful the snitch was such a thin worm of a person. With a slight grunt, Max hauled the man over his shoulder and took the quickest route back to his room.

Once Charlie was secured in Max's room, the detective locked him in and headed to the ward.

"How the tables have turned," Max said when his prisoner woke. He looked at Charlie, each limb tied to a bedpost and his torso bound to the mattress, and smiled.

Charlie thrashed, his screams muffled by the gag.

"I don't get it. I mean, you asked me to come after you, Charlie. Was I too quick? Because this was easy." Max reveled at the gleam of anguish in Charlie's eyes. "Can I take the gag out? Is that what you're asking? Are you going to scream?"

Charlie scowled but shook his head, and Max pulled out the

bunched-up cloth.

"No point in screamin' anyway," Charlie said once the gag was out.

"No?"

"Who's gonna care?"

"You think I'm going to kill you?" Max asked.

"I would, if the roles was reversed."

"I've been thinking about that a lot recently," Max said. That thrill of absolute power swelled in Max again. It was even better than it had been with Zeke. Not that he condoned what happened in The City's shows, but Max could finally appreciate why so many men came here to watch and engage in dominating acts. "All this time on homicide and you start to block out the concept of death. Death is a job. And it's my task to assign death a cause. Stripping the human element from death helped me block it from my mind. I've been able to block a lot of things I didn't want to deal with."

"Tell it to someone who cares."

"You should humor me, Charlie. After all, I'm the key to how much pain you're gonna experience."

Charlie lifted his head, stared back with his beady eyes, lips pursed.

"What do you think happens when you die?"

Charlie lay his head down on the mattress. "Your body rots."

"And what of your soul?"

"You don't seem like a soul-believing kind of guy, Max."

"Like I said, for a long time, I wasn't. Thanks to you, it's been on my mind as of late."

"You remember anything before you was born?" Charlie said.

"No. One day I just...*was*."

"And that's what it's like when ya die," Charlie said. "'Cause there's no such thing as a soul."

Max pulled a black rectangular case, similar to an eyeglass case, from his trench coat. "I think you're wrong. I may not know what happens to that conscious part of a human at death, or if some of us can ever be redeemed for the ills we inflict upon each other, but I have some ideas." Max paused. "I was wrong last year, and I'm sorry Brittny paid the price." Max pounded his fist against the wall. "Damn, I'm sorry. But that doesn't justify your revenge. You went beyond an eye for an eye, killed so many more innocents…and all to make a drug."

Charlie sneered up at him. "Go on and finish me."

"No. Death is too good for you. I want you to taste the fear that my daughter went through when you raped her. Know the pain my wife and your victims felt when you sliced their flesh from the bones."

"Think that's gonna help your soul?" Charlie spat.

"I told you I don't know how the afterlife works…I'm hoping that the end justifies the means." Max stepped forward and opened the case. "You ever been to that giant building at the border? Turns out they call it a ward, not a hospital."

Charlie struggled, the bed creaked.

"They house some fascinating things…like skin puppets. You know what those are, right?"

Charlie swallowed, his eyes darted around the room.

"Then you know how careful one should be when interacting with a puppet. Bites and scratches result in a fifty/fifty chance of contracting the virus."

Max stood over the bed; there was fear in Charlie's eyes now. Not on the surface, but just beneath his false front. Max smiled, breathing in Charlie's uncertainty like a Mara. Then he grabbed the wrist of Charlie's outstretched right arm.

"What the fuck are you doing?" Charlie tried to wiggle his arm away, but the bonds held fast.

"I really need this to work, so I'm hedging my bets." Max plucked a syringe from the case, then let the case fall to the floor.

Charlie's eyes grew larger. "What's that?"

Max held up the metal syringe, the cylinder full of a reddish-black liquid. "They just leave you alone with those things to do whatever. Punch, fuck, anything really. A quick stick and now—" He held the needle in front of Charlie's eyes, a dirty-red drop of skin-puppet blood bubbling up from the tip. "Can't get more direct contact than this."

"Ya son of a bitch."

Max sunk the needle into the bulging vein in the crook of Charlie's elbow. He pressed the plunger and the tainted blood disappeared. Charlie screamed and thrashed around on the bed. Max tried to replace the gag, but Charlie bit at his fingers.

"What's the matter with you?" Max mocked. "You just gonna return to the nothingness before your birth."

"Ya fucking bastard!"

"I know we have souls," Max said. "But I hope Henry's wrong about puppets. I pray you get stuck inside there, Charlie. I've got big plans for you."

At first, Charlie flopped against his restraints, howling in pain, cursing and frothing. But as the tantrum subsided, Max got the impression that the display was more of fear and shock than actual pain.

Max checked his watch. Two minutes had passed. Charlie seemed to be fighting to keep control of his breathing. Then his body started to twitch, and this time the spasms didn't appear to be under his control. Tremors gripped his face, twisting it into a mask of anguish.

Max didn't care. Didn't blink. Just watched Charlie writhe. "Life as you know it is over. How does that feel?"

Charlie's breathing turned ragged. "You know the only difference between you and me?" His speech was choppy, jaw clenching and releasing with forceful rigors.

Max held his tongue.

Charlie raised his head, glaring. "Only difference is they gave you a badge." Charlie let his head drop back to the mattress with a sigh.

VI

"**I TAKE IT** this isn't just a friendly visit," Tom Proctor's patented smile was present, but this version had an empathic hint to it.

McCloud shifted in the leather seat opposite Tom in his city hall office. "Last time we spoke, you made it sound like things were taking off for the juvenile courts movement. What else has happened recently?"

Tom nodded. "We finally got Senator Flint on board once he saw the results in Cook County, Illinois, and he knew that we had done the leg work. We now have houses of refuge, out-of-home placement, probation, and the rest coming together." Tom's smile changed to pride and some relief. "There's going to be a specialized treatment plan, case by case. Probation over incarceration."

Even though he'd left the battle years ago, McCloud remembered how hard it was to lay groundwork that changed juvies from being tried as adults and the rigid adherence to due process. "I'm happy for you, Tom. You and the other advocates have done a hell of a job."

"Hey, you earned this too. The time you spent gathering statics so we could prove our stance was invaluable. And how are you?"

"I don't know. I guess I wanted to get some things off my chest, but now that I'm here, I feel like I can't."

"This is a safe place, John."

"I made it to homicide detective."

"Yes. I noticed you in the papers. Appalling case; the city is lucky you're on it."

"Maybe. It's just...I got information and the force wants to bury it because there's not enough proof. They say that once we have the suspect, Charlie Willis, in custody, they'll work on confirmation of my other lead. But I don't think they will. I think if they can make the case stick with Willis, they'll peg it all on him so the problem goes away."

"Are you being ordered to lie?"

"More like omit."

"So you aren't *certain* this suspect committed all the crimes in question?" Tom asked.

"I don't feel certain of anything anymore. It just feels unethical. But I don't know if it's a fellow detective lying or the lieutenant."

"That's too bad to hear. Wish you had come to me sooner. Now with the press out...I understand your confliction."

"I didn't come to you because I didn't want to put the idea in my head that you were right. That maybe I don't belong in this position after all the fighting I went through to get it."

"It's going to be hard to fit in wherever you go, because you'll always expect more from yourself and others than they expect of themselves."

"Great, so you're saying I'm eternally doomed to this 'grass is always greener' disease where I dislike my current position and regret leaving previous career paths."

"Are you saying you want to come back?" Tom steepled his fingers.

"I told you, I'm not sure of anything. Who's to say I won't have the same experience with the juvies as I do with homicide. Who can guarantee the population won't get to the point where we haven't the manpower to remain effective with these kids, that funds won't be cut a year later, that it won't end up as just one big political game."

"There are no guarantees in life," Tom said. "But the grass is never greener. It's only different. And the real sad part is the truth they keep secret: there is no green grass. Anywhere. Everything has problems. It's all politics. And it all has duality built in. For you to make progress in any avenue, you'll have to fight tooth and nail for it. So make sure that whatever you take a stand for, it's worth dedicating your life to."

McCloud leaned back in the chair. He couldn't keep changing his job path every few years, but he had to know. "Talk to me about the probation aspect. How many officers do you need?"

VII

For TWENTY-FOUR HOURS, Max watched the life drain from Charlie Willis. His skin grew clammy, and a day later, his chest ceased to rise. Max didn't take any chances. He prepared a muzzle and mobile restraints, including a black leather collar, its leash made of thick metal links. Then he waited.

Three days later, the man came to in a fit of grunts, rattling the chain leash.

"My God." Max leaned in, staying out of biting distance, and stared into Charlie's eyes. "It worked."

Max had a quick meal and packed. After his belongings were settled, he fitted Charlie into his walking restraints—leg and hand cuffs and gloves to match the muzzle. Still keeping a vigilant eye despite the precautions, Max stood Charlie up, and with two tugs of the metal leash, he got the man to shuffle forward.

"We got a lot to do, Charlie." Max put on his fedora and opened the door. "Follow me." And with jerky movements, they headed out into the street.

Max walked his skin puppet down the cobblestone paths. Like a perverse giant pet, he guided Charlie's husk past the ward and the various red shows he'd forced himself to sit through. And then he saw it. The street sign with the triangle emblem.

He moved with caution, Charlie keeping a sluggish gait by his side. Businesses ceased and a few errant roads wrapped around the last row of buildings, converging with the triangle path. The path widened and terminated at the entrance to Gehanna: a small arched bridge curved over a narrow moat that set the border of this city within a city. Modest-sized bonfires burned in stone pits on either side of the wooden walkway. As Max and Charlie drew closer, acrid smoke and heat clung to Max's body, making him sweat.

Closer still and now the remains of charred skulls and femurs appeared within the leaping flames, mixed in amongst the logs. Music and voices from beyond the bridge were carried to him on clouds of rancid smoke.

Sensing something rush behind him, Max glanced around, but there was nothing there. A scream came from the north, though muffled in an instant, and hair rose on Max's neck. Even Charlie shifted. Max squinted into the darkness between the buildings. Dampened, frantic yells erupted along with the kicking and scraping of hands and feet against stone. Max turned, pretending not to hear them—or the sickening whoosh as a blade ripped fabric and sunk into flesh—and he walked on.

The flames were now close enough to sting his face as Max pulled Charlie over the three-foot high bridge. He looked down into the thin gaps between the wooden planks at the two-foot wide moat of redirected water. Max's eyes followed the manmade pipeline up to the high rock ceiling. They stepped onto the other side and he felt relief from the blaze.

Not only had all paths converged to meet the bridge, but the monstrous cave that The City was dug into was also coming to an end. Even in the misleading waver of firelight, Max could see the

232

concave walls closing in. In the far distance, The City's structures became one with the rock.

There were no obelisks to bless him with guiding light or symbols to memorize for direction. The only light source came from torches and oil bowls burning in front of brick and stone establishments. People moved in the flickering glow; their dress was too hard to distinguish from this distance in the dancing shadows, but Max knew it would be as varied as anywhere in The City, if not more so.

Having processed his initial impression, Max dragged Charlie forward. To their left a gallows pole was erected, and a suspension cell hung from its highest point. The legs and arms of a dead man dangled from the rusted bars; he slumped against a metal brace, but his mouth, visible below the bars, hung open. In the flames, Max could see insects crawling over the placid face, and a thick snake slithered from his mouth and disappeared behind the bar, probably into the prisoner's empty eye socket. Crouched behind the corpse was another man, naked and laughing.

Max paused, staring at the long-haired and unwashed man. As if sensing observation, the man's laughter ceased; he looked up and found Max's gaze. Dirty, cracked fingers wrapped around the iron bars and the man brought his face to the opening. A hollow chuckle began in the man's belly, shaking loose folds of flesh and his flaccid penis. The prisoner reared back, then smashed his head against the bar. Max cringed at the sick, cracking sound his skull made as it connected with the metal. But he couldn't turn away. He watched as the man continued to smash his skull against the cell, over and over, his laughter never ceasing. Even as blood dribbled down his face, he laughed louder and louder until he forced his head against the bar so hard that Max swore he could hear the cranium split in two. The man fell limp against his fellow prisoner.

Max looked away; if his information was right, there was a boarding house just up ahead. He pulled Charlie along.

"Come see her secrets," a man in a red *keffiyeh* and black and gold robes announced. Beside him a woman wrapped in a shimmering *bedlah* swayed her hips, slow and sensual. "She is not all human. Not all animal. Discover her secrets."

Above the baggy pants was a flowing vest, then a face covered in wraps, a thin veil over the small opening for her eyes. The fabric around her midriff seemed to pulsate while she danced, as if something was attempting to poke through, and Max was certain a hissing sound emanated from her clothed stomach.

"Come." The man pointed at Max. "Bring your puppet."

The woman's eyes floated in the sliver of exposed cream-colored flesh of her face, like a separate entity standing out against the dark bold colors that enshrouded the rest of her body. The hissing intensified, and before Max hustled past them, he noticed a long, thick black antenna creep out from underneath a fabric fold near her abdomen.

The next torch-lit building was the boarding house. Max was thankful he didn't need to coerce Charlie farther into Gehanna. It would be hard enough keeping an eye on his own well-being; not that Charlie had any well-being anymore. But Max couldn't afford to lose his commodity yet.

Inside, a desk built up from the ground separated Max from the Mara behind it. The creature was leaning upright against the wall, head cast downward, with a light smile hinting on his reptilian lips. Max set his hands on the desk but didn't speak for fear of interrupting the intensity the humanoid was using to focus on something below the desk.

Then the creature inhaled with loud gusts of air. Its head swiveled, vertical lids blinking over shark eyes. The smile that was too wicked to be playful fell on Max. The thing reached below the desk and pushed something aside, eliciting a soft, feminine grunt.

"One moment." The Mara looked down. "Don't go anywhere." He straightened his puffy dress shirt and adjusted his suspenders and waist line, then opened a ledger to the ribboned page. "How long?"

"I'd like a room for two weeks."

The Mara cackled. "Might as well put you down for permanent residence." He pushed a pen into the paper, scribbling in a language that Max couldn't read.

"Is that not long enough to enjoy the pleasures of Gehanna?"

The Mara laid the pen down. "After forty-eight hours, you'll either have left or you'll never want to leave…or you're dead." He turned the book around and pushed it to Max. "We'll start with two weeks for now though to make you happy. Sign here."

A thick talon tapped a line on the cream paper, and Max signed. Charlie remained dazed at his side, like a drunkard swaying back and forth, looking at everything yet understanding little.

"Take those stairs." The Mara pointed left at two men passed out, leaning against each other on a bench next to the staircase. "Leave your puppet in your room when you go out."

"Okay."

The Mara tossed him a key and looked back under the desk at his unseen companion. "Where were we?"

Max didn't stick around to hear the wet, gagging sounds that ensued. He headed up the stairs, watching the two motionless men, smelling like vomit, head and shoulders against each other, never taking his eyes off them until halfway up the stairs when the floor blotted them from his craned neck. "Never can be too careful. Right, Charlie?"

Max chuckled, scanning for the room number that matched his key. By the time he reached door VIII, his light chuckle had turned into uncontrollable fits of laughter. He thought of the prisoner in his hanging cell, laughing as he bashed his own brains out. Because if you had to accept your fate, it was best to do so with a smile.

Laugh, and the world laughs with you;
Weep, and you weep alone.

Eve had shown him that poem.

Max opened the door and pulled Charlie into the small room. There was a bed only a few feet from a washroom. At least there was a desk and an oil lamp. Max spent fifteen minutes making sure Charlie was secure. Once he felt confident, he took off the muzzle and fed him some scraps he bought at a vendor before leaving She'ol.

"We gotta keep you looking fresh, Charlie boy." Max clamped a palm down on Charlie's thigh, giving him an enthusiastic shake.

Charlie didn't seem to be laughing with him.

Once they had both eaten, Max replaced the muzzle. "Wish me

luck." And he left to examine the shows. He'd be systematic. Chart everything in his notebook. And he'd be able to handle everything now. Just like he handled Zeke. And the puppet at the ward. And if it did become too much, he could always laugh.

VIII

"Evening, John."

Seeing Harris looking so cheerful disgusted McCloud. "Sir." He nodded solemnly as the lieutenant walked up to John's desk. McCloud had noticed the man's disposition improving a little every day since the meeting with the mayor.

Conversely, McCloud's moods had gotten more sour.

"Didn't expect you to be here after the night shift clocked in." Harris examined the clutter on John's normally pristine desk. "Everything all right?"

"Things are as good as can be expected, I suppose." McCloud pointed to a manila envelope. "Considering I was just handed the Mancito case and I'm still no closer to finding Charlie Willis or—"

"You were tailing Barnes on that one, right?"

"It's a dead end." McCloud sighed, scratched the stubble on his normally smooth-shaved cheek. "I'm convinced Barnes is looking for Charlie just as much as we are, and sadly, he's got about as much clue to his whereabouts as us. He's taking odd jobs to scrape by, but nothing illegal…yet. Meanwhile—"

"May I?" The wooden chair scraped loudly in the quiet police hall as Harris pulled it up to McCloud's desk and sat. "You're looking at this all wrong." He smiled in a warmer than usual way, the crow's feet making him look like a wise father. "You solved the case already. We know Charlie is guilty. It's just gonna take some time to physically find him."

"Is that why you're so calm?" John hoped the edge in his voice cut into Harris's demeanor.

"Lord knows I'm never calm. But is it why I haven't been on edge lately? Yes."

McCloud opened his mouth, but Harris raised his hand and continued. "People die every day. It's your job to figure out the murderer. Once we got that, it's a whole different ball game. You're doing it right. We put out flyers, talk to the public, follow up on tips. You can't always find the culprit, even when you know who they are. Oftentimes they leave the state. We only fail if we can't determine who the criminal is. Besides, it's out of our hands after the arrest is made anyway. We give it to the courts after that. And I can't tell you how many times I've seen guilty bastards walk away. You can't take it personal. You're doing a good job."

McCloud looked away. Harris may have been right. But it didn't feel like a job well done. It felt like something was lacking. He had so many questions about the Digger case that he just couldn't bring up yet. And if this was how the game was played, he didn't like it.

"You started in juvie. Homicide is a different beast."

"You're right." McCloud began arranging the strewn papers on his desk.

"All departments are cogs in this clock of justice and you have to remember you're doing your part here at homicide." Harris rose and put his palm gently on McCloud's shoulder. "Go home. Rest."

"Will do, sir."

Once his desk was organized, McCloud headed to the street, again opting to walk rather than take a trolley or cab. He couldn't help but contemplate if the homicide department of the machine was better served by *preventing* crimes rather than pointing a finger at the accused. And to prevent crimes, there was only one source to go to: start with the kids.

אׁ

BACK ON THE street, the cold nipped at Max when not passing by one of the small fires. Between buildings, a long series of canopies jutted out from the rocks, about seven feet off the ground and stretching almost twenty feet long. Beneath the canopy were carpets full of artifacts, jewelry, pottery, statues, and paintings. Yellowish liquid preserved small creatures that floated lifeless in mason jars. Some looked like shrunken heads and hearts. Max wanted to stop at the flea market bazaar, wanted to speak to the woman in the tight *mekhela sador* dress who seemed to be the owner, the silent one with dark-painted oval eyes, like an Egyptian's. If she did speak, Max imagined her voice would be as mysterious as her beauty. And he scowled to himself that he'd never know what stories she could have shared of the treasures sold at her feet.

Past the woman's canopy store was a theatre; at least he assumed that's what it was. All the largest buildings seemed to have that in common: a stage where they would act out everything from ballet to sex to murder, and the audience sat and watched like it was merely the newest play on Broadway. But this structure was a feat of engineering masterpiece compared to the rest. Polished stone pillars connected with a smoothed-rock overhang that reached upward, sanded straight for fifteen feet before turning to the jagged rocks of the cavernous crust of the earth.

In the polished wall was a familiar sigil. He removed the black business card he got from the hunchback in the alley and matched up the third seal to the structure's engraving. The front door was cut into the stone below the overhang, the workmanship accomplished with razor precision.

The building seemed to have an energy wafting off it, different than any of the other theatres and buildings. Those had looked like any building in San Fran. But this structure before Max was different. It carried the ominous weight of a pyramid or a divine Aztec temple.

Max walked inside. The initial temperature dropped, sending a shiver up his spine. His shoes echoed in the stone dwelling. Torches burned bright within the entrance, the flames illuminating a female Mara standing behind a granite podium.

The Mara wore a hooded cloak, like a monk, and though there were no breasts discernable above the rope belt tied about her waist, Max was sure it was feminine. Her scaly features were somehow softer, smoothed and more curved. It made perfect sense that there would be a female of the species, but Max had almost come to associate the creature with masculinity. Nowhere in the streets of She'ol or the West End had he encountered anything but male Maras. A question on sexual habits stabbed at his brain, however Max knew that now was not the time. Beyond her, small groups of humans had collected. Some were boisterous and flamboyant, others solemn and reserved.

She tapped her long talons against the rock podium.

Max was often less intimidated when dealing with ladies of the human race; he felt in control. But this creature's femininity did not put Max at any more ease than when he dealt with the males. If anything, he felt more nervous.

"Is this a theatre?" Max asked.

"Let me see your left forearm," the creature said, her demand powerful without sounding masculine.

Max couldn't chance taking off the coat and exposing his gun, so he undid the wrist button and rolled the sleeve up as far as he could. Food scarcity and insomnia had shrunk most of the extra muscle and fat from his arms, and the sleeve rolled up farther than it ever had. Max wondered if he'd have the strength for a fight. He bet on adrenaline taking over if it came to that; a mania would build as it had with Zeke.

The creature took his arm in her slender, powerful hand and Max shifted uneasy against the scaly texture. She eyed him, amused, then released. "There are seven clubs in Gehanna. You may visit each once or in any combination until seven visits are reached. Stay as long as you want. Every club has food and rooms, *mogjiŭ* and *sĭ fĕn*."

"Are the seven clubs all there is in this part of The City?"

"No. There are a few other establishments and services unique to Gehanna. You experience those as you wish. The Seven Stone Clubs will always be carved from the rocks of the earth." From an unseen sheath, the creature drew a dagger and placed it on the podium. "And they'll always ask for payment."

"I have Ameri—"

She inserted the dagger into the flames of the touch. "Our clubs do not accept money. We deal in flesh." The fire danced in her eyes as the metal of the knife glowed. "We are offering you knowledge. Experience on a plane that doesn't exist above ground. But the price is not fleeting; it's permanent. Like The City's seal on your palm, it's binding." She removed the thin blade, lightly blackened from the heat. "Raise your sleeve again."

Max took a breath. He raised his sleeve and winced, grunting and grinding his teeth as the burning blade sliced into his flesh. It was over before he knew, much easier than branding, and he was left with a cauterized hash mark down his forearm. Max blew on the sensitive flesh. He heard a sloshing of water, and the Mara brought a damp rag from behind the podium. She wrapped it over Max's arm, then pulled the sleeve from his hand and gently brought it back down to his wrist.

"This is your home now. For as long as you choose. Find one of us if you require something and we will direct you, even if that means you will be visiting another club." She gestured with an open arm. "There is lots to explore here, pleasure and pain. You can make of these experiences what you want. But when you leave…"

"Then I have only six chances left." He patted gingerly at the coat over the damp rag and wound.

"Precisely."

Max passed the small, stagnant crowd of humans and there were two hallways. Small numbers of people filed back and forth between one path and the next. None looked much interested in speaking and Max was happy with chance telling him where to go. He pulled Ming's photo out of his pocket, deciding that if her face was pointed at him, he'd go left. If the side facing him was the blank back, he'd go right.

Ming's snarky smile sealed the deal and Max headed to the left. The hallway sloped downward and opened into a massive Romanesque amphitheater. Three tiers were cut into the stone. Tables and chairs covered each level, an aisle between each leading down to a circular stage. The audience was positioned mostly in the lower two levels in a horseshoe-shape around the stage. The rock wall behind the stage was alive with a hundred torches, lighting up the performers and keeping the crowd in low visibility.

Max watched his step as he moved through the crowd. There was a naked woman who was bent over on the stage, her head and wrists through a wooden stockade, her legs trembling. Max could see her head and chest hitching against the wooden device, her moans audible over the steaming hiss arising from some kind of machine behind her. At her side was a man in a suit with long coattails.

Max slipped into an empty table and could now see that the stage itself was rotating at a rate so slow it was near imperceptible. As the contraption rotated, each angle of the crowd got to see the steam powered machine that sat on a tall table behind the woman. With its water barrel, hoses, and gear pulleys, it reminded Max of the Manipulator, the anti-feminine-hysteria tool. He'd seen rejected patent prototypes in magazines, but nothing as bronze and mechanical as this. As the vibrator whirled, the long tube of rubber was thrust in and out, wriggling like a snake in the woman's vagina. Hanging from hooks in the table were a top hat and cape; the man was a magician of the woman's flesh.

The magician turned along the edge of the stage, keeping pace with the rotation so that his eyes always faced the crowd. When the woman's knees began to buckle and she threatened to collapse, he thrashed her left buttocks with an ungloved hand. She squealed and he pummeled her more until she straightened her legs. When the circling stage placed Max's view at her ass, he could see liquid trickling down her thighs, and he wasn't sure if it was excitement or urine.

The woman shuddered and grunted, her face reddened with climax, but the man did not turn off the machine. Instead, he looked to the audience. "This prototype increases power two times that of any model you've previously seen." With the crank of a knob, the machine whistled and the thick tube worked faster and harder into her vaginal orifice, her moans oscillating, the force pushing her against the wooden stock. The man slipped on a sleek black glove, then donned a hand-held machine over his fingers. "Watch the Oyster Company my friends." His handheld device buzzed to life at the touch of a button and he pressed it to the woman's puckered anus. A series of "ohs" from the woman turned into mindless rambling as both her holes were filled with unrelenting vibrations.

He looked to the crowd and in the low light could make out a bit of the row above him. There was a man in his forties, slouched in his chair, trousers open, and it took Max a minute to register what was happening. Free from the confines of his pants and underwear, the man massaged his penis watching the orgasmic woman, unconcerned about the audience around him.

Max sat up and turned to examine the rest of the crowd. Several people were manipulating their genitals in their seats or using a companion's touch with someone at their table, though most were clothed.

"Stopstopstopstopstopstop." The woman's quavering voice was stuck on a loop. Her pleas of protest were only interrupted by loud, shuddering orgasms that she seemed to have no control over. "G-g-god!"

The bound woman collapsed unconscious against the stocks, gagging as her body weight pulled against her secured head. The magician turned off his machines. "The Oyster Company." He raised the handheld glove, in no hurry to alleviate the woman's choking. Once he had his cape and hat donned, he undid the clasps and pulled her from the confines. Her breaths came hard and she looked at the crowd in a daze before they disappeared together through the stage door in the back.

The front lights dimmed and in their absence, the audience was even more shadowed. He could hear clothing zipping back up, and couples released each other's embrace. The male masturbator had removed his hands and was blowing on his swollen member, coaxing it to go down and rest before the next show. Servers weaved between tables taking orders for *mogjiǔ*, no doubt, unfazed by the sex-crazed couples, some of whom appeared to be of the same gender.

There was movement on the stage, and at the front of the floor a spotlight emerged. From a pulley high in the cave ceiling, descending at a controlled pace down the shaft of brightness, was a woman clinging to some sort of flowing fabric. Two segments actually; long strips of satin sheets that hung past her feet. She grasped the fabric with either hand, and had both feet wrapped in the separate sections, helping to support her. She was dressed in the leggings and exaggerated bra and panties of a trapeze artist.

Still about ten feet from the stage floor below, the woman's descent stopped. Music, sad and slow, poured out from what Max thought were violins, though it could have been a recording. The woman swayed in the air to the melody. Flipping herself around the hanging fabric, twirling, dropping through the air, catching herself at the dramatic last moment, only to climb again and repeat the process with even more impressive variations of the routine.

Max had never seen such aerial gymnastics before. She had such brute power and strength to complete the routine, yet the unknown woman still executed the moves with grace and femininity.

Behind her, moving in the shadows behind the spotlight, were shadowed figures pushing objects around. Preparing the stage for the next show, no doubt. After ten minutes of amazing acrobatics, the music ended. The woman repelled to the floor, landing whisper quiet. The lights faded to black. The brief moment of darkness ended as the lights flared up from the gap between the stage, illuminating the magician standing between a life-sized bronze bull and what looked like a saw horse. Behind him was a bed on the rotating part of the stage that held the stockade prior.

"Sex and death," the magician said. "Juxtaposed together in a way that only Gehanna can bring you." The magician drifted to the right and a massive man stepped from side stage left, dragging a male and female slave behind him. Size was hard to determine, but if the male slave was average height, the captor was maybe six-foot nine with at least a forty-two-inch waist, though his body appeared to be more fat than muscle in the tight black clothes. Over his face was a hood, jagged holes for the eyes cut into the covering. Max shivered at the resemblance to medieval executioners.

The two slaves trailed behind him from a few feet of coarse-looking rope. They were naked, cut and bruised. The executioner held one rope for each, the other end tied around their necks. But the rope was not in contact with their skin. Instead the rope was cinched around the fabric of a black hood that covered not only the man and woman's heads, but down past their necks and to the tops of their sternums. Unlike the executioner, there were no cutouts for air or sight in their hoods. The beast of a man led his slave train—shuffling against the ankle cuffs and arms tied to their waists—to a halt beside the bronze bull statue.

The magician regarded the cowering slaves. "*Sǐ fěn* thieves from She'ol. Both of them. Why steal what the Mara provides free of charge? Greed is the only answer. They wanted to sell our pleasures to the surface."

The executioner let go of the woman's rope and she fell to her knees. She tried to curl over and inward, hiding her nude breasts as best she could with her hands bound. However, she didn't try to run; she must have known that escape was futile. Max willed himself to not identify with how the woman might feel, blind to her surroundings, the only sound being the hot panting of her breath and pulsing temples inside the heavy hood, fear of the unknown coursing through her veins.

The executioner left her and came up behind the man next. Tearing off the slave's hood, he took him from behind in a giant bear hug. The man slammed his head against the stocky chest with little effect. An extra hard squeeze to his midsection and the fight was crushed from his lungs.

Breathless, and unable to resist, the giant grabbed the slave's hand and ankle cuffs and carried him to the bronze bull. A small hatch in the statue's chest was open, yawning with anticipation. Effortlessly, the slave was slid inside the bull and the door was latched with a hollow echo. Max detected the faintest whoosh of breathing from the bull's amplified mouth and snout as the man regained his lung capacity and panicked in his new prison.

Max wasn't sure what the bull symbolized, if anything, or what would happen next. He looked over at the woman, shivering on her knees, hands and feet bound.

"Smoke. Drink. Eat. Play. Do as thou wilt," the magician said. "But do not steal the secrets of the Mara. Embrace in the tips they provide you. Invest in monetary and personal gain with the confidence of advanced foresight. But do not profit off the knowledge which is forbidden."

The female thief's sobs did not falter the executioner. Just as fast, he removed her hood, exposing her wet, scared eyes, and grabbed her by the shoulders. Max cringed as the executioner lifted the naked woman and positioned her over the saw horse, the wedge of wood sanded and sharp. The magician walked over and took one of her limp legs. He spread them apart and guided her body as the executioner lowered her so that the wooden top slipped between her vaginal lips.

"Please, I didn't do it. I didn't!" She cried and shook her head, but the motion drove the wedge into her crotch and she gave up, keeping her hitching sobs at a minimum to lessen the pain. With the executioner's bear-size paws securing her body, Max watched the magician tie weights around the woman's ankles. Once gravity took over, the magician stood up. "Enjoy." And with that, he left the stage.

The woman from the aerial show marched onto the stage, a baton in her right hand, both ends engulfed in flames. Chopin's "Marcha fúnebre" piped into the amphitheater, but soft, so you could still hear the flaming baton whoosh as it twirled about her head. A second woman entered the stage wearing a corset and dark stockings, her hair pinned up, no panties. She laid on the bed as the baton twirler passed the flame from hand to hand, years of skill shown in her adept routine.

Meanwhile the executioner added more weight to the saw horse prisoner's ankles, and the sad piano of Chopin was no match for her screams. Over the beautiful music and fire show the woman's pleas of innocence changed to those of guilt and promises of penance.

"Please, anything you want!" she screamed. "I'll do anything!"

The baton woman sashayed over to the bronze bull, and as her torch illuminated more of the background, Max knew what was in store for the trapped man. With an elegant bow, she touched her flaming wand to a pyramid of sticks and kindling underneath the hollow statue. She then doused the baton in a bucket of water as the fire licked the bull's belly. Abandoning the baton, she joined the corseted woman on the bed, exploring her naked sex.

Max closed his eyes, but it didn't stop the tumbling and screams that echoed from the bull's facial openings. Short gasps, some from the cooking man, some the passion of the women now feverishly rubbing each other's crotches and grinding their bodies together on the bed, and plenty from the audience filled the theatre. Sex and death were not meant to coexist like this. In the crowd, males and females explored themselves and those around them.

As the fire below the bronze bull grew, the man's gasps turned to shrieks, bloodcurdling and shrill. Meanwhile, the panting of the corseted woman also grew as the baton lady sucked her labia. The corset wearer's squeals of ecstasy were momentarily overshadowed by a painful howl from the saw horse rider as her vaginal lips tore, the weight spreading her wider, pulling at her ankles like a wishbone.

Max noticed that the male masturbator in the crowd was no longer a solo act; another well-groomed Victorian man had seated himself there and was tugging on his companion's cock while they both watched the murderous entertainment.

A symphony of death harmonized in the strangest way as the burning man's screams turned to air raid sirens in the hollow bull and the saw horse woman's vocal cords ripped, her yells for mercy became little more than wet, cracking yelps. Steam poured from the bronze bull's snout. Chopin continued, but the volume gradually lowered, allowing the other sounds, including the two lovers writhing over each other on the bed, to become more pronounced.

Then above it all came a bone-crunching crack as the female

prisoner's pelvis gave way. A dark splash of blood and excrement slid down the sharp wooden planks to the stage. At the same time, the woman on the bed shuddered, releasing an orgasmic wail; her voice oscillated with pleasure, chanting and rolling her head from side to side. The music ended following the death and sex crescendo, leaving only the constant, maddening drip as blood dropped into the puddle on the floor and the crackle of fire and hiss of steam echoed from inside the bronze bull.

א

BACK IN HIS room at the boarding house, Max sat on the bed and examined the hash mark on his forearm from the dagger. He looked up; Charlie's dead eyes were fixated on him. They looked so much like the Mara's eyes. It was both unnerving and mesmerizing. Max pulled off the pillowcase and stuck it over Charlie's head. "Light's out. Unless you're eating, you're staying covered."

Max ran sweaty hands over the beard that had sprouted since his arrival. It made him feel dirty and haggard, more like the filthy attendees of Gehanna. And in a way, he was like them. Max could have easily asked the Mara if there were slave records available or opportunities to buy a prisoner's freedom. Instead, he'd chosen to sit there and absorb the show. He'd watched in curiosity as those women pleased themselves while the slaves were tortured to death.

Max ran a finger around the burnt, scabbing incision from the dagger. Electric pins pressed into his arm, but not enough to make him wince. Max pulled his sleeve down. This wasn't going to work. Not just because he risked slipping into his patterns of addiction being exposed to such sights, but logistically too. Even with only seven clubs, she could be on stage during any time of the day in any location. He removed Ming's picture and wondered if it was too risky to show a Mara and inquire about buying her. After a few minutes of contemplating, he decided to try a brothel first. It'd helped him find Leigh Anne. It might help again.

When he woke from his nap, Max ate a rushed breakfast, fed Charlie some scraps, then crossed the street from his boarding house to the only brothel in Gehanna. It was as large as the casino in She'ol with an illuminated sign, constructed from what looked like molded glass tubes. The light announced the business name in vibrant, glowing lines: *Kitch*. The tubular lights reminded him of a newspaper article he'd recently seen about Geissler tubes and something called neon being at the Paris Motor Show. But this stuff wasn't anywhere in California or the States as far as he knew. The City seemed to have a technological head start on humans.

Inside, the layout and procedure nearly mimicked his first brothel experience. A single, burly Mara sat behind a large concierge desk. He was the most well-groomed of the species he'd seen in Gehanna, but he was also the most dismissive. "Photo albums are on the table. Let me know when you've selected."

Max assumed the indifferent Mara was the owner; possibly Kitch. The lobby had a long coffee table with two red photo albums laid on its surface and a third in the possession of a black man with a short Mohawk.

Max picked up one of the books and sat down. He opened the leather-bound album and gazed into the dark eyes of a young woman. She wore a formal dress, but her face lacked the elegance that accompanies such an attire. Below was a second photo, similar age and eyes displaying the same voided expression. Max flipped through page after page, noting the despair that hung in each picture. Max had done enough profiling and missing person descriptions to properly assess age. The women in those photos were all around the age of twenty.

Max looked up at Kitch. The creature was watching him now, his scaly brows narrowed.

Max closed the book, glanced at the Mohawk man, then selected another album. This time the black and white photos contained boys too and was more what Max was looking for. The youngest girl appeared to be thirteen and the oldest maybe seventeen. These teenagers did not try to fake their calmness as their older counterparts had. Rather than despair, their eyes were full of stark terror. Even the grainy film could not hide the tear streaks that messed their adult makeup. He flipped through the entire pageant of tragedy, but Ming was nowhere to be found.

There was one album left and the Mohawk man was taking his sweet time with each page. Max found himself studying the décor of the brothel as he waited. The architecture here was different. It wasn't the plain wooden generic rooms of the East End. There were Greek and Roman statues, tapestries from all cultures and time periods, text and symbols ran along the walls in a hodgepodge of artistic works from around the world. If it wasn't for the sex trafficking, they could open a museum. Charlie was right: the Mara had been here for a very long time. They'd adapted over the ages and somehow had influence from—*or to*—every culture Max had ever heard studied. And their current tie-in with American language and society was unbelievable.

Bam!

Mohawk man slammed his album down on the table and picked up Max's discarded ones. Max didn't bother acknowledging him. He grabbed the final album and searched through pages of placid faces and lifeless eyes. With each grainy black and white horror show that passed, the weight of the book was shifting from right to left. His stomach coiled. *She's not gonna be in here*, he thought grimly.

The Mohawked man pulled a photo and walked to Kitch. "See something you like?" Max heard him ask.

Three pages left until the end and still nothing. Then Max's hand bounced back from the final page, as if burned by the last photo.

Unlike the other girls, her eyes were closed and she looked peaceful, as if she were sleeping. He ran the pads of his fingers over the photo, his breathing and heart heavy. "Ming."

Max looked at Kitch. The Mara had finished with Mohawk and sent him to his desires. Pulling Ming's photo, Max took his turn at the desk.

"Ready?"

Max handed him the photo.

Kitch took it and his face went a bit sour. "Ah, not this one."

"What? Why not?"

"She ain't with us no more. Sent to the Seventh Club for disposal." He ripped the photo a few times and tossed it behind the desk.

Max felt his stomach rent with each tear of the laminate paper. "Where's the Seventh Club?"

"End of the line."

Max barely recalled leaving Kitch's or if there was further conversation. He made it to the street and headed west, ignoring all buildings and people. His attention focused on the distant horizon, the termination of The City.

The main street led him right to the massive stone cut doors. Even in the distance he could see that this club was more impressive than the first he visited. If the last club had inspired feelings of ancient altars and temples, then this was the great pyramid itself. But it was not a pyramid in the true sense. Only its slanted, front-facing surface was triangular. It was a one-sided pyramid, its giant stone bricks chiseled directly into the rocky cave, little discernment from where the rock stopped and The City began. Passing the stone entrance would take him inside the rock wall and the end of The City.

Like the club before, there was no barrier or door to the giant entrance in the pyramid. Instead of pillars, this club had two enormous spires, slightly thicker in diameter than a spear. Their material was a polished onyx, their shafts curved and pointed like an elephant's tusk but ten times as long. Impaled halfway down the shaft of the right spire was a naked woman. The giant pole traveled through her anus, then reemerged from the cracked jaws of her mouth. Life had left her body long ago, but gravity continued to slide her down the black shaft to four other dead bodies waiting below, each stacked on top of each other.

Max passed between the impaling spires and into the stone entrance yawning with shadows and flames. Torch holders lit his path to another female Mara waiting by a podium. Behind her a reflecting pool shimmered and the sandstone walls were carved with imagery of humans and Maras, mountains and tunnels. Painted scenes had humans trekking down inside a mountain, while a few Mara journeyed upward. The reflecting pool gave Max the impression that the Mara were the shadows of people, anti-humans. And the hieroglyphs left impressions that over the centuries Mara had both helped and harmed humans throughout their evolution.

The paintings reminded Max of Tarot cards he'd seen on exhibit once. The deck had been expertly hand painted. And the longer you studied a card, the more you noticed little details in the imagery, and it gave you a more pronounced feeling. These stone paintings were created with as much care and probably held the entire history of civilization in allegory.

Max approached the podium and pulled out his photo of Ming. "I've been told this slave is owned by your club. I would like to buy her."

"Let me see your arm." Her voice was venomous.

Max popped the cuff button and raised his sleeve. She removed her dagger, sterilized it in the flames, and drew it down Max's forearm an inch from the previous cut.

Adrenaline helped deaden the burn and block the pain. "The slave. Can you sell her to me?"

"Do you know what this club is?"

Max looked past her at the wall of sacred knowledge but remained silent. How could such acts of depravity be captured in such reverence-inspiring structures and artwork?

"We are the end. The Recyclers. We created the *sĭ fĕn*, and here you have a chance to learn that knowledge."

"I thought humans weren't supposed to know those secrets."

"Those who enter this temple shall learn the full truth. However, they may not sell the secret. The knowledge itself must be enough. They also use the *fĕn* afterward to seek further wisdom."

"Never mind. Just tell me if she's alive."

"Perhaps." Her lips snarled, both disgusted and amused. "You'll have to find out for yourself." She pointed past the reflecting pool to a point where the ceiling and walls condensed to a small chamber door. A robed man stood guard.

Max walked to the wooden door and the man raised his head. The flickering torch revealed the man's eyes and mouth had been sewn shut. The stitched-up man reached for the door handle and swung the chamber open.

The screams came instantly; the smell took another few seconds to reach him.

The door was shut behind him and Max entered a square floor cut into the ground. Two thick walls rose up around him in a border that was chest level. Altars were built atop the walls. To his left and his right, humans were laid out on the sacrificial stones. On the east altars, Mara chemists shed the skin of recently deceased bodies, their knives moving with the swiftness of a honed craft. To the west, the humans were still alive, kicking, screaming, held down by two Maras while a third carved into the slaves. Their anguished cries echoed off the walls, creating a vibration of suffering. Once a human was skinned, the organs were sorted and carted away by short slaves and another body was quick to replace the prior.

Max lowered his head and walked quickly through the macabre chamber to a set of stone stairs, also lit by torches.

The stairs brought him to another chamber. This time there were a few men already inside. These men did not wear suits. They wore loose *shalwar kameez* and robes and stared in wild abandon at a large altar. The shrine was framed by pillars and more hieroglyphs, mosaics of medieval wars, peasant butchers and inquisition tortures.

A Mara on the altar stage looked out at Max. "You're just in time." Nude except for a loin cloth, the creature's red-skinned body rippled with muscle. "You are about to witness the most glorious of rituals."

The Mara smiled to a woman who was chained to the wall behind the altar. Her arms were pulled over her head and affixed at the wrist by iron manacles fastened into the stone. Her flesh was tan and taut. "When a human asks to die, to give themselves freely without fear, actually welcoming the moment of death...that will be the most powerful *sǐ fěn* you will ever know."

This club was revealing every aspect of the *sǐ fěn* process. Here the focus was on various ways to secure bones—the deceased, the unwilling, and now those wanting to die. Next was sure to be the transfer of human into hallucinogenic powder.

The near-naked Mara produced a scimitar. The woman flushed, ecstatic and thankful. Greedy for death.

Max backed out through the exit to the chamber and down a flight of stairs. He had to find a Mara he could talk to, not one who was skinning a human...or about to.

"Hello?" Max called down the stairwell. His voice echoed off the walls as he descended. "I want to bargain. I want to buy a slave."

He hustled down the stairs and entered a concave room. A handful of men and three women sat cross-legged and shirtless at the base of a table supporting the setup of something from an alchemist laboratory. The chemistry experiment contained an alembic still, boiling near heating beakers and subliming alludes. Blue flames licked, water steamed, and powder dried. Gas poured into the room from the chemical processes, and Max felt a tingle in his feet and euphoria building in his head. The seated humans swayed like marionettes in the thick smoke.

Max heard the distant purr, the voice of an old friend, and faint murmurs vibrating in the room. There was room here if he wanted to stay. Max stilled against desire and forced himself from the area, concentrating his will as he pushed on through the narrow passageway, the hum and purr of the dead following close behind.

Time was distorting again, similar to at Peek-a-Boos, and Max's nerves felt shattered. Ming was here, and at any moment, she could be the next human sacrifice. He had to find a Mara to talk to.

The narrow hall opened into a giant bath house. Instead of showers and tubs, there were stone pools that were shallow yet dark, wooden recliners, benches, and pillows. Males and females lounged in the resort atmosphere. The room was much more engulfed by *fěn* smoke than the chemical chamber, but at least here, in the large space, there was enough fresh air to breathe freely below the thick clouds hanging unnaturally above everyone's head.

Finally, Max saw them just outside the flickering, peaceful glow of the torches, watching with vigilance as the humans lazed. These robed watchers, like their female counterparts at the entrance, were not the Mara of She'ol, nor were they the derelict brood of the West. Max could tell the temple clubs held a different breed of Mara. They seemed older and wiser than the rest.

"Excuse me." Max approached a robed Mara, ignoring the inebriated humans who rolled in their own ecstasy, garbling speech as they tried to interact with their hallucinations. "I want to buy this slave." Max held up Ming's photo.

By now, Max was used to the Mara's roving dead eyes, the sniffing. But there was nothing so theatrical this time. The temple Mara pulled back his hood and spoke. "You're asking to pick the one you smoke?"

"No. I want to buy her, alive."

The Mara looked to his right and, with his scaly head, signaled at another member of the clergy several feet away. "Why this one?" the Mara asked, turning back to Max.

Max glanced over at the figure who was now walking over to join them. "She...she..." Max looked at the photo. "She wronged me and I've been traveling across Gehanna hoping to find her being humiliated. But if she's to die, I'd pay to be the one to do it."

"You would?" The figure the Mara had signaled was tall and elegant as he removed the hood from his scaly head. "I am Valbas," the creature said. "Come with me."

Max followed him to a quiet room. The only furniture was a small table and two stone chairs. When they sat across from each other, Max looked into Valbas's eyes and knew the creature recognized Ming.

This was his final chance.

א

"**W**HY SUCH OVERWHELMING interest in this particular human?" Valbas held up Ming's photograph.

"Overwhelming interest?" Anxiety fought to undermine his acting. It was time for his greatest act. "That bitch cheated me. I can't get back the money lost. So I got plans at my boarding house to take it out of her hide… If you give your approval."

"I see, Mister…"

"Elliot. Max Elliot."

"Mr. Elliot." The monster grinned, and Max realized why their act of smiling was so unnerving to him. It was like seeing a wild animal suddenly take on human characteristics. A dog or wolf, lips pulled back and upward, unnatural and wicked. An image of something that should not be possible.

"How about thirty-five American dollars," Max offered.

"Money is not the issue."

"But she is alive?" he kept his voice calm.

Valbas nodded.

"What if I trade a commodity for a commodity? I can offer

you a male skin puppet. American. Late thirties. White. Plus the money."

"If we want a puppet, we'll get one from our many wards."

"Of course," Max said. "But this is not a regular puppet. He's cheated the Mara in the past. I felt you may want him for your personal collection."

"Cheated us?" The Mara sat up straighter, his scaly expression no longer indifferent. "Who is this mysterious puppet that you feel has slipped through our fingers of justice?"

"Charlie Willis. He was selling *sǐ fěn* in San Francisco. Set up his partner to take the blame." Max saw no point in holding back. Either Valbas would take the bait or Ming was lost forever. "And when Charlie snitched to the Mara about his partner as the sole culprit, he even got compensated monetarily."

"I do recognize that name, but you are obviously not said partner. So, why do you find it your task to turn him over to us?"

"I have my reasons. For one it's nice to have a bargaining chip down here. I'm sure you can appreciate that." Max felt confident he had turned the tide back to his favor.

"Would you excuse me?" Valbas asked, rising from his chair.

"Of course."

Valbas left the room and Max was alone with thoughts of Ming's uncertain fate. Everything rested on this decision.

Though maybe not. There was always another option…

When the thought entered his head, it came with a sense of peace, that same electric calmness he felt when seeing Leigh Anne's hands at Arthur's. It may have lasted only a second or two, but in that heartbeat, Max had faith he would save Ming. Yet in his heart's next contraction, the consequences of the idea bit into his resolve and the energy field dissipated. This wasn't some empty choice. The implications were real, harsh, and irreversible.

Valbas's footsteps floated into the room and Max tabled his thought. The Mara sat across from Max again. "You say you have reasons." Valbas's tone was punitive. "Would vengeance be among the list?"

"Well…yes. I very much want to take my vengeance out on her."

"No. I mean vengeance against Charlie Willis."

Max was reduced to a blank stare at the wolfish grin that

returned to Valbas's face.

Valbas leaned forward. "The stench of *our* blood permeates your weak flesh." The unnatural smile left, and Max knew it was over for him. Something bottomed out in his stomach, his bowels tightened and he felt like passing out.

The weight of his weapons suddenly felt unbearable. Max considered drawing the gun. Sweat beaded on his forehead and his trigger hand ached. The Mara bore into him with dark, cold eyes. Max imagined that the creature could read his mind and it sent his pulse racing faster.

Max felt his hand moving toward the holster. He had killed Lakzo, he could do it again.

No. He steadied his hand. There were only four bullets left, and even if he used them to get out, what of Ming? There would be no guarantee of finding her and getting her out safely if he started a fight.

"Everything I said about Charlie is true. He's a double-crosser—"

"And you're the assassin of a Mara!" The creature slammed his hands on the table, claws chipping the stone. "Both your names are known by the council. There are several humans whose dealings make us take note—"

"Wait!" Max tried to say more, but it was like a part of him died. His mouth was open, hands trembling, though he couldn't speak.

Then something slipped into his grip. He was flooded with peace again as he realized it was Leigh Anne he felt. Sober hallucination or not, she was back, and it was pure strength. Max tightened his grip on her tiny hand and felt Leigh Anne return with a squeeze of her own. "Let me sweeten the deal. In addition to Charlie, I offer myself." Max felt a rebirth in the words. "Let me take Ming's place. She had nothing to do with my actions against Lakzo."

"Wasn't that the point of the council's decis—"

"Charlie and I for the girl," Max said. "Two for the price of one. Your people's council would be happy with that, right? Two enemies of The City for some girl who will truly never escape the memories of what happened here, no matter where she goes or how much time passes."

"I don't know. I was quite looking forward to her demise. She was making problems at shows. Her will was quite bothersome—it wouldn't break properly."

"Death's too good for her then. Might as well let her go free. Let her be haunted. That can be her punishment. And me—"

"Your selfless act seems meaningless though. We already have you."

"But if you release her, I'll go freely. No fighting, no casualties. No unbreakable will like Ming. I'll submit to whatever you wish, but she's left alone."

"The council expressed much to me in the short time I left you, none of which much resonates with what you're asking. But they did not foresee your choice of free will." A curl began at the corners of his scaly mouth. "I have a feeling that I won't regret this pact should I make it."

"Just let me see Ming one last time. That's all I ask. Once she's gone, I'm yours, and—" He produced the boarding room key from his pocket. "You can find Charlie here." The emblem from the street sign was stamped onto a leather fob attached to the key ring.

Valbas took the key. "Agreed. She'll have six hours to leave The City—for good. If not, she will be recycled."

Max ignored the implications to his own life and instead felt the elation of success. He bordered on tears of joy and relief from over a month of torment. Leigh Anne's hand was no longer in his grip, but he still felt her. "Thank you."

"Don't thank me." Valbas narrowed his eyes. "We'll make sure you are never thankful for sacrificing yourself."

A chill passed up and down his spine, but Max still tasted bliss.

Valbas stood and pocketed the key in a fold of his robe. "Follow me."

Max trailed the Mara on shaky legs down a hallway. They stopped at a locked door. Max's head throbbed and his stomach roiled in a mixture of fear and anxiety while Valbas unlocked the door. It creaked open and they took a staircase down. There were only thirteen steps—Max counted them, hoping they would last forever. The closer he got to seeing Ming in person, the more nervous he became. The issue was no longer belief that the plan could succeed; now the fear was looking into Ming's eyes.

When the steps ended, Valbas led him down a wide corridor; rooms built into the rocky walls were closed off with large wooden doors. Valbas stopped at the eleventh door on the right-hand side.

Valbas unlocked the door and stepped to the side. "You have ten minutes, Mr. Elliot."

"Then she walks out of here unharmed?"

Valbas nodded. "And you stay…freely. That is the agreement we are bound by." The Mara reached out his scaly hand.

There was little hesitation before Max reached out and took the handshake. There was no fear of being clawed; they wanted him alive. But still, his hand felt strange and numb in the creature's grasp. He was repulsed, yet somehow the shake helped him trust Valbas.

As twisted and demented as these creatures were, the Mara still had some kind of hideous honor code, and this was it. They'd buy a human to do mortifying things with, but they'd *buy* them. Not steal. They'd kill, but never without a reason. Somehow Max was certain of it all.

Or maybe I'm just trying to convince myself.

No. Somehow, he knew. These things liked watching human torture. And it was better when the humans made the choice to endure the pain, to participate. These Mara didn't use the drugs, the women, the shows. Humans did. The Mara just gave mankind a playing field. And Max knew his surrender was just what they wanted. They'd abide by the agreement. And he'd have all the time in the world to come to understand their twisted psychology and contemplate their true purpose, because it was much more than just offering up a sinful city, a playground for perverted adults. There was something here, something deeper, but Max didn't know what.

Valbas released his grip. Max turned from him and walked into the room. The Mara pulled the door shut behind him.

XII

Ming sat on a wooden chair. The chains of the shackles were affixed to the legs of the seat, and a hood had been placed over her head. A tight white shirt clung to her torso and only a pair of long underpants covered her lower body. Both articles of clothing were streaked with dirt. Her feet were bare. Stringy black hair hung down from under the hood.

Max stood no more than five feet from her, but he couldn't speak.

"Who's there?" Her words were laced with bravery and Max knew it was more than he could have produced in her situation.

"It's me." Max's voice sounded alien to himself.

"Mister Elliot?"

"You remember me, right?" *Of course she remembers, you idiot. You caused all her pain.*

"T-take me home," she whimpered. "Please."

The sudden sadness in her voice broke the spell over Max and he rushed to Ming, though he couldn't bear to remove the hood and see her hurt eyes. Kneeling on the ground, he took her hands in his, the metal shackles rattling.

"You're going home, kiddo." He took a deep breath. "But I can't be the one to escort you. I have to stay here." He didn't even take a second breath; he just kept on talking because he couldn't bear to hear her sad voice again. "You'll be safe though. I have money for you and weapons—"

"They'll find me and—"

"No they won't, Ming. I took care of everything. I promise. I just need you to trust me. I even have a place for you to live for now. Please listen to me. We don't have much time."

Max saw the table in the corner, a silver key on its surface. He let go of Ming's hands and snatched the key. "When I unlock you, you're a free woman. But I want you to go straight home. If anyone tries to stop you, I want you to kill them." He removed the revolver and placed it in her lap.

"The Mara will—"

"It's not to use against the Mara. It's in case any scum on the West End attack you as you try to get home. The Mara will let you go. But there is plenty of other filth down here that will take advantage of you in this compromised state."

"What do you mean, the Mara will let me go? Do you know how crazy that sounds? What's going on—"

"I don't have time to explain. You just get home. And when you get there, open the puzzle box on Arthur's living room shelf. You know the one?"

"Yes, but—"

"Just do it. You'll find what you need in there." Max undid the locks and the shackles fell to the ground. "You're a guide, you're tough…I know you can find your way back to the surface safely. And then you'll be free. The Mara won't come after you. But you have to move quick. This deal only lasts for six hours. Grab what you need and then leave immediately."

"What deal?"

Full explanations and parting words were not a luxury Max had time for. "I know you don't want help, but you can't live down here anymore, ever. At least let what's in the box get you back on your feet. Then you can move on if you want. But please, give it a chance…"

He unlocked the cuffs and Ming went to remove the hood.

Max placed his hands over hers, stopping her. "What about you?" she said.

"I won't be coming with you. I...I have to stay here. That's why you need to go to the surface. Okay?"

She nodded under the hood.

"I promised Arthur, just like he promised your sister," Max said. "Now promise me you'll leave."

"I promise."

"Good. Then get out of here." He pulled her up and guided her hands so that she was pushing the revolver into the waist band of her underpants. "Better if it's slightly hidden." He guided her, still hooded, toward the door and then slumped down into the wooden chair she had just occupied.

Ming pulled off the hood. Her face was smeared with dirt and tears and Max had to look away.

"Thank you," Max said, still facing the dirt floor. "You'll never know how much you've given me back. I'm sorry that things turned out this way. Sorry for everything. I wasn't worthy of your loyalty and help, and I understand if you hate me. But you taught me a lot in a short period of time. I feel at peace now."

Max felt pressure as Ming's arms wrapped around him and squeezed. She nuzzled her head into his neck. Max could feel hot wet tears roll from her cheeks down his rough skin and pool on his collar. Her dry, cracked lips kissed his stubble.

"I knew you'd come for me."

Max felt more hot tears, but this time, they were his. "Of course," he choked out. "Now get moving."

He looked up from the ground and Ming pulled back from his neck. Her eyes were no drier now, but there was a new look in them. Gratitude, respect...maybe it was love. Max wasn't sure. He felt like he hadn't seen a real human in ages, didn't know how they felt anymore. But the look made him wish he could go with her. That they could just disappear together.

"Please," Max said, looking away.

The wooden door opened. Valbas stood in the frame. "Time's up, little one."

"You know where to go, Ming," Max said. "I came back for you. Now do this for me."

A fire ignited behind Ming's eyes. She nodded, and in that

moment Max knew then that she'd make it.

Ming stood, hands around her frail body, covering the revolver, and strode out of the room.

"How noble of you, Mister Elliot," Valbas said. "I have someone fetching Willis now. Before long the two of you will be reunited here, where you belong."

There wasn't much fear in Max now; that would come later. There was just relief in completing the mission. Case solved. Ming would be fine, and that was as good an ending as he could hope for.

"I'll be back when our skin puppet arrives." Valbas went to leave but paused. He turned back to Max. "She was worth giving up the rest of your life to us? All the earthly pleasures of The City, of home, of freedom were not enough to convince you otherwise?"

"Some things have no price tag."

"Everything comes at a price."

"Then I guess I paid the ultimate cost," Max said. "I can't think of a single thing I've been more attached to than myself."

"How very interesting. You are quite a puzzle yourself, Max Elliot. Quite a puzzle indeed."

"We have sentries watching her," a tall, skinny Mara said to Valbas in the privacy of a meeting hall.

"No need. I made the deal because I wanted her to leave."

"Do you think the council will be upset with your decision?"

"No. We all agreed to do away with her, but with this new development...let's just say that I find her almost as intriguing as Elliot. She will do more for us alive now than dead. I will explain everything to the counsel and take responsibility," Valbas said. "Though I believe this will not be the last we see of little Ming. She'll drift to us eventually. I'm sure of it."

"Very well," the Mara said.

Valbas thought he still detected a hint of uncertainty in the other's voice.

"Don't lose sight of our true task," Valbas reminded. "A part of me actually wants to see Elliot released as well."

"Elliot? Released?"

"Yes. I promise you, he will be of more use to us free than as a slave. A magnificent weapon for us. All in due time...all in due time."

XIII

I T WAS SATURDAY evening and John McCloud had settled down with a book. He was done with newspapers. There was enough misery at work without reading more at home. After two more meetings to discuss his options as a parole officer and mentor, Tom Proctor had turned him on to Jules Verne, and McCloud now was halfway through *20,000 Leagues Under the Sea*. This fantasy genre was perfect to wash away the distaste of an unproductive day at homicide. And as Tom explained, such books were an invaluable resource in getting wayward teens interested in beneficial hobbies such as reading and proper thinking. But for it to effectively work, McCloud had to have read a book prior to lending it to a kid.

If things went as planned, maybe there wouldn't be many more days of homicide left.

There was a knock at the door.

John stiffened. He moved toward the door and listened for a few seconds before opening it a bit.

An Asian teenager stood on his door step, a sad smile on her lips. "Mr. McCloud?"

"How can I help you?"

"It's a bit hard to explain. I'm…I'm a friend of Max Elliot. I came here to deliver a letter and ask if…uh…if you'd be so gracious as to let me spend the evening in your home. Unfortunately, I have nowhere else to stay tonight and I'm not used to this place."

John opened the door wider and the teen handed him a sealed letter. "Please come in." He stepped aside as the young girl entered. "What's your name, young lady?"

"Ming, sir."

"Ming." John smiled. "Please have a seat, Ming."

She settled softly on the couch, while McCloud took the chair. He opened the letter.

> *McCloud,*
>
> *If you're reading this, chances are I'm dead. I hope you're still considering my suggestion about juvenile services. They need people with police backgrounds, but with the patience, wisdom, and love of a teacher. And I believe you're just the candidate.*
>
> *Perhaps you can start honing your mentor skills on the young woman I sent over. She's no baby, but she needs help. She's seen horrors at the hands of Charlie and narrowly escaped being killed herself. She has the heart of a fighter, but she's sixteen, and even though she doesn't want to ask for help, she needs it. All her family is dead. Please take care of her. I know she's not your flesh and blood. But she is a good person.*
>
> *Thank you,*
> *Max*

John folded the letter up and looked at the girl. "It's very nice to meet you, Ming." He used the same voice he had used when interning as a teacher. "Welcome to my home." John paused. "Max was a good man. And I'd like you to consider this your home too. For as long as you need."

"Thank you, sir. I hope I won't inconvenience you long."

"It's no trouble at all."

"It's just that sixteen-year-olds can do a bit more where I'm from. Not too many job opportunities for me up here." She tried to smile.

"Don't worry, Ming, everything's gonna be fine. I promise."

"I know everything will work out." She smiled, though her bottom lip began to tremble. There was love and sadness in her voice. "Because Max promised me too."

THE END

Made in the USA
Middletown, DE
22 November 2022